THE WALLET OF KAI LUNG

THE WALLET
OF KAI LUNG

Ernest Bramah

HONG KONG   OXFORD
OXFORD UNIVERSITY PRESS
1986

Oxford University Press

Oxford   New York   Toronto
Petaling Jaya   Singapore   Hong Kong   Tokyo
Delhi   Bombay   Calcutta   Madras   Karachi
Nairobi   Dar es Salaam   Cape Town
Melbourne   Auckland

and associated companies in
Beirut   Berlin   Ibadan   Nicosia

First published by Grant Richards 1900
First issued, with permission, in Oxford Paperbacks 1986

ISBN 0 19 584050 X

Printed in Hong Kong by Kings Time Printing Press Ltd.
Published by Oxford University Press, Warwick House, Hong Kong

CONTENTS

CHAPTER ONE

THE TRANSMUTATION OF LING

*

§ I

INTRODUCTION

THE sun had dipped behind the western mountains before Kai Lung, with twenty li or more still between him and the city of Knei Yang, entered the camphor-laurel forest which stretched almost to his destination. No person of consequence ever made the journey unattended; but Kai Lung professed to have no fear, remarking with extempore wisdom, when warned at the previous village, that a worthless garment covered one with better protection than that afforded by an army of bowmen. Nevertheless, when within the gloomy aisles, Kai Lung more than once wished himself back at the village, or safely behind the mud walls of Knei Yang; and, making many vows concerning the amount of prayer-paper which he would assuredly burn when he was actually through the gates, he stepped out more quickly, until suddenly, at a turn in the glade, he stopped altogether, while the watchful expression into which he had unguardedly dropped at once changed into a mask of impassiveness and extreme unconcern. From behind the next tree projected a long straight rod, not unlike a slender bamboo at the distance, but, to Kai Lung's all-seeing eye, in reality the barrel of a matchlock, which would come into line with his breast if he took another step. Being a prudent man, more accustomed to guile and subservience to destiny than to force, he therefore waited, spreading out his hands in proof of his peaceful acquiescence, and smiling cheerfully until it should please

7

the owner of the weapon to step forth. This the unseen did a moment later, still keeping his gun in an easy and convenient attitude, revealing a stout body and a scarred face, which in conjunction made it plain to Kai Lung that he was in the power of Lin Yi, a noted brigand of whom he had heard much in the villages.

'O illustrious person,' said Kai Lung very earnestly, 'this is evidently an unfortunate mistake. Doubtless you were expecting some exalted Mandarin to come and render you homage, and were preparing to overwhelm him with gratified confusion by escorting him yourself to your well-appointed abode. Indeed, I passed such a one on the road, very richly apparelled, who inquired of me the way to the mansion of the dignified and upright Lin Yi. By this time he is perhaps two or three li towards the east.'

'However distinguished a Mandarin he may be, it is fitting that I should first attend to one whose manners and accomplishments betray him to be of the Royal House,' replied Lin Yi, with extreme affability. 'Precede me, therefore, to my mean and uninviting hovel, while I gain more honour than I can reasonably bear by following closely in your elegant footsteps, and guarding your Imperial person with this inadequate but heavily loaded weapon.'

Seeing no chance of immediate escape, Kai Lung led the way, instructed by the brigand, along a very difficult and bewildering path, until they reached a cave hidden among the crags. Here Lin Yi called out some words in the Miaotze tongue, whereupon a follower appeared, and opened a gate in the stockade of prickly mimosa which guarded the mouth of the den. Within the enclosure a fire burned, and food was being prepared. At a word from the chief, the unfortunate Kai Lung found his hands seized and tied behind his back, while a second later a rough hemp rope was fixed round his neck, and the other end tied to an overhanging tree

Lin Yi smiled pleasantly and critically upon these preparations, and when they were complete dismissed his follower.

'Now we can converse at our ease and without restraint,' he remarked to Kai Lung. 'It will be a distinguished privilege for a person occupying the important public position which you undoubtedly do; for myself, my instincts are so degraded and low-minded that nothing gives me more gratification than to dispense with ceremony.'

To this Kai Lung made no reply, chiefly because at that moment the wind swayed the tree, and compelled him to stand on his toes in order to escape suffocation.

'It would be useless to try to conceal from a person of your inspired intelligence that I am indeed Lin Yi,' continued the robber. 'It is a dignified position to occupy, and one for which I am quite incompetent. In the sixth month of the third year ago, it chanced that this unworthy person, at that time engaged in commercial affairs at Knei Yang, became inextricably immersed in the insidious delights of quail-fighting. Having been entrusted with a large number of taels with which to purchase elephant's teeth, it suddenly occurred to him that if he doubled the number of taels by staking them upon an exceedingly powerful and agile quail, he would be able to purchase twice the number of teeth, and so benefit his patron to a large extent. This matter was clearly forced upon his notice by a dream, in which he perceived one whom he then understood to be the benevolent spirit of an ancestor in the act of stroking a particular quail, upon whose chances he accordingly placed all he possessed. Doubtless evil spirits had been employed in the matter; for, to this person's great astonishment, the quail in question failed in a very discreditable manner at the encounter. Unfortunately, this person had risked not only the money which had been entrusted to him, but all that he had himself become possessed of by some years of honourable toil and assiduous courtesy as a professional witness in law cases. Not doubting that his patron would see that he was himself greatly to blame in confiding so large a sum of money to a comparatively young man of whom he knew little, this person placed the matter before him, at the same time showing him that he would suffer in the eyes of the virtuous if he did not restore this person's savings, which but for the presence of the larger sum, and a generous desire to benefit his patron, he would never have risked in so uncertain a venture as that of quail-fighting. Although the facts were laid in the form of a dignified request instead of a demand by legal means, and the reasoning carefully drawn up in columns on fine parchment by a very illustrious writer, the reply which this person received showed him plainly that a wrong view had been taken of the matter, and that the time had arrived when it became necessary for him to make a suitable rejoinder by leaving the city without delay.'

'It was a high-minded and disinterested course to take,' said Kai Lung with great conviction, as Lin Yi paused. 'Without doubt evil will shortly overtake the avaricious-souled person at Knei Yang.'

'It has already done so,' replied Lin Yi. 'While passing through this forest in the season of Many White Vapours, the spirits of his bad deeds appeared to him in misleading and symmetrical shapes, and drew him out of the path and away from his bowmen. After suffering many torments, he found his way here, where, in spite of our continual care, he perished miserably and in great bodily pain. . . . But I cannot conceal from myself, in spite of your distinguished politeness, that I am becoming intolerably tiresome with my commonplace talk.'

'On the contrary,' replied Kai Lung, 'while listening to your voice I seemed to hear the beating of many gongs of the finest and most polished brass. I floated in the Middle Air, and for the time I even became unconscious of the fact that this honourable appendage, though fashioned, as I perceive, out of the most delicate silk, makes it exceedingly difficult for me to breathe.'

'Such a thing cannot be permitted,' exclaimed Lin Yi, with some indignation, as with his own hands he slackened the rope, and, taking it from Kai Lung's neck, fastened it round his ankle. 'Now, in return for my uninviting confidences, shall not my senses be gladdened by a recital of the titles and honours borne by your distinguished family? Doubtless, at this moment many Mandarins of the highest degree are anxiously awaiting your arrival at Knei Yang, perhaps passing the time by outdoing one another in protesting the number of taels each would give rather than permit you to be tormented by fire-brands, or even to lose a single ear.'

'Alas!' replied Kai Lung, 'never was there a truer proverb than that which says, "It is a mark of insincerity of purpose to spend one's time in looking for the sacred Emperor in the low-class tea-shops." Do Mandarins or the friends of Mandarins travel in mean garments and unattended? Indeed, the person who is now before you is none other than the outcast Kai Lung, the story-teller, one of degraded habits and no very distinguished or reputable ancestors. His friends are few and mostly of the criminal class; his wealth is not more than some six or eight cash, concealed in his left sandal; and his entire stock-in-trade consists of a few unendurable and badly told stories, to which, however, it is his presumptuous intention shortly to add a dignified narrative of the high-born Lin Yi, setting out his domestic virtues and the honour which he has reflected upon his house, his valour in war, the destruction of his enemies, and, above all, his great benevolence and the protection which he extends to the poor and those engaged in the distinguished arts.'

'The absence of friends is unfortunate,' said Lin Yi thoughtfully, after he had possessed himself of the coins indicated by Kai Lung, and also of a much larger amount concealed elsewhere among the story-teller's clothing. 'My followers are mostly outlawed Miaotze, who have been driven from their own tribes in Yun Nan for man-eating and disregarding the sacred laws of hospitality. They are somewhat rapacious, and in this way it has become a custom that they should have as their own, for the purpose of exchanging for money, persons such as yourself, whose insatiable curiosity has led them to this place.'

'The wise and all-knowing Emperor Fohy instituted three degrees of attainment: Being poor, to obtain justice; being rich, to escape flattery; and being human, to avoid the passions,' replied Kai Lung. 'To these the practical and enlightened Kang added yet another, the greatest: Being lean, to yield fatness.'

'In such cases,' observed the brigand, 'the Miaotze keep

an honoured and very venerable rite, which chiefly consists in suspending the offender by the pigtail from a low tree, and placing burning twigs of hemp-palm between his toes. To this person it seems a foolish and meaningless habit; but it would not be well to interfere with their religious observances, however trivial they may appear.'

'Such a course must inevitably end in great loss,' suggested Kai Lung; 'for undoubtedly there are many poor yet honourable persons who would leave with them a bond for a large number of taels and save the money with which to redeem it, rather than take part in a ceremony which is not according to one's own Book of Rites.'

'They have already suffered in that way on one or two occasions,' replied Lin Yi; 'so that such a proposal, no matter how nobly intended, would not gladden their faces. Yet they are simple and docile persons, and would, without doubt, be moved to any feeling you should desire by the recital of one of your illustrious stories.'

'An intelligent and discriminating assemblage is more to a story-teller than much reward of cash from hands that conceal open mouths,' replied Kai Lung with great feeling. 'Nothing would confer more pleasurable agitation upon this unworthy person than an opportunity of narrating his entire stock to them. If also the accomplished Lin Yi would bestow renown upon the occasion by his presence, no omen of good would be wanting.'

'The pleasures of the city lie far behind me,' said Lin Yi, after some thought, 'and I would cheerfully submit myself to an intellectual accomplishment such as you are undoubtedly capable of. But as we have necessity to leave this spot before the hour when the oak-leaves change into night-moths, one of your amiable stories will be the utmost we can strengthen our intellects with. Select which you will. In the meantime, food will be brought to refresh you after your benevolent exertions in conversing with a person of my vapid understanding. When you have partaken, or thrown it away as utterly unendurable, the time will have arrived, and this person, together with all his accomplices, will put themselves in a position to be subjected to all the most dignified emotions.'

§ 2

'The story which I have selected for this gratifying occasion,' said Kai Lung, when, an hour or so later, still pinioned, but released from the halter, he sat surrounded by the brigands, 'is entitled "Good and Evil," and it is concerned with the adventures of one Ling, who bore the honourable name of Ho. The first, and indeed the greater, part of the narrative, as related by the venerable and accomplished writer of history Chow-Tan, is taken up by showing how Ling was assuredly descended from an enlightened Emperor of the race of Tsin; but as the no less omniscient Ta-lin-hi proves beyond doubt that the person in question was in no way connected with any but a line of hereditary ape-worshippers, who entered China from an unknown country many centuries ago, it would ill become this illiterate person to express an opinion on either side, and he will in consequence omit the first seventeen books of the story, and only deal with the three which refer to the illustrious Ling himself.'

THE TRANSMUTATION OF LING

THE STORY OF LING

Ling was the youngest of three sons, and from his youth upwards proved to be of a mild and studious disposition. Most of his time was spent in reading the sacred books, and at an early age he found the worship of apes to be repulsive to his gentle nature, and resolved to break through the venerable traditions of his family by devoting his time to literary pursuits, and presenting himself for the public examinations at Canton. In this his resolution was strengthened by a rumour that an army of bowmen was shortly to be raised from the Province in which he lived, so that if he remained he would inevitably be forced into an occupation which was even more distasteful to him than the one he was leaving.

Having arrived at Canton, Ling's first care was to obtain particulars of the examinations, which he clearly perceived, from the unusual activity displayed on all sides, to be near at hand. On inquiring from passers-by, he received very conflicting information; for the persons to whom he spoke were themselves entered for the competition, and therefore naturally misled him in order to increase their own chances of success. Perceiving this, Ling determined to apply at once, although the light was past, to a Mandarin who was concerned in the examinations, lest by delay he should lose his chance for the year.

'It is an unfortunate event that so distinguished a person should have selected this day and hour on which to overwhelm us with his affable politeness!' exclaimed the porter at the gate of the Yamên, when Ling had explained his reason for going. 'On such a day, in the reign of the virtuous Emperor Hoo Chow, a very benevolent and un-assuming ancestor of my good lord the Mandarin was destroyed by treachery, and ever since his family has observed the occasion by fasting and no music. This person would certainly be punished with death if he entered the inner room from any cause.'

At these words, Ling, who had been simply brought up, and chiefly in the society of apes, was going away with many expressions of self-reproach at selecting such a time, when the gate-keeper called him back.

'I am overwhelmed with confusion at the position in which I find myself,' he remarked, after he had examined his mind for a short time. 'I may meet with an ungraceful and objectionable death if I carry out your estimable instructions, but I shall certainly merit and receive a similar fate if I permit so renowned and versatile a person to leave without a fitting reception. In such matters a person can only trust to the intervention of good spirits; if, therefore, you will permit this unworthy individual to wear, while making the venture, the ring which he perceives upon your finger, and which he recognizes as a very powerful charm against evil, misunderstandings, and extortion, he will go without fear.'

Overjoyed at the amiable porter's efforts on his behalf, Ling did as he was desired, and the other retired. Presently the door of the Yamên was opened by an attendant of the house, and Ling bidden to enter. He was covered with astonishment to find that this person was entirely unacquainted with his name or purpose.

'Alas!' said the attendant, when Ling had explained his object, 'well said the renowned and inspired Ting Fo,

"When struck by a thunderbolt it is unnecessary to consult the Book of Dates as to the precise meaning of the omen." At this moment my noble-minded master is engaged in conversation with all the most honourable and refined persons in Canton, while singers and dancers of a very expert and nimble order have been sent for. The entertainment will undoubtedly last far into the night, and to present myself even with the excuse of your graceful and delicate inquiry would certainly result in very objectionable consequences to this person.'

'It is indeed a day of unprepossessing circumstanes,' replied Ling, and, after many honourable remarks concerning his own intellect and appearance, and those of the person to whom he was speaking, he had turned to leave when the other continued:

'Ever since your dignified presence illumined this very ordinary chamber, this person has been endeavouring to bring to his mind an incident which occurred to him last night while he slept. Now it has come back to him with a diamond clearness, and he is satisfied that it was as follows: While he floated in the Middle Air a benevolent spirit in the form of an elderly and toothless vampire appeared, leading by the hand a young man, of elegant personality. Smiling encouragingly upon this person, the spirit said, "O Fou, recipient of many favours from Mandarins and of innumerable taels from gratified persons whom you have obliged, I am, even at this moment, guiding this exceptional young man towards your presence; when he arrives do not hesitate, but do as he desires, no matter how great the danger seems or how inadequately you appear to be rewarded on earth." The vision then melted, but I now clearly perceive that, with the exception of the embroidered cloak which you wear, you are the person thus indicated to me. Remove your cloak, therefore, in order to give the amiable spirit no opportunity of denying the fact, and I will advance your wishes; for, as the Book of Verses indicates, "The person who patiently awaits a sign from the clouds for many years, and yet fails to notice the earthquake at his feet, is devoid of intellect." '

Convinced that he was assuredly under the especial protection of the Deities, and that the end of his search was in view, Ling gave his rich cloak to the attendant, and was immediately shown into another room, where he was left alone.

After a considerable space of time the door opened and there entered a person whom Ling at first supposed to be the Mandarin. Indeed, he was addressing him by his titles when the other interrupted him. 'Do not distress your incomparable mind by searching for honourable names to apply to so inferior a person as myself,' he said agreeably. 'The mistake is, nevertheless, very natural; for, however miraculous it may appear, this unseemly individual, who is in reality merely a writer of spoken words, is admitted to be exceedingly like the dignified Mandarin himself, though somewhat stouter, clad in better garments, and, it is said, less obtuse of intellect. This last matter he very much doubts, for he now finds himself unable to recognize by name one who is undoubtedly entitled to wear the Royal Yellow.'

With this encouragement Ling once more explained his position, narrating the events which had enabled him to reach the second chamber of the Yamên. When he had finished the secretary was overpowered with a high-minded indignation.

'Assuredly those depraved and rapacious persons who have both misled and robbed you shall suffer bow-stringing when the whole matter is brought to light,' he exclaimed. 'The noble Mandarin neither fasts nor receives guests, for, indeed, he has slept since the sun went down. This person would unhesitatingly break his slumber for so commendable a purpose were it not for a circumstance of intolerable unavoidableness. It must not even be told in a low breath beyond the walls of the Yamên, but my benevolent and high-born lord is in reality a person of very miserly instincts, and nothing will call him from his natural sleep but the sound of taels shaken beside his bed In an unexpected manner it comes about that this person is quite unsupplied with anything but thin printed papers of a thousand taels each, and these are quite useless for the purpose.'

'It is unendurable that so obliging a person should be put to such inconvenience on behalf of one who will certainly become a public laughing-stock at the examinations,' said Ling, with deep feeling; and taking from a concealed spot in his garments a few taels, he placed them before the secretary for the use he had indicated.

Ling was again left alone for upwards of two strokes of the gong, and was on the point of sleep when the secretary returned with an expression of dignified satisfaction upon his countenance. Concluding that he had been successful in the manner of awakening the Mandarin, Ling was opening his mouth for a polite speech, which should contain a delicate allusion to the taels, when the secretary warned him, by affecting a sudden look of terror, that silence was exceedingly desirable, and at the same time opened another door and indicated to Ling that he should pass through.

In the next room Ling was overjoyed to find himself in the presence of the Mandarin, who received him graciously, and paid many estimable compliments to the name he bore and the country from which he came. When at length Ling tore himself from this enchanting conversation, and explained the reason of his presence, the Mandarin at once became a prey to the whitest and most melancholy emotions, even plucking two hairs from his pigtail to prove the extent and conscientiousness of his grief.

'Behold,' he cried at length, 'I am resolved that the extortionate and many-handed persons at Pekin who have control of the examination rites and customs shall no longer grow round-bodied without remark. This person will un-hesitatingly proclaim the true facts of the case without regarding the danger that the versatile Chancellor or even the sublime Emperor himself may, while he speaks, be concealed in some part of this unassuming room to hear his words; for, as it is wisely said, "When marked out by destiny, a person will assuredly be drowned, even though he passes the whole of his existence among the highest branches of a date tree." '

'I am overwhelmed that I should be the cause of such an engaging display of polished agitation,' said Ling, as the Mandarin paused. 'If it would make your own stomach less heavy, this person will willingly follow your estimable example, either with or without knowing the reason.'

'The matter is altogether on your account, O most un-obtrusive young man,' replied the Mandarin, when a voice without passion was restored to him. 'It tears me internally with hooks to reflect that you, whose refined ancestors I might reasonably have known had I passed my youth in another Province, should be a victim to the cupidity of the ones in authority at Pekin. A very short time before you arrived there came a messenger in haste from those persons, clearly indicating that a legal toll of sixteen taels was to be made on each printed paper setting forth the times and manner of the examinations, although, as you may see, the paper is undoubtedly marked, "Persons are given notice that they are defrauded of any sum which they may be induced to exchange for this matter." Furthermore, there is a legal toll of nine taels on all persons who have previously been examined –'

'I am happily escaped from that,' exclaimed Ling with some satisfaction as the Mandarin paused.

' – and twelve taels on all who present themselves for the first time. This is to be delivered over when the paper is purchased, so that you, by reason of this unworthy proceeding at Pekin, are required to forward to that place, through this person, no less than thirty-two taels.'

'It is a circumstance of considerable regret,' replied Ling; 'for had I only reached Canton a day earlier I should, it appears, have avoided this evil.'

'Undoubtedly it would have been so,' replied the Mandarin, who had become engrossed in exalted meditation. 'However,' he continued a moment later, as he bowed to Ling with an accomplished smile, 'it would certainly be a more pleasant thought for a person of your refined intelligence that had you delayed until to-morrow the insatiable persons at Pekin might be demanding twice the amount.'

Pondering the deep wisdom of this remark, Ling took his departure; but in spite of the most assiduous watchfulness he was unable to discern any of the three obliging persons to whose efforts his success had been due.

§ 3

It was very late when Ling again reached the small room which he had selected as soon as he reached Canton, but without waiting for food or sleep he made himself fully acquainted with the times of the forthcoming examinations and the details of the circumstances connected with them. With much satisfaction he found that he had still a week in which to revive his intellect on the most difficult subjects. Having become relieved on these points, Ling retired for a few hours' sleep, but rose again very early, and gave the whole day with great steadfastness to contemplation of the sacred classics Y-King, with the exception of a short period spent in purchasing ink, brushes, and writing-leaves. The following day, having become mentally depressed through witnessing unaccountable hordes of candidates thronging the streets of Canton, Ling put aside his books, and passed the time in visiting all the most celebrated tombs in the neighbourhood of the city. Lightened in mind by this charitable and agreeable occupation, he returned to his studies with a fixed resolution, nor did he again falter in his purpose.

On the evening of the examination, when he was sitting alone, reading by the aid of a single light, as his custom was, a person arrived to see him, at the same time manifesting a considerable appearance of secrecy and reserve. Inwardly sighing at the interruption, Ling nevertheless received him with distinguished consideration and respect, setting tea before him, and performing towards it many honourable actions with his own hands. Not until some hours had sped in conversation relating to the health of the Emperor, the unexpected appearance of a fiery dragon outside the city, and the insupportable price of opium, did the visitor allude to the object of his presence.

'It has been observed,' he remarked, 'that the accomplished Ling, who aspires to a satisfactory rank at the examinations, has never before made the attempt. Doubtless in this case a preternatural wisdom will avail much, and its fortunate possessor will not go unrewarded. Yet it is as precious stones among ashes for one to triumph in such circumstances.'

'The fact is known to this person,' replied Ling sadly, 'and the thought of the years he may have to wait before he shall have passed even the first degree weighs down his soul with bitterness from time to time.'

'It is no infrequent thing for men of accomplished perseverance, but merely ordinary intellects, to grow venerable within the four walls of the examination cell,' continued the other. 'Some, again, become afflicted with various malignant evils, while not a few, chiefly those who are presenting themselves for the first time, are so overcome on perceiving the examination paper, and understanding the inadequate nature of their own accomplishments, that they become an easy prey to the malicious spirits which are ever on the watch in those places; and, after covering their leaves with unpresentable remarks and drawings of men and women of distinguished rank, have at length to be forcibly carried away by the attendants and secured with heavy chains.'

'Such things undoubtedly exist,' agreed Ling; 'yet by a due regard paid to spirits, both good and bad, a proper esteem for one's ancestors, and a sufficiency of charms about the head and body, it is possible to be closeted with all manner of demons and yet to suffer no evil.'

'It is undoubtedly possible to do so, according to the Immortal Principles,' admitted the stranger; 'but it is not an undertaking in which a refined person would take intelligent pleasure; as the proverb says, "He is a wise and enlightened suppliant who seeks to discover an honourable Mandarin, but he is a fool who cries out, 'I have found one.'" However, it is obvious that the reason of my visit is understood, and that your distinguished confidence in yourself is merely a graceful endeavour to obtain my services for a less amount of taels than I should otherwise have demanded. For half the usual sum, therefore, this person will take your place in the examination cell, and enable your versatile name to appear in the winning lists, while you pass your moments in irreproachable pleasures elsewhere.'

Such a course had never presented itself to Ling. As the person who narrates this story has already remarked, he had passed his life beyond the influence of the ways and manners of towns, and at the same time he had naturally been endowed with an unobtrusive highmindedness. It appeared to him, in consequence, that by accepting this engaging offer, he would be placing those who were competing with him at a disadvantage. This person clearly sees that it is a difficult matter for him to explain how this could be, as Ling would undoubtedly reward the services of the one who took his place, nor would the number of the competitors be in any way increased; yet in such a way the thing took shape before his eyes. Knowing, however, that few persons would be able to understand this action, and being desirous of not injuring the estimable emotions of the obliging person who had come to him, Ling made a number of polished excuses in declining, hiding the true reason within himself. In this way he earned the powerful malignity of the person in question, who would not depart until he had effected a number of very disagreeable prophecies connected with unpropitious omens and internal torments, all of which undoubtedly had a great influence on Ling's life beyond that time.

Each day of the examination found Ling alternately elated or depressed, according to the length and style of the essay which he had written while enclosed in his solitary examination cell. The trials each lasted a complete day, and long before the fifteen days which composed the full examination were passed, Ling found himself half regretting that he had not accepted his visitor's offer, or even reviling the day on which he had abandoned the hereditary calling of his ancestors. However, when, after all was over, he came to deliberate with himself on his chances of attaining a degree, he could not disguise from his own mind that he had well-formed hopes; he was not conscious of any undignified errors, and, in reply to several questions, he had been able to introduce curious knowledge which he possessed by means of his exceptional circumstances – knowledge which it was unlikely that any other candidate would have been able to make himself master of.

At length the day arrived on which the results were to be made public; and Ling, together with all the other competitors and many distinguished persons, attended at the great Hall of Intellectual Coloured Lights to hear the reading of the lists. Eight thousand candidates had been examined, and from this number less than two hundred were to be selected for appointments. Amid a most distinguished silence the winning names were read out. Waves of most undignified but inevitable emotion passed over those assembled as the list neared its end, and the chances of success became less at each spoken word. Nevertheless, Ling hoped till the last name was given forth; and then, finding that his was not among them, together with the greater part of those present, he became a prey to very inelegant thoughts, which were not lessened by the refined cries of triumph of the successful persons. Among this confusion the one who had read the lists was observed to be endeavouring to make his voice known, whereupon, in the expectation that he had omitted a name, the tumult was quickly subdued by those who again had pleasurable visions.

'There was among the candidates one of the name of Ling,' said he, when no noise had been obtained. 'The written leaves produced by this person are of a most versatile and conflicting order, so that, indeed, the accomplished examiners themselves are unable to decide whether they are very good or very bad. In this matter, therefore, it is clearly impossible to place the expert and inimitable Ling among the foremost, as his very uncertain success may have been brought about with the assistance of evil spirits; nor would it be safe to pass over his efforts without reward, as he may be under the protection of powerful but exceedingly ill-advised deities. The estimable Ling is told to appear again at this place after the gong has been struck three times, when the matter will have been looked at from all round.'

At this announcement there arose another great tumult, several crying out that assuredly their written leaves were either very good or very bad; but no further proclamation was made, and very soon the hall was cleared by force.

At the time stated Ling again presented himself at the Hall, and was honourably received.

'The unusual circumstances of the matter have already been put forth,' said an elderly Mandarin of engaging appearance, 'so that nothing remains to be made known except the end of our despicable efforts to come to an agreeable conclusion. In this we have been successful, and now desire to notify the result. A very desirable and not unremunerative office, rarely bestowed in this manner, is lately vacant, and taking into our minds the circumstances of the event, and the fact that Ling comes from a Province very esteemed for the warlike instincts of its inhabitants, we have decided to appoint him commander of the valiant and blood-thirsty band of archers now stationed at Si-chow, in the Province of Hu Nan. We have spoken. Let three guns go off in honour of the noble and invincible Ling, now and henceforth a commander in the ever-victorious Army of the Sublime Emperor, Brother of the Sun and Moon, and Upholder of the Four Corners of the World.'

§ 4

Many hours passed before Ling, now more downcast in mind than the most unsuccessful student in Canton, returned to his room and sought his couch of dried rushes. All his efforts to have his distinguished appointment set aside had been without avail, and he had been ordered to reach Si-chow within a week. As he passed through the streets, elegant processions in honour of the winners met him at every corner, and drove him into the outskirts for

27

the object of quietness. There he remained until the beating of paper drums and the sound of exulting voices could be heard no more; but even when he returned lanterns shone in many dwellings, for two hundred persons were composing verses, setting forth their renown and undoubted accomplishments, ready to affix to their doors and send to friends on the next day.

Not giving any portion of his mind to this desirable act of behaviour, Ling flung himself upon the floor, and, finding sleep unattainable, plunged himself into profound meditation of a very uninviting order.

'Without doubt,' he exclaimed, 'evil can only arise from evil, and as this person has always endeavoured to lead a life in which his devotions have been equally divided between the sacred Emperor, his illustrious parents, and his venerable ancestors, the fault cannot lie with him. Of the excellence of his parents he has full knowledge; regarding the Emperor, it might not be safe to conjecture. It is therefore probable that some of his ancestors were persons of abandoned manner and inelegant habits, to worship whom results in evil rather than good. Otherwise, how could it be that one, whose chief delight lies in the passive contemplation of the Four Books and the Five Classics, should be selected by destiny to fill a position calling for great personal courage and an aggressive nature? Assuredly it can only end in a mean and insignificant death, perhaps not even followed by burial.'

In this manner of thought he fell asleep, and after certain very base and impressive dreams, from which good omens were altogether absent, he awoke, and rose to begin his preparations for leaving the city.

After two days spent chiefly in obtaining certain safe-

guards against treachery and the bullets of foemen, purchasing opium and other gifts with which to propitiate
the soldiers under his charge, and in consulting well-
disposed witches and readers of the future, he set out, and
by travelling in extreme discomfort reached Si-chow
within five days. During his journey he learned that the
entire Province was engaged in secret rebellion, several
towns, indeed, having declared against the Imperial army
without reserve. Those persons to whom Ling spoke
described the rebels, with respectful admiration, as fierce
and unnaturally skilful in all methods of fighting, revenge-
ful and merciless towards their enemies, very numerous
and above the ordinary height of human beings, and
endowed with qualities which made their skin capable of
turning aside every kind of weapon. Furthermore, he was
assured that a large band of the most abandoned and best
trained was at that moment in the immediate neighbourhood of Si-chow.

Ling was not destined long to remain in any doubt
concerning the truth of these matters, for as he made his
way through a dark cypress wood, a few li from the houses
of Si-chow, the sounds of a confused outcry reached his
ears, and on stepping aside to a hidden glade some distance
from the path, he beheld a young and elegant maiden of
incomparable beauty being carried away by two persons
of most repulsive and undignified appearance, whose dress
and manner clearly betrayed them to be rebels of the
lowest and worst-paid type. At this sight Ling became
possessed of feelings of a savage yet agreeable order, which
until that time he had not conjectured to have any place
within his mind, and without even pausing to consider
whether the planets were in favourable positions for the

enterprise to be undertaken at that time, he drew his sword, and ran forward with loud cries. Unsettled in their intentions at this unexpected action, the two persons turned and advanced upon Ling with whirling daggers, discussing among themselves whether it would be better to kill him at the first blow or to take him alive, and, when the day had become sufficiently cool for the full enjoyment of the spectacle, submit him to various objectionable tortures of so degraded a nature that they were rarely used in the army of the Emperor except upon the persons of barbarians. Observing that the maiden was not bound, Ling cried out to her to escape and seek protection within the town, adding, with a magnanimous absence of vanity:

'Should this person chance to fall, the repose which the presence of so lovely and graceful a being would undoubtedly bring to his departing spirit would be outbalanced by the unendurable thought that his commonplace efforts had not been sufficient to save her from the two evilly disposed individuals who are, as he perceives, at this moment, neglecting no means within their power to accomplish his destruction.'

Accepting the discernment of these words, the maiden fled, first bestowing a look upon Ling which clearly indicated an honourable regard for himself, a high-minded desire that the affair might end profitably on his account, and an amiable hope that they should meet again, when these subjects could be expressed more clearly between them.

In the meantime Ling had become at a disadvantage, for the time occupied in speaking and in making the necessary number of bows in reply to her entrancing glance had given the other persons an opportunity of arranging their charms and sacred written sentences to greater advantage, and of occupying the most favourable ground for the encounter. Nevertheless, so great was the force of the new emotion which had entered into Ling's nature that, without waiting to consider the dangers or the best method of attack, he rushed upon them, waving his sword with such force that he appeared as though surrounded by a circle of very brilliant fire. In this way he reached the rebels, who both fell unexpectedly at one blow, they, indeed, being under the impression that the encounter had not commenced in reality, and that Ling was merely menacing them in order to inspire their minds with terror and raise his own spirits. However much he regretted this act of the incident which he had been compelled to take, Ling could not avoid being filled with intellectual joy at finding that his own charms and omens were more distinguished than those possessed by the rebels, none of whom, as he now plainly understood, he need fear.

Examining these things within his mind, and reflecting on the events of the past few days, by which he had been thrown into a class of circumstances greatly differing from anything which he had ever sought, Ling continued his journey, and soon found himself before the southern gate of Si-chow. Entering the town, he at once formed the resolution of going before the Mandarin for Warlike Deeds and Arrangements, so that he might present, without delay, the papers and seals which he had brought with him from Canton.

'The noble Mandarin Li Keen?' replied the first person to whom Ling addressed himself. 'It would indeed be a difficult and hazardous conjecture to make concerning his sacred person. By chance he is in the strongest and best-concealed cellar in Si-chow, unless the sumptuous attractions of the deepest dry well have induced him to make a short journey'; and, with a look of great unfriendliness at Ling's dress and weapons, this person passed on.

'Doubtless, he is fighting single-handed against the armed men by whom the place is surrounded,' said another; 'or perhaps he is constructing an underground road from the Yamên to Pekin, so that we may all escape when the town is taken. All that can be said with certainty is that the Heaven-sent and valorous Mandarin has not been seen outside the walls of his well-fortified residence since the trouble arose; but, as you carry a sword of conspicuous excellence, you will doubtless be welcome.'

Upon making a third attempt Ling was more successful, for he inquired of an aged woman, who had neither a reputation for keen and polished sentences to maintain, nor any interest in the acts of the Mandarin or of the rebels. From her he learned how to reach the Yamên, and accordingly turned his footsteps in that direction.

When at length he arrived at the gate, Ling desired his tablets to be carried to the Mandarin with many expressions of an impressive and engaging nature, nor did he neglect to reward the porter. It was therefore with the expression of a misunderstanding mind that he received a reply setting forth that Li Keen was unable to receive him. In great doubt he prevailed upon the porter, by means of a still larger reward, again to carry in his message, and on this occasion an answer in this detail was placed before him.

'Li Keen,' he was informed, 'is indeed awaiting the arrival of one Ling, a noble and valiant Commander of Bowmen. He is given to understand, it is true, that a certain person claiming the same honoured name is standing in somewhat undignified attitudes at the gate, but he is unable in any way to make these two individuals meet within his intellect. He would further remind all persons that the refined observances laid down by the wise and exalted Board of Rites and Ceremonies have a marked and irreproachable significance when the country is in a state of disorder, the town surrounded by rebels, and every breathing-space of time of more than ordinary value.'

Overpowered with becoming shame at having been connected with so unseemly a breach of civility, for which his great haste had in reality been accountable, Ling hastened back into the town, and spent many hours in endeavouring to obtain a chair of the requisite colour in which to visit the Mandarin. In this he was unsuccessful, until it was at length suggested to him that an ordinary chair, such as stood for hire in the streets of Si-chow, would be acceptable if covered with blue paper. Still in some doubt as to what the nature of his reception would be, Ling had no choice but to take this course, and accordingly he again reached the Yamên in such a manner, carried by two persons whom he had obtained for the purpose. While yet hardly at the residence a salute was suddenly fired; all the gates and doors were, without delay, thrown open with embarrassing and hospitable profusion, and the Mandarin himself passed out, and would have assisted Ling to step down from his chair had not that person, clearly perceiving that such a course would be too great an honour, evaded him by an unobtrusive display of versatile dexterity. So numerous and profound were the graceful remarks which each made concerning the habits and accomplishments of the other that more than the space of an hour was passed in traversing the small enclosed ground which led up to the principal door of the Yamên. There an almost greater time was agreeably spent, both Ling and the Mandarin having determined that the other should enter first. Undoubtedly Ling, who was the more powerful of the two, would have conferred this courteous distinction upon Li Keen had not that person summoned to his side certain attendants who succeeded in frustrating Ling in his high-minded intentions, and in forcing him through the doorway in spite of his conscientious protests against the unsurmountable obligation under which the circumstance placed him.

Conversing in this intellectual and dignified manner, the strokes of the gong passed unheeded; tea had been brought into their presence many times, and night had fallen before the Mandarin allowed Ling to refer to the matter which had brought him to that place, and to present his written papers and seals.

'It is a valuable privilege to have so intelligent a person as the illustrious Ling occupying this position,' remarked the Mandarin, as he returned the papers; 'and not less so on account of the one who preceded him proving himself to be a person of feeble attainments and an unendurable deficiency of resource.'

'To one with the all-knowing Li Keen's mental acquisitions, such a person must indeed have become excessively offensive,' replied Ling delicately; 'for, as it is truly said, "Although there exist many thousand subjects for elegant conversation, there are persons who cannot meet a cripple without talking about feet."'

'He to whom I have referred was such a one,' said Li Keen, appreciating with an expression of countenance the fitness of Ling's proverb. 'He was totally inadequate to the requirements of his position; for he possessed no military knowledge, and was placed in command by those at Pekin as a result of his taking a high place at one of the examinations. But more than this, although his three years of service were almost completed, I was quite unsuccessful in convincing him that an unseemly degradation probably awaited him unless he could furnish me with the means with which to propitiate the persons in authority at Pekin. This he neglected to do with obstinate pertinacity, which compelled this person to inquire within himself whether one of so little discernment could be trusted with an important and arduous office. After much deliberation, this person came to the decision that the Commander in question was not a fit person, and he therefore reported him to the Imperial Board of Punishment at Pekin as one subject to frequent and periodical eccentricities, and possessed of less than ordinary intellect. In consequence of this act of justice, the Commander was degraded to the rank of common bowman, and compelled to pay a heavy fine in addition.'

'It was a just and enlightened conclusion of the affair,' said Ling, in spite of a deep feeling of no enthusiasm, 'and one which surprisingly bore out your own prophecy in the matter.'

'It was an inspired warning to persons who should chance to be in a like position at any time,' replied Li Keen. 'So grasping and corrupt are those who control affairs in Pekin that I have no doubt they would scarcely hesitate in debasing even one so immaculate as the exceptional Ling, and placing him in some laborious and ill-paid civil department should he not accede to their extortionate demands.'

35

This suggestion did not carry with it the unpleasurable emotions which the Mandarin anticipated it would. The fierce instincts which had been aroused within Ling by the incident in the cypress wood had died out, while his lamentable ignorance of military affairs was ever before his mind. These circumstances, together with his naturally gentle habits, made him regard such a degradation rather favourably than otherwise. He was meditating within himself whether he could arrange such a course without delay when the Mandarin continued:

'That, however, is a possibility which is remote to the extent of at least two or three years; do not, therefore, let so unpleasing a thought cast darkness upon our brows or remove the unparalleled splendour of so refined an occasion. . . . Doubtless the accomplished Ling is a master of the art of chess-play, for many of our most thoughtful philosophers have declared war to be nothing but such a game; let this slow-witted and cumbersome person have an opportunity, therefore, of polishing his declining faculties by a pleasant and dignified encounter.'

§ 5

On the next day, having completed his business at the Yamên, Ling left the town, and without desiring any ceremony quietly betook himself to his new residence within the camp, which was situated among the millet fields some distance from Si-chow. As soon as his presence became known all those who occupied positions of command, and whose years of service would shortly come to an end, hastened to present themselves before him, bringing with them offerings according to the rank they held, they themselves requiring a similar service from those

36

beneath them. First among these, and next in command to Ling himself, was the Chief of Bowmen, a person whom Ling observed with extreme satisfaction to be very powerful in body and possessing a strong and dignified countenance which showed unquestionable resolution and shone with a tiger-like tenaciousness of purpose.

'Undoubtedly,' thought Ling, as he observed this noble and prepossessing person, 'here is one who will be able to assist me in whatever perplexities may arise. Never was there an individual who seemed more worthy to command and lead; assuredly to him the most intricate and prolonged military positions will be an enjoyment; the most crafty stratagems of the enemy as the full moon rising from behind a screen of rushes. Without making any pretence of knowledge, this person will explain the facts of the case to him and place himself without limit in his hands.'

For this purpose he therefore detained the Chief of Bowmen when the others departed, and complimented him, with many expressive phrases, on the excellence of his appearance, as the thought occurred to him that by this means, without disclosing the full measure of his ignorance, the person in question might be encouraged to speak unrestrainedly of the nature of his exploits, and perchance thereby explain the uses of the appliances employed and the meaning of the various words of order, in all of which details the Commander was as yet most disagreeably imperfect. In this, however, he was disappointed, for the Chief of Bowmen, greatly to Ling's surprise, received all his polished sentences with somewhat foolish smiles of great self-satisfaction, merely replying from time to time as he displayed his pigtail to greater advantage or rearranged his gold-embroidered cloak:

'This person must really pray you to desist; the honour is indeed too great.'

Disappointed in his hope, and not desiring after this circumstance to expose his shortcomings to one who was obviously not of a highly refined understanding, no matter how great his valour in war or his knowledge of military affairs might be, Ling endeavoured to lead him to converse of the bowmen under his charge. In this matter he was more successful, for the Chief spoke at great length and with evilly inspired contempt of their inelegance, their undiscriminating and excessive appetites, and the frequent use which they made of low words and gestures. Desiring to become acquainted rather with their methods of warfare than with their domestic details, Ling inquired of him what formation they relied upon when receiving the foemen.

'It is a matter which has not engaged the attention of this one,' replied the Chief, with an excessive absence of interest. 'There are so many affairs of intelligent dignity which cannot be put aside, and which occupy one from beginning to end. As an example, this person may describe how the accomplished Li-Lu, generally depicted as the Blue-eyed Dove of Virtuous and Serpent-like Attitudes, has been scattering glory upon the Si-chow Hall of Celestial Harmony for many days past. It is an enlightened display which the high-souled Ling should certainly endeavour to dignify with his presence, especially at the portion where the amiable Li-Lu becomes revealed in the appearance of a Pekin sedan-chair bearer and describes the manner and likenesses of certain persons – chiefly high-priests of Buddha, excessively round-bodied merchants who feign to be detained within Pekin on affairs of commerce, maidens who attend at the tables of tea-houses, and those of both sexes who are within the city for the first time to behold its temples and open spaces – who are conveyed from place to place in the chair.'

'And the bowmen?' suggested Ling, with difficulty restraining an undignified emotion.

'Really, the elegant Ling will discover them to be persons of deficient manners, and quite unworthy of occupying his well-bred conversation,' replied the Chief. 'As regards their methods – if the renowned Ling insists – they fight by means of their bows, with which they discharge arrows at the foemen, they themselves hiding behind trees and rocks. Should the enemy be undisconcerted by the cloud of arrows, and advance, the bowmen are instructed to make a last endeavour to frighten them back by uttering loud shouts and feigning the voices of savage beasts of the forest and deadly snakes.'

'And beyond that?' inquired Ling.

'Beyond that there are no instructions,' replied the Chief. 'The bowmen would then naturally take to flight, or, if such a course became impossible, run to meet the enemy, protesting that they were convinced of the justice of their cause, and were determined to fight on their side in the future.'

'Would it not be of advantage to arm them with cutting weapons also?' inquired Ling; 'so that when all their arrows were discharged they would still be able to take part in the fight, and not be lost to us?'

'They would not be lost to *us*, of course,' replied the Chief, 'as we should still be with them. But such a course as the one you suggest could not fail to end in dismay. Being as well armed as ourselves, they would then turn upon us, and, having destroyed us, proceed to establish leaders of their own.'

As Ling and the Chief of Bowmen conversed in this enlightened manner, there arose a great outcry from among the tents, and presently there entered to them a spy who had discovered a strong force of the enemy not more than ten or twelve li away, who showed every indication of marching shortly in the direction of Si-chow. In numbers alone, he continued, they were greatly superior to the bowmen, and all were well armed. The spreading of this news threw the entire camp into great confusion, many protesting that the day was not a favourable one on which to fight, others crying out that it was their duty to fall back on Si-chow and protect the women and children. In the midst of this tumult the Chief of Bowmen returned to Ling, bearing in his hand a written paper which he regarded in uncontrollable anguish.

'Oh, illustrious Ling,' he cried, restraining his grief with difficulty, and leaning for support upon the shoulders of two bowmen, 'how prosperous indeed are you! What greater misfortune can engulf a person who is both an ambitious soldier and an affectionate son, than to lose such a chance of glory and promotion as only occurs once within the lifetime, and an affectionate and venerable father upon the same day? Behold this mandate to attend, without a moment's delay, at the funeral obsequies of one whom I left, only last week, in the fullness of health and power. The occasion being an unsuitable one, I will not call upon the courteous Ling to join with me in sorrow; but his own devout filial piety is so well known that I conscientiously rely upon an application for absence to be only a matter of official ceremony.'

40

'The application will certainly be regarded as merely official ceremony,' replied Ling, without resorting to any delicate pretence of meaning, 'and the refined scruples of the person who is addressing me will be fully met by the official date of his venerated father's death being fixed for a more convenient season. In the meantime, the unobtrusive Chief of Bowmen may take the opportunity of requesting that the family tomb be kept unsealed until he is heard from again.'

Ling turned away, as he finished this remark, with a dignified feeling of not inelegant resentment. In this way he chanced to observe a large body of soldiers which was leaving the camp accompanied by their lesser captains, all crowned with garlands of flowers and creeping plants. In spite of his very inadequate attainments regarding words of order, the Commander made it understood by means of an exceedingly short sentence that he was desirous of the men returning without delay.

'Doubtless the accomplished Commander, being but newly arrived in this neighbourhood, is unacquainted with the significance of this display,' said one of the lesser captains pleasantly. 'Know, then, O wise and custom-respecting Ling, that on a similar day many years ago this valiant band of bowmen was engaged in a very honourable affair with certain of the enemy. Since then it has been the practice to commemorate the matter with music and other forms of delight within the large square at Si-chow.'

'Such customs are excellent,' said Ling affably. 'On this occasion, however, the public square will be so insufferably thronged with the number of timorous and credulous villagers who have pressed into the town that insufficient justice would be paid to your entrancing display. In consequence of this, we will select for the purpose some convenient spot in the neighbourhood. The proceedings will be commenced by a display of arrow-shooting at moving objects, followed by racing and dancing, in which this person will lead. I have spoken.'

At these words many of the more courageous among the bowmen became destructively inspired, and raised shouts of defiance against the enemy, enumerating at great length the indignities which they would heap upon their prisoners. Cries of distinction were also given on behalf of Ling, even the most terrified exclaiming:

'The noble Commander Ling will lead us! He has promised, and assuredly he will not depart from his word. Shielded by his broad and sacred body, from which the bullets glance aside harmlessly, we will advance upon the enemy in the stealthy manner affected by ducks when crossing the swamp. How altogether superior a person our Commander is when likened unto the leaders of the foemen — they who go into battle completely surrounded by their archers!'

Upon this, perceiving the clear direction in which matters were turning, the Chief of Bowmen again approached Ling.

'Doubtless the highly favoured person whom I am now addressing has been endowed with exceptional authority direct from Pekin,' he remarked, with insidious politeness. 'Otherwise this narrow-minded individual would suggest that such a decision does not come within the judgment of a Commander.'

In his ignorance of military matters, it had not entered the mind of Ling that his authority did not give him the power to commence an attack without consulting other and more distinguished persons. At the suggestion, which he accepted as being composed of truth, he paused, the enlightened zeal with which he had been inspired dying out as he plainly understood the difficulties by which he was enclosed. There seemed a single expedient path for him in the matter; so directing a person of exceptional trustworthiness to prepare himself for a journey, he inscribed a communication to the Mandarin Li Keen, in which he narrated the facts and asked for speedy directions, and then despatched it with great urgency to Si-chow.

§ 6

When these matters were arranged, Ling returned to his tent, a victim to feelings of a deep and confused doubt, for all courses seemed to be surrounded by extreme danger, with the strong probability of final disaster. While he was considering these things attentively, the spy who had brought word of the presence of the enemy again sought him. As he entered, Ling perceived that his face was the colour of a bleached linen garment, while there came with him the odour of sickness.

'There are certain matters which this person has not made known,' he said, having first expressed a request that he might not be compelled to stand while he conversed. 'The bowmen are as an inferior kind of jackal, and they who lead them are pigs, but this person has observed that the Heaven-sent Commander has internal organs like steel hardened in a white fire and polished by running water. For this reason he will narrate to him the things he has seen — things at which the lesser ones would undoubtedly perish in terror without offering to strike a blow.'

43

'Speak,' said Ling, 'without fear and without conceal-ment.'

'In numbers the rebels are as three to one with the bowmen, and are, in addition, armed with matchlocks and other weapons; this much I have already told,' said the spy. 'Yesterday they entered the village of Ki without resistance, as the dwellers there were all peaceable persons, who gain a living from the fields, and who neither under-stood nor troubled about the matters between the rebels and the army. Relying on the promises made by the rebel chiefs, the villagers even welcomed them, as they had been assured that they came as buyers of their corn and rice. To-day not a house stands in the street of Ki, not a person lives. The men they slew quickly, or held for torture, as they desired at the moment; the boys they hung from the trees as marks for their arrows. Of the women and children this person, who has since been sub-ject to several attacks of fainting and vomiting, desires not to speak. The wells of Ki are filled with the bodies of such as had the good fortune to be warned in time to slay themselves. The cattle drag themselves from place to place on their forefeet; the fish in the Heng-Kiang are dying, for they cannot live in water thickened into blood. All these things this person has seen.'

When he had finished speaking, Ling remained in deep and funereal thought for some time. In spite of his mild nature, the words which he had heard filled him with an inextinguishable desire to slay in hand-to-hand fighting. He regretted that he had placed the decision of the matter before Li Keen.

'If only this person had a mere handful of brave and expert warriors, he would not hesitate to fall upon those savage and barbarous characters, and either destroy them to the last one, or let his band suffer a like fate,' he murmured to himself.

The return of the messenger found him engaged in reviewing the bowmen, and still in this mood, so that it was with a commendable feeling of satisfaction, no less than virtuous contempt, that he learned of the Mandarin's journey to Pekin as soon as he understood that the rebels were certainly in the neighbourhood.

'The wise and ornamental Li Keen is undoubtedly consistent in all matters,' said Ling, with some refined bitterness. 'The only information regarding his duties which this person obtained from him chanced to be a likening of war to skilful chess-play, and to this end the accomplished person in question has merely availed himself of a common expedient which places him at the remote side of the divine Emperor. Yet this act is not unwelcome, for the responsibility of deciding what course is to be adopted now clearly rests with this person. He is, as those who are standing by may perceive, of under the usual height, and of no particular mental or bodily attainments. But he has eaten the rice of the Emperor, and wears the Imperial sign embroidered upon his arm. Before him are encamped the enemies of his master and of his land, and in no way will he turn his back upon them. Against brave and skilful men, such as those whom this person commands, rebels of a low and degraded order are powerless, and are, moreover, openly forbidden to succeed by the Forty-second Mandate in the Sacred Book of Arguments. Should it have happened that into this assembly any person of a perfidious or uncourageous nature has gained entrance by guile, and has been undetected and driven forth by his

45

outraged companions (as would certainly occur if such a person were discovered), I, Ling, Commander of Bowmen, make an especial and well-considered request that he shall be struck by a molten thunderbolt if he turns to flight or holds thoughts of treachery.'

Having thus addressed and encouraged the soldiers, Ling instructed them that each one should cut and fashion for himself a graceful but weighty club from among the branches of the trees around, and then return to the tents for the purpose of receiving food and rice spirit.

When noon was passed, allowing such time as would enable him to reach the camp of the enemy an hour before darkness, Ling arranged the bowmen in companies of convenient numbers, and commenced the march, sending forward spies, who were to work silently and bring back tidings from every point. In this way he penetrated to within a single li of the ruins of Ki, being informed by the spies that no outposts of the enemy were between him and that place. Here the first rest was made to enable the more accurate and bold spies to reach them with trustworthy information regarding the position and movements of the camp. With little delay there returned the one who had brought the earliest tidings, bruised and torn with his successful haste through the forest, but wearing a complacent and well-satisfied expression of countenance. Without hesitation or waiting to demand money before he would reveal his knowledge, he at once disclosed that the greater part of the enemy were rejoicing among the ruins of Ki, they having discovered there a quantity of opium and a variety of liquids, while only a small guard remained in the camp with their weapons ready. At these words Ling sprang from the ground in gladness, so great was his certainty of destroying the invaders utterly. It was, however, with less pleasurable emotions that he considered how he should effect the matter, for it was in no way advisable to divide his numbers into two bands. Without any feeling of unendurable conceit, he understood that no one but himself could hold the bowmen before an assault, however weak. In a similar manner he determined that it would be more advisable to attack those in the village first. These he might have reasonable hopes of cutting down without warning the camp, or, in any event, before those from the camp arrived. To assail the camp first would assuredly, by the firing, draw down upon them those from the village, and in whatever evil state these might arrive, they would, by their numbers, terrify the bowmen, who without doubt would have suffered some loss from the matchlocks.

Waiting for the last light of the day, Ling led on the men again, and sending forward some of the most reliable, surrounded the place of the village silently and without detection. In the open space, among broken casks and other inconsiderable matters, plainly shown by the large fires at which burned the last remains of the houses of Ki, many men moved or lay, some already dull or in heavy sleep. As the darkness dropped suddenly, the signal of a peacock's shriek, three times uttered, rang forth, and immediately a cloud of arrows, directed from all sides, poured in among those who feasted. Seeing their foemen defenceless before them, the archers neglected the orders they had received, and throwing away their bows, they rushed in with uplifted clubs, uttering loud shouts of triumph. The next moment a shot was fired in the wood, drums beat, and in an unbelievably short space of time a small but well-armed band of the enemy was among them. Now that all need of caution was at an end, Ling rushed forward with raised sword, calling to his men that victory was certainly theirs, and dealing discriminating and inspiriting blows whenever he met a foeman. Three times he formed the bowmen into a figure emblematic of triumph, and led them against the line of matchlocks. Twice they fell back, leaving mingled dead under the feet of the enemy. The third time they stood firm, and Ling threw himself against the waving rank in a noble and inspired endeavour to lead the way through. At that moment, when a very distinguished victory seemed within his hand, his elegant and well-constructed sword broke upon an iron shield, leaving him defenceless and surrounded by the enemy.

'Chief among the sublime virtues enjoined by the divine Confucius,' began Ling, folding his arms and speaking in an unmoved voice, 'is an intelligent submission —' but at that word he fell beneath a rain of heavy and unquestionably well-aimed blows.

§ 7

Between Si-chow and the village of Ki, in a house completely hidden from travellers by the tall and black trees which surrounded it, lived an aged and very wise person whose ways and manner of living had become so distasteful to his neighbours that they at length agreed to regard him as a powerful and ill-disposed magician. In this way it became a custom that all very unseemly deeds committed by those who, in the ordinary course, would not be guilty of such behaviour, should be attributed to his influence, so that justice might be effected without

persons of assured respectability being put to any inconvenience. Apart from the feeling which resulted from
this just decision, the uncongenial person in question had
become exceedingly unpopular on account of certain
definite actions of his own, as that of causing the greater
part of Si-chow to be burned down by secretly breathing
upon the seven sacred water-jugs to which the town owed
its prosperity and freedom from fire. Furthermore, although possessed of many taels, and able to afford such
food as is to be found upon the tables of Mandarins, he
selected from choice dishes of an objectionable nature; he
had been observed to eat eggs of unbecoming freshness,
and the *Si-chow Official Printed Leaf* made it public that
he had, on an excessively hot occasion, openly partaken
of cow's milk. It is not a matter for wonder, therefore,
that when unnaturally loud thunder was heard in the
neighbourhood of Si-chow the more ignorant and credulous persons refused to continue in any description of work
until certain ceremonies connected with rice spirit, and the
adherence to a reclining position for some hours, had been
conscientiously observed as a protection against evil.

Not even the most venerable person in Si-chow could
remember the time when the magician had not lived there,
and as there existed no written record narrating the
incident, it was with well-founded probability that he was
said to be incapable of death. Contrary to the most general
practice, although quite unmarried, he had adopted no
son to found a line which would worship his memory in
future years, but had instead brought up and caused to
be educated in the most difficult varieties of embroidery a
young girl, to whom he referred, for want of a more suitable description, as the daughter of his sister, although he

would admit without hesitation, when closely questioned, that he had never possessed a sister, at the same time, however, alluding with some pride to many illustrious brothers, who had all obtained distinction in various employments.

Few persons of any high position penetrated into the house of the magician, and most of these retired with inelegant haste on perceiving that no domestic altar embellished the great hall. Indeed, not to make conceal-ment of the fact, the magician was a person who had entirely neglected the higher virtues in an avaricious pursuit of wealth. In that way all his time and a very large number of taels had been expended, testing results by means of the four elements, and putting together things which had been inadequately arrived at by others. It was confidently asserted in Si-chow that he possessed every manner of printed leaf which had been composed in what-soever language, and all the most precious charms, including many snake-skins of more than ordinary rarity, and the fang of a black wolf which had been stung by seven scorpions.

On the death of his father the magician had become possessed of great wealth, yet he contributed little to the funeral obsequies, nor did any suggestion of a durable and expensive nature for conveying his enlightened name and virtues down to future times cause his face to become gladdened. In order to preserve greater secrecy about the enchantments which he certainly performed, he employed only two persons within the house, one of whom was blind and the other deaf. In this ingenious manner he hoped to receive attention and yet be unobserved – the blind one being unable to see the nature of the incantations which he undertook, and the deaf one being unable to hear the words. In this, however, he was unsuccessful, as the two persons always contrived to be present together, and to explain to one another the nature of the various matters afterwards; but as they were of somewhat deficient understanding, the circumstance was unimportant.

It was with more uneasiness that the magician perceived one day that the maiden whom he had adopted was no longer a child. As he desired secrecy above all things until he should have completed the one important matter for which he had laboured all his life, he decided with extreme unwillingness to put into operation a powerful charm towards her, which would have the effect of diminishing all her attributes until such time as he might release her again. Owing to his reluctance in the matter, however, the magic did not act fully, but only in such a way that her feet became naturally and without binding the most perfect and beautiful in the entire province of Hu Nan, so that ever afterwards she was called Pan Fei Mian, in delicate reference to that Empress whose feet were so symmetrical that a golden lily sprang up wherever she trod. Afterwards the magician made no further essay in the matter, chiefly because he was ever convinced that the accomplishment of his desire was within his grasp.

The rumours of armed men in the neighbourhood of Si-chow threw the magician into an unendurable condition of despair. To lose all, as would most assuredly happen if he had to leave his arranged rooms and secret preparations and take to flight, was the more bitter because he felt surer than ever that success was even standing by his side. The very subtle liquid, which would mix itself into the component parts of the living creature which drank it, and by an insidious and harmless process so work that, when the spirit departed, the flesh would become resolved into a figure of pure and solid gold of the finest quality, had engaged the refined minds of many of the most expert individuals of remote ages. With most of these inspired persons, however, the search had been undertaken in pure-minded benevolence, their chief aim being an honourable desire to discover a method by which one's ancestors might be permanently and effectively preserved in a fit and becoming manner to receive the worship and veneration of posterity. Yet, in spite of these amiable motives, and of the fact that the magician merely desired the possession of the secret to enable him to become excessively wealthy, the affair had been so arranged that it should come into his possession.

The matter which concerned Mian in the dark wood, when she was only saved by the appearance of the person who is already known as Ling, entirely removed all pleasurable emotions from the magician's mind, and on many occasions he stated in a definite and systematic manner that he would shortly end an ignoble career which seemed to be destined only to gloom and disappointment. In this way an important misunderstanding arose, for when, two days later, during the sound of matchlock firing, the magician suddenly approached the presence of Mian with an uncontrollable haste and an entire absence of dignified demeanour, and fell dead at her feet without expressing himself on any subject whatever, she deliberately judged that in this manner he had carried his remark into effect; nor did the closed vessel of yellow liquid which he held in his hand seem to lead away from this decision. In reality, the magician had fallen owing to the heavy and conflicting emotions which success had engendered in an intellect already greatly weakened by his continual disregard of the higher virtues; for the bottle, indeed, contained the perfection of his entire life's study, the very expensive and three-times-purified gold liquid.

On perceiving the magician's condition, Mian at once called for the two attendants, and directed them to bring from an inner chamber all the most effective curing substances, whether in the form of powder or liquid. When these proved useless, no matter in what way they were applied, it became evident that there could be very little hope of restoring the magician, yet so courageous and grateful for the benefits which she had received from the person in question was Mian, that, in spite of the uninviting dangers of the enterprise, she determined to journey to Ki to invoke the assistance of a certain person who was known to be very successful in casting out malicious demons from the bodies of animals, and from casks and barrels, in which they frequently took refuge, to the great detriment of the quality of the liquid placed therein.

Not without many hidden fears Mian set out on her journey, greatly desiring not to be subjected to an encounter of a nature similar to the one already recorded; for in such a case she could hardly again hope for the inspired arrival of the one whom she now often thought of in secret as the well-formed and symmetrical young sword-user. Nevertheless, an event of equal significance was destined to prove the wisdom of the well-known remark concerning thoughts which are occupying one's intellect and the unexpected appearance of a very formidable evil spirit; for as she passed along, quickly yet with so dignified a motion that the moss received no impression beneath her footsteps, she became aware of a circumstance which caused her to stop by imparting to her mind two definite and greatly dissimilar emotions.

In a grassy and open space, on the verge of which she stood, lay the dead bodies of seventeen rebels, all disposed in very degraded attitudes, which contrasted strongly with the easy and unbecoming position adopted by the eighteenth — one who bore the unmistakable emblems of the Imperial army. In this brave and noble-looking personage Mian at once saw her preserver, and not doubting that an inopportune and treacherous death had overtaken him, she ran forward and raised him in her arms, being well assured that however indiscreet such an action might appear in the case of an ordinary person, the most select maiden need not hesitate to perform so honourable a service in regard to one whose virtues had by that time undoubtedly placed him among the Three Thousand Pure Ones. Being disturbed in this providential manner, Ling opened his eyes, and faintly murmuring, 'Oh, sainted and adorable Koon Yam, Goddess of Charity, intercede for me with Buddha!' he again lost possession of himself in the Middle Air. At this remark, which plainly proved Ling to be still alive, in spite of the fact that both the maiden and the person himself had thoughts to the contrary, Mian found herself surrounded by a variety of embarrassing circumstances, among which occurred a remembrance of the dead magician and the wise person at Ki whom she had set out to summon; but on considering the various natural and sublime laws which bore directly on the alternative before her, she discovered that her plain destiny was to endeavour to retain the breath in the person who was still alive rather than engage on the very unsatisfactory chance of attempting to call it back to the body from which it had so long been absent.

Having been inspired to this conclusion — which, when she later examined her mind, she found not to be repulsive to her own inner feelings — Mian returned to the house with dexterous speed, and calling together the two attendants, she endeavoured by means of signs and drawings to explain to them what she desired to accomplish. Succeeding in this after some delay (for the persons in question, being very illiterate and narrow-minded, were unable at first to understand the existence of any recumbent male person other than the dead magician, whom they thereupon commenced to bury in the garden with expressions of great satisfaction at their own intelligence in comprehending Mian's meaning so readily), they all journeyed to the wood, and bearing Ling between them, they carried him to the house without further adventure.

§ 8

It was in the month of Hot Dragon Breaths, many weeks after the fight in the woods of Ki, that Ling again opened his eyes, to find himself in an unknown chamber, and to recognize in the one who visited him from time to time the incomparable maiden whose life he had saved in the cypress glade. Not a day had passed in the meanwhile on which Mian had neglected to offer sacrifices to Chang-Chung, the deity interested in drugs and healing substances, nor had she wavered in her firm resolve to bring Ling back to an ordinary existence even when the two attendants had protested that the person in question might without impropriety be sent to the Restoring Establishment of the Last Chance, so little did his hope of recovering rest upon the efforts of living beings.

After he had beheld Mian's face and understood the circumstances of his escape and recovery, Ling quickly shook off the evil vapours which had held him down so long, and presently he was able to walk slowly in the courtyard and in the shady paths of the wood beyond, leaning upon Mian for the support he still required.

'Oh, graceful one,' he said on such an occasion, when little stood between him and the full powers which he had known before the battle, 'there is a matter which has been pressing upon this person's mind for some time past. It is as dark after light to let the thoughts dwell around it, yet the thing itself must inevitably soon be regarded, for in this life one's actions are for ever regulated by conditions which are neither of one's own seeking nor within one's power of controlling.'

At these words all brightness left Mian's manner, for she at once understood that Ling referred to his departure, of which she herself had lately come to think with unrestrained agitation.

'Oh, Ling,' she exclaimed at length, 'most expert of sword-users and most noble of men, surely never was a maiden more inelegantly placed than the one who is now by your side. To you she owes her life, yet it is unseemly for her even to speak of the incident; to you she must look for protection, yet she cannot ask you to stay by her side. She is indeed alone. The magician is dead, Ki has fallen, Ling is going, and Mian is undoubtedly the most unhappy and solitary person between The Wall and the Nan Hai.'

'Beloved Mian,' exclaimed Ling, with inspiring vehemence, 'and is not the utterly unworthy person before you indebted to you in a double measure that life is still within him? Is not the strength which now promotes him to such exceptional audacity as to aspire to your lovely hand, of your own creating? Only encourage Ling to entertain a well-founded hope that on his return he shall not find you partaking of the wedding feast of some wealthy and exceptionally round-bodied mandarin, and this person will accomplish the journey to Canton and back as it were in four strides.'

'Oh, Ling, reflection of my ideal, holder of my soul, it would indeed be very disagreeable to my own feelings to make any reply save one,' replied Mian, scarcely above a breath-voice. 'Gratitude alone would direct me, were not it that the great love which fills me leaves no resting-place for any other emotion than itself. Go if you must, but return quickly, for your absence will weigh upon Mian like a dragon-dream.'

'Violet light of my eyes,' exclaimed Ling, 'even in surroundings which with the exception of the matter before us are uninspiring in the extreme, your virtuous and retiring encouragement yet raises me to such a commanding eminence of demonstrative happiness that I fear I shall become intolerably self-opinionated towards my fellow-men in consequence.'

'Such a thing is impossible with my Ling,' said Mian, with conviction. 'But must you indeed journey to Canton?'

'Alas!' replied Ling, 'gladly would this person decide against such a course did the matter rest with him, for as The Verses say, "It is needless to apply the ram's head to the unlocked door. But Ki is demolished, the unassuming Mandarin Li Keen has retired to Pekin, and of the fortunes of his bowmen this person is entirely ignorant.'

'Such as survived returned to their homes,' replied Mian, 'and Si-chow is safe, for the scattered and broken rebels fled to the mountains again; so much this person has learned.'

'In that case Si-chow is undoubtedly safe for the time, and can be left with prudence,' said Ling. 'It is an unfortunate circumstance that there is no mandarin of authority between here and Canton who can receive from this person a statement of past facts and give him instructions for the future.'

'And what will be the nature of such instructions as will be given at Canton?' demanded Mian.

'By chance they may take the form of raising another company of bowmen,' said Ling, with a sigh, 'but, indeed, if this person can obtain any weight by means of his past service, they will tend towards a pleasant and unambitious civil appointment.'

'Oh, my artless and noble-minded lover!' exclaimed Mian, 'assuredly a veil has been before your eyes during your residence in Canton, and your naturally benevolent mind has turned all things into good, or you would not thus hopefully refer to your brilliant exploits in the past. Of what commercial benefit have they been to the sordid and miserly persons in authority, or in what way have they diverted a stream of taels into their insatiable pockets? Far greater is the chance that had Si-chow fallen many of its household goods would have found their way into the Yamêns of Canton. Assuredly in Li Keen you will have a friend who will make many delicate allusions to your ancestors when you meet, and yet one who will float many barbed whispers to follow you when you have passed; for you have planted shame before him in the eyes of those who would otherwise neither have eyes to see nor tongues to discuss the matter. It is for such a reason that this person mistrusts all things connected with the journey, except your constancy, oh, my true and strong one.'

'Such faithfulness would alone be sufficient to assure my safe return if the matter were properly represented to the supreme Deities,' said Ling. 'Let not the thin curtain of bitter water stand before your lustrous eyes any longer, then, the events which have followed one another in the past few days in a fashion that can only be likened to thunder following lightning are indeed sufficient to distress one with so refined and swan-like an organization, but they are now assuredly at an end.'

'It is a hope of daily recurrence to this person,' replied Mian, honourably endeavouring to restrain the emotion which openly exhibited itself in her eyes; 'for what maiden would not rather make successful offerings to the Great mother Kum-Fa than have the most imposing and verbose Triumphal Arch erected to commemorate an empty and unsatisfying constancy?'

In this amiable manner the matter was arranged between Ling and Mian, as they sat together in the magician's garden drinking peach-tea, which the two attendants — not without discriminating and significant expressions between themselves — brought to them from time to time. Here Ling made clear the whole manner of his life from his earliest memory to the time when he fell in dignified combat, nor did Mian withhold anything, explaining in particular such charms and spells of the magician as she had knowledge of, and in this graceful manner materially assisting her lover in the many disagreeable encounters and conflicts which he was shortly to experience.

It was with even more objectionable feelings than before that Ling now contemplated his journey to Canton, involving as it did the separation from one who had become as the shadow of his existence, and by whose side he had an undoubted claim to stand. Yet the necessity of the undertaking was no less than before, and the full possession of all his natural powers took away his only excuse for delaying in the matter. Without any pleasurable anticipations, therefore, he consulted the Sacred Flat and Round Sticks, and learning that the following day would be propitious for the journey, he arranged to set out in accordance with the omen.

When the final moment arrived at which the invisible threads of constantly passing emotions from one to the other must be broken, and when Mian perceived that her lover's horse was restrained at the door by the two attendants, who with unsuspected delicacy of feeling had taken this opportunity of withdrawing, the noble endurance which had hitherto upheld her melted away, and she became involved in very melancholy and obscure meditations until she observed that Ling also was quickly becoming affected in a similar gloom.

'Alas!' she exclaimed, 'how unworthy a person I am thus to impose upon my lord a greater burden than that which already weighs him down! Rather ought this one to dwell upon the happiness of that day, when, after successfully evading or overthrowing the numerous bands of assassins which infest the road from here to Canton, and after escaping or recovering from the many deadly pestilences which invariably reduce that city at this season of the year, he shall triumphantly return. Assuredly there is a highly polished surface united to every action in life, no matter how funereal it may at first appear. Indeed, there are many incidents compared with which death itself is welcome, and to this end Mian has reserved a farewell gift.' Speaking in this manner the devoted and magnanimous maiden placed in Ling's hands the transparent vessel of liquid which the magician had grasped when he fell. 'This person,' she continued, speaking with difficulty, 'places her lover's welfare incomparably before her own happiness, and should he ever find himself in a situation which is unendurably oppressive, and from which death is the only escape – such as inevitable tortures, the infliction of violent madness, or the subjection by magic to the will of some designing woman – she begs him to accept this means of freeing himself without regarding her anguish beyond expressing a clearly defined last wish that the two persons in question may be in the end happily reunited in another existence.'

Assured by this last evidence of affection, Ling felt that he had no longer any reason for internal heaviness; his spirits were immeasurably raised by the fragrant incense of Mian's great devotion, and under its influence he was even able to breathe towards her a few words of similar comfort as he left the spot and began his journey.

§ 9

On entering Canton, which he successfully accomplished without any unpleasant adventure, the marked absence of any dignified ostentation which had been accountable for many of Ling's misfortunes in the past, impelled him again to reside in the same insignificant apartment that he had occupied when he first visited the city as an unknown and unimportant candidate. In consequence of this, when Ling was communicating to any person the signs by which messengers might find him, he was compelled to add, 'the neighbourhood in which this contemptible person resides is that officially known as "the mean quarter favoured by the lower class of those who murder by treachery,"' and for this reason he was not always treated with the regard to which his attainments entitled him, or which he would have unquestionably received had he been able to describe himself as of 'the partly drained and uninfected area reserved to Mandarins and their friends.'

It was with an ignoble feeling of mental distress that Ling exhibited himself at the Chief Office of Warlike Deeds and Arrangements on the following day; for the many disadvantageous incidents of his past life had repeated themselves before his eyes while he slept, and the not unhopeful emotions which he had felt when in the inspiring presence of Mian were now altogether absent. In spite of the fact that he reached the office during the early gong strokes of the morning, it was not until the withdrawal of light that he reached any person who was in a position to speak with him on the matter, so numerous were the lesser ones through whose chambers he had to pass in the process. At length he found himself in the presence of an upper one who had the appearance of being acquainted with the circumstances, and who received him with dignity, though not with any embarrassing exhibition of respect or servility.

'"The hero of the illustrious encounter beyond the walls of Si-chow,"' exclaimed that official, reading the words from the tablet of introduction which Ling had caused to be carried in to him, and at the same time examining the person in question closely. 'Indeed, no such one is known to those within this office, unless the words chance to point to the courteous and unassuming Mandarin Li Keen, who, however, is at this moment recovering his health at Pekin as set forth in the amiable and impartial report which we have lately received from him.'

At these words Ling plainly understood that there was little hope of the past events becoming profitable on his account.

'Did not the report to which allusion has been made bear reference to one Ling, Commander of Archers, who thrice led on the fighting men, and who was finally successful in causing the rebels to disperse towards the mountains?' he asked, in a voice which somewhat trembled.

'There is certainly reference to one of the name you mention,' said the other; 'but regarding the terms – perhaps this person would better protect his own estimable time by displaying the report within your sight.'

With these words the upper one struck a gong several times, and after receiving from an inner chamber the parchment in question, he placed it before Ling, at the same time directing a lesser one to interpose between it and the one who read it a large sheet of transparent substance, so that destruction might not come to it, no matter in what way its contents affected the reader. Thereon Ling perceived the following facts, very skilfully inscribed with the evident purpose of inducing persons to believe, without question, that words so elegantly traced must of necessity be truthful also:

'*A Benevolent Example of the Intelligent Arrangement by which the most Worthy Persons outlive those who are Incapable.*

'The circumstances connected with the office of the valuable and accomplished Mandarin of Warlike Deeds and Arrangements at Si-chow have, in recent times, been of anything but a prepossessing order. Owing to the very inadequate methods adopted by those who earn a livelihood by conveying necessities from the more enlightened portions of the Empire to that place, it so came about that for a period of five days the Yamên was entirely unsupplied with the fins of sharks or even with goats' eyes. To add to the polished Mandarin's distress of mind the barbarous and slow-witted rebels who infest those parts took this opportunity to destroy the town and most of its inhabitants, the matter coming about as follows:

'The feeble and commonplace person named Ling who commanded the bowmen had but recently been elevated to that distinguished position from a menial and degraded occupation (for which, indeed, his stunted intellect more aptly fitted him); and being in consequence very greatly puffed out in self-gratification, he became an easy prey to the cunning of the rebels, and allowed himself to be beguiled into a trap, paying for his contemptible stupidity with his life. The town of Si-chow was then attacked, and being in this manner left defenceless through the weakness – or treachery – of the person Ling, who had contrived to encompass the entire destruction of his unyielding company, it fell after a determined and irreproachable resistance; the Mandarin Li Keen being told, as covered with the blood of the foemen, he was dragged away from the thickest part of the unequal conflict by his followers, that

64

he was the last person to leave the town. On his way to Pekin with news of this valiant defence, the Mandarin was joined by the Chief of Bowmen, who had understood and avoided the very obvious snare into which the stagnant-minded Commander had led his followers, in spite of dis-interested advice to the contrary. For this intelligent per-ception, and for general nobility of conduct when in battle, the versatile Chief of Bowmen is by this written paper strongly recommended to the dignity of receiving the small metal Embellishment of Valour.

'It has been suggested to the Mandarin Li Keen that the bestowal of the Crystal Button would only be a fit and graceful reward for his indefatigable efforts to uphold the dignity of the sublime Emperor; but to all such persons the Mandarin has sternly replied that such a proposal would more fitly originate from the renowned and valuable Office of Warlike Deeds and Arrangements, he well knowing that the wise and engaging persons who conduct that indispensable and well-regulated department are grace-fully voracious in their efforts to reward merit, even when it is displayed, as in the case in question, by one who from his position will inevitably soon be urgently petitioning in a like manner on their behalf.'

When Ling had finished reading this elegantly arranged but exceedingly misleading parchment, he looked up with eyes from which he vainly endeavoured to restrain the signs of undignified emotion, and said to the upper one:

'It is difficult employment for a person to refrain from unendurable thoughts when his unassuming and really conscientious efforts are represented in a spirit of no satis-faction, yet in this matter the very expert Li Keen appears to have gone beyond himself; the Commander Ling, who is herein represented as being slain by the enemy, is, indeed, the person who is standing before you, and all the other statements are in a like exactness.'

'The short-sighted individual who for some hidden desire of his own is endeavouring to present himself as the corrupt and degraded creature Ling, has overlooked one important circumstance,' said the upper one, smiling in a very intolerable manner, at the same time causing his head to move slightly from side to side in the fashion of one who rebukes with assumed geniality; and, turning over the written paper, he displayed upon the under side the Imperial vermilion Sign. 'Perhaps,' he continued, 'the omniscient person will still continue in his remarks, even with the evidence of the Emperor's unerring pencil to refute him.'

At these words and the undoubted testimony of the red mark, which plainly declared the whole of the written matter to be composed of truth, no matter what might afterwards transpire, Ling understood that very little prosperity remained with him.

'But the town of Si-chow,' he suggested, after examining his mind; 'if any person in authority visited the place, he would inevitably find it standing and its inhabitants in agreeable health.'

'The persistent person who is so assiduously occupying my intellectual moments with empty words seems to be unaccountably deficient in his knowledge of the customs of refined society and of the meaning of the Imperial Signet,' said the other, with an entire absence of benevolent consideration. 'That Si-chow has fallen and that Ling is dead are two utterly uncontroversial matters truthfully recorded. If a person visited Si-chow, he might find it rebuilt or even inhabited by those from the neighbouring villages or by evil spirits taking the forms of the ones who formerly lived there; as in a like manner, Ling might be restored to existence by magic, or his body might be found and possessed by an outcast demon who desired to revisit the earth for a period. Such circumstances do not in any way disturb the announcement that Si-chow has without question fallen, and that Ling has officially ceased to live, of which events notifications have been sent to all who are concerned in the matter.'

As the upper one ceased speaking, four strokes sounded upon the gong, and Ling immediately found himself carried into the street by the current of both lesser and upper ones who poured forth at the signal.

The termination of this conversation left Ling in a more unenviable state of dejection than any of the many preceding misfortunes had done, for with enlarged inducements to possess himself of a competent appointment he seemed to be even further removed from this attainment than he had been at any time in his life. He might, indeed, present himself again for the public examinations; but in order to do even that it would be necessary for him to wait almost a year, nor could he assure himself that his efforts would again be likely to result in an equal success. Doubts also arose within his mind of the course which he should follow in such a case; whether to adopt a new name, involving as it would certain humiliation and perhaps disgrace if detection overtook his footsteps, or still to possess the title of one who was in a measure dead, and hazard the likelihood of having any prosperity which he might obtain reduced to nothing if the fact should become public.

As Ling reflected upon such details he found himself

without intention before the house of a wise person who
had become very wealthy by advising others on all matters,
but chiefly on those connected with strange occurrences and
such events as could not be settled definitely either one way
or the other until a remote period had been reached. Becoming assailed by a curious desire to know what manner
of evils particularly attached themselves to such as were
officially dead but who nevertheless had an ordinary existence, Ling placed himself before this person, and after
arranging the manner of reward, related to him so many of
the circumstances as were necessary to enable a full understanding to be reached, but at the same time in no way
betraying his own interest in the matter.

'Such inflictions are to no degree frequent,' said the wise
person after he had consulted a polished sphere of the finest
red jade for some time; 'and this is in a measure to be
regretted, as the hair of these persons – provided they die a
violent death, which is invariably the case – constitutes a
certain protection against being struck by falling stars, or
becoming involved in unsuccessful law cases. The persons
in question can be recognized with certainty in the public
ways by the unnatural pallor of their faces and by the
general repulsiveness of their appearance, but as they soon
take refuge in suicide, unless they have the fortune to be
removed previously by accident, it is an infrequent matter
that one is gratified by the sight. During their existence
they are subject to many disorders from which the gener-
ality of human beings are benevolently preserved; they
possess no rights of any kind, and if by any chance they are
detected in an act of a seemingly depraved nature, they are
liable to judgment at the hands of the passers-by without
any form whatever, and to punishment of a more severe

order than that administered to commonplace criminals. There are many other disadvantages affecting such persons when they reach the Middle Air, of which the chief –'

'This person is immeasurably indebted for such a clear explanation of the position,' interrupted Ling, who had a feeling of not desiring to penetrate further into the detail; 'but as he perceives a line of anxious ones eagerly waiting at the door to obtain advice and consolation from so expert and amiable a wizard, he will not make himself uncongenial any longer with his very feeble topics of conversation.'

By this time Ling plainly comprehended that he had been marked out from the beginning – perhaps, for all the knowledge which he had to the opposite effect, from a period in the life of a far-removed ancestor – to be an object of marked derision and the victim of all manner of malevolent demons in whatever actions he undertook. In this condition of understanding his mind turned gratefully to the parting gift of Mian, whom he had now no hope of possessing; for the intolerable thought of uniting her to so objectionable a being as himself would have been dismissed as utterly inelegant even had he been in a manner of living to provide for her adequately, which itself seemed clearly impossible. Disregarding all similar emotions, therefore, he walked without pausing to his abode, and stretching his body upon the rushes, drank the entire liquid unhesitatingly, and prepared to pass beyond with a tranquil mind entirely given up to thoughts and images of Mian.

§ 10

Upon a certain occasion, the particulars of which have already been recorded, Ling had judged himself to have passed into the form of a spirit on beholding the ethereal form of Mian bending over him. After swallowing the entire liquid, which had cost the dead magician so much to distil and make perfect, it was with a well-assured determination of never again awakening that he lost the outward senses and floated in the Middle Air, so that when his eyes next opened upon what seemed to be the bare walls of his own chamber, his first thought was a natural conviction that the matter had been so arranged either out of a charitable desire that he should not be overcome by a too sudden transition to unparalleled splendour, or that such a reception was the outcome of some dignified jest on the part of certain lesser and more cheerful spirits. After waiting in one position for several hours, however, and receiving no summons or manifestation of a celestial nature, he began to doubt the qualities of the liquid, and applying certain tests, he soon ascertained that he was still in the lower world and unharmed. Nevertheless, this circumstance did not tend in any way to depress his mind, for, doubtless owing to some hidden virtue in the fluid, he felt an enjoyable emotion that he still lived; all his attributes appeared to be purified, and he experienced an inspired certainty of feeling that an illustrious and highly remunerative future lay before one who still had an ordinary existence after being both officially killed and self-poisoned.

In this intelligent disposition thoughts of Mian recurred to him with unreproved persistence, and in order to convey to her an account of the various matters which had engaged him since his arrival at the city, and a well-considered declaration of the unchanged state of his own feelings towards her, he composed and despatched with impetuous haste the following delicate verses:

'CONSTANCY

'About the walls and gates of Canton
Are many pleasing and entertaining maidens;
Indeed, in the eyes of their friends and of the passers-by
Some of them are exceptionally adorable.
The person who is inscribing these lines, however,
Sees before him, as it were, an assemblage of deformed and
      unprepossessing hags,
Venerable in age and inconsiderable in appearance;
For the dignified and majestic image of Mian is ever
      before him,
Making all others very inferior.

'Within the houses and streets of Canton
Hang many very bright lanterns.
The ordinary person who has occasion to walk by night
Professes to find them highly lustrous.
But there is one who thinks contrary facts,
And when he goes forth he carries two long curved poles
To prevent him from stumbling among the dark and
      hidden places;
For he has gazed into the brilliant and pellucid orbs of Mian,
And all other lights are dull and practically opaque.

'In various parts of the literary quarter of Canton
Reside such as spend their time in inward contemplation.
In spite of their generally uninviting exteriors
Their reflections are often of a very profound order.
Yet the unpopular and persistently abused Ling
Would unhesitatingly prefer his own thoughts to theirs,
For what makes this person's thoughts far more pleasing
Is that they are invariably connected with the virtuous and
      ornamental Mian.'

Becoming very amiably disposed after this agreeable occupation, Ling surveyed himself at the disc of polished metal, and observed with surprise and shame the rough and uninviting condition of his person. He had, indeed, although it was not until some time later that he became aware of the circumstance, slept for five days without interruption, and it need not therefore be a matter of wonder or of reproach to him that his smooth surfaces had become covered with short hair. Reviling himself bitterly for the appearance which he conceived he must have exhibited when he conducted his business, and to which he now in part attributed his ill-success, Ling went forth without delay, and quickly discovering one of those who remove hair publicly for a very small sum, he placed himself in the chair, and directed that his face, arms, and legs should be denuded after the manner affected by the ones who make a practice of observing the most recent customs.

'Did the illustrious individual who is now conferring distinction on this really worn-out chair by occupying it express himself in favour of having the face entirely denuded?' demanded the one who conducted the operation; for these persons have become famous for their elegant and persistent ability to discourse, and frequently assume ignorance in order that they themselves may make reply, and not for the purpose of gaining knowledge. 'Now, in the objectionable opinion of this unintelligent person, who has a presumptuous habit of offering his very undesirable advice, a slight covering on the upper lip, delicately arranged and somewhat fiercely pointed at the extremities, would bestow an appearance of — how shall this illiterate person explain himself? — dignity? — matured reflection? — doubtless the accomplished nobleman before me will understand what is intended with a more knife-like accuracy than this person can describe it – but confer that highly desirable effect upon the face of which at present it is entirely destitute. . . . "Entirely denuded?" Then without fail it shall certainly be so, O incomparable personage. . . . Does the versatile mandarin now present profess any concern as to the condition of the rice plants? . . . Indeed, the remark is an inspired one; the subject is totally devoid of interest to a person of intelligence. . . . A remarkable and gravity-removing event transpired within the notice of this unassuming person recently A discriminating individual had purchased from him a portion of his justly renowned Thrice-extracted Essence of Celestial Herb Oil – a preparation which in this experienced person's opinion, indeed, would greatly relieve the undoubted afflictions from which the one before him is evidently suffering – when after once anointing himself –'

A lengthy period containing no words caused Ling, who had in the meantime closed his eyes and lost Canton and all else in delicate thoughts of Mian, to look up. That which met his attention on doing so filled him with an intelligent wonder, for the person before him held in his hand what had the appearance of a tuft of bright yellow hair, which shone in the light of the sun with a most engaging splendour, but which he nevertheless regarded with a most undignified expression of confusion and awe.

'Illustrious demon,' he cried at length, kowtowing very respectfully, 'have the extreme amiableness to be of a benevolent disposition, and do not take an unworthy and entirely unremunerative revenge upon this very unimportant person for failing to detect and honour you from the beginning.'

73

'Such words indicate nothing beyond an excess of hemp spirit,' answered Ling, with signs of displeasure. 'To gain my explicit esteem, make me smooth without delay, and do not exhibit before me the lock of hair which, from its colour and appearance, has evidently adorned the head of one of those maidens whose duty it is to quench the thirst of travellers in the long narrow rooms of this city.'

'Majestic and anonymous spirit,' said the other, with extreme reverence, and an entire absence of the appearance of one who has gazed into many vessels, 'if such be your plainly expressed desire, this superficial person will at once proceed to make smooth your peach-like skin, and with a carefulness inspired by the certainty that the most unimportant wound would give forth liquid fire, in which he would undoubtedly perish. Nevertheless, he desires to make it evident that this hair is from the head of no maiden, being, indeed, the uneven termination of your own sacred pigtail, which this excessively self-confident salve took the inexcusable liberty of removing, and which changed in this manner within his hand in order to administer a fit reproof for his intolerable presumption.'

Impressed by the mien and unquestionable earnestness of the remover of hair, Ling took the matter which had occasioned these various emotions in his hand and examined it. His amazement was still greater when he perceived that—in spite of the fact that it presented every appearance of having been cut from his own person—none of the qualities of hair remained in it; it was hard and wire-like, possessing, indeed, both the nature and the appearance of a metal.

As he gazed fixedly and with astonishment, there came back into the remembrance of Ling certain obscure and little-understood facts connected with the limitless wealth possessed by the Yellow Emperor — of which the great gold life-like image in the Temple of Internal Symmetry at Pekin alone bears witness now — and of his lost secret. Many very forcible prophecies and omens in his own earlier life, of which the rendering and accomplishment had hitherto seemed to be dark and incomplete, passed before him, and various matters which Mian had related to him concerning the habits and speech of the magician took definite form within his mind. Deeply impressed by the exact manner in which all these circumstances fitted together, one into another, Ling rewarded the person before him greatly beyond his expectation, and hurried without any delay to his own chamber.

§ 11

For many hours Ling remained in his room, examining in his mind all passages, either in his own life or in the lives of others, which might by any chance have influence on the event before him. In this thorough way he became assured that the competition and its results, his journey to Si-chow with the encounter in the cypress wood, the flight of the incapable and treacherous Mandarin, and the battle at Ki, were all, down to the matter of the smallest detail, parts of a symmetrical and complete scheme, tending to his present condition, in which he had become involved. Cheered and upheld by this proof of the fact that very able deities were at work on his behalf, he turned his intellect from the entrancing subject to a contemplation of the manner in which his condition would enable him to frustrate the un-inventive villainies of the obstinate person Li Keen and to provide a suitable house and mode of living to which he would be justified in introducing Mian, after adequate marriage ceremonies had been observed between them. In this endeavour he was less successful than he had imagined would be the case, for when he had first fully understood that his body was of such a substance that nothing was wanting to transmute it into fine gold but the absence of the living spirit, he had naturally, and without deeply examining the detail, assumed that so much gold might be considered as in his possession. Now, however, a very definite thought arose within him that his own wishes and interests would have been better secured had the benevolent spirits who undertook the matter placed the secret within his knowledge in such a way as to enable him to administer the fluid to some very heavy and inexpensive animal, so that the issue which seemed inevitable before the enjoyment of the riches could be entered upon should not have touched his own comfort so closely. To a person of Ling's refined imagination it could not fail to be a subject of internal reproach that while he would become the most precious dead body in the world, his value in life might not be very honourably placed even by the most complimentary one who should require his services. Then came the thought, which, however degraded, he found himself unable to put quite beyond him, that if in the meantime he were able to gain a sufficiency for Mian and himself, even her pure and delicate love might not be able to bear so offensive a test as that of seeing him grow old and remain intolerably healthy — perhaps with advancing years actually becoming lighter day by day, and thereby lessening in value before her eyes — when the natural infirmities of age and the presence of an ever-increasing posterity would make even a moderate amount of taels of inestimable value.

No doubt remained in Ling's mind that the process of frequently making smooth his surfaces would yield an amount of gold enough to suffice for his own needs, but a brief consideration of the matter convinced him that this source would be inadequate to maintain an entire household even if he continually denuded himself to an almost ignominious extent. As he fully weighed these varying chances the certainty became more clear to him with every thought that for the virtuous enjoyment of Mian's society one great sacrifice was required of him. This act, it seemed to be intimated, would without delay provide for an affluent and lengthy future, and at the same time would influence all the spirits — even those who had been hitherto evilly disposed towards him — in such a manner that his enemies would be removed from his path by a process which would expose them to public ridicule, and he would be assured in founding an illustrious and enduring line. To accomplish this successfully necessitated the loss of at least the greater part of one entire member, and for some time the disadvantages of going through an existence with only a single leg or arm seemed more than a sufficient price to pay even for the definite advantages which would be made over to him in return. This unworthy thought, however, could not long withstand the memory of Mian's steadfast and high-minded affection, and the certainty of her enlightened gladness at his return even in the imperfect condition which he anticipated. Nor was there absent from his mind a dimly understood hope that the matter did not finally rest with him, but that everything which he might be inspired to do was in reality only a portion of the complete and arranged system into which he had been drawn, and in which his part had been assigned to him from the beginning without power for him to deviate, no matter how much to the contrary the thing should appear.

As no advantage would be gained by making any delay, Ling at once sought the most favourable means of putting his resolution into practice, and after many skilful and insidious inquiries he learnt of an accomplished person who made a consistent habit of cutting off limbs which had become troublesome to their possessors either through accident or disease. Furthermore, he was said to be of a sincere and charitable disposition, and many persons declared that on no occasion had he been known to make use of the helpless condition of those who visited him in order to extort money from them.

Coming to the ill-considered conclusion that he would be able to conceal within his own breast the true reason for the operation, Ling placed himself before the person in question, and exhibited the matter to him so that it would appear as though his desires were promoted by the presence of a small but persistent sprite which had taken its abode within his left thigh, and there resisted every effort of the most experienced wise persons to induce it to come forth again. Satisfied with this explanation of the necessity of the deed, the one who undertook the matter proceeded, with Ling's assistance, to sharpen his cutting instruments and to heat the hardening irons; but no sooner had he made a shallow mark to indicate the lines which his knife should take, than his subtle observation at once showed him that the facts had been represented to him in a wrong sense, and that his visitor, indeed, was composed of no common substance. Being of a gentle and forbearing disposition, he did not manifest any indication of rage at the discovery, but amiably and unassumingly pointed out that such a course was not respectful towards himself, and that, moreover, Ling might incur certain well-defined and highly undesirable maladies as a punishment for the deception.

Overcome with remorse at deceiving so courteous and noble-minded a person, Ling fully explained the circumstances to him, not even concealing from him certain facts which related to the actions of remote ancestors, but which, nevertheless, appeared to have influenced the succession of events. When he had made an end of the narrative, the other said:

'Behold now, it is truly remarked that every mandarin has three hands and every soldier a like number of feet, yet it is a saying which is rather to be regarded as manifesting the deep wisdom and discrimination of the speaker than as an actual fact which can be taken advantage of when one is so minded — least of all by so valiant a Commander as the one before me, who has clearly proved that in time of battle he has exactly reversed the position.'

'The loss would undoubtedly be of considerable inconvenience occasionally,' admitted Ling, 'yet none the less the sage remark of Huai Mei-shan, "When actually in the embrace of a voracious and powerful wild animal, the desirability of leaving a limb is not a matter to be subjected to lengthy consideration," is undoubtedly a valuable guide for general conduct. This person has endured many misfortunes and suffered many injustices; he has known the wolf-gnawings of great hopes, which have withered and daily grown less when the difficulties of maintaining an honourable and illustrious career have unfolded themselves within his sight. Before him still lie the attractions of a moderate competency to be shared with the one whose absence would make even the Upper Region unendurable, and after having this entrancing future once shattered by the tiger-like cupidity of a depraved and incapable mandarin, he is determined to welcome even the sacrifice which you condemn rather than let the opportunity vanish through indecision.'

'It is not an unworthy or abandoned decision,' said the one whose aid Ling had invoked, 'nor a matter from which this person would refrain taking part, were there no other and more agreeable means by which the same results may be attained. A circumstance has occurred within this superficial person's mind, however: A brother of the one who is addressing you is by profession one of those who purchase large undertakings for which they have not the money to pay, and who thereupon by various expedients gain the ear of the thrifty, enticing them by fair offers in return to entrust their savings for the purpose of paying off the debt. These persons are ever on the watch for transactions by which they inevitably prosper without incurring any obligation, and doubtless my brother will be able to gather together a community which would in some way endow you with a just share of the value of your highly remunerative body without submitting you to the insufferable annoyance of losing a great part of it prematurely.'

Without clearly understanding how so inviting an arrangement could be effected, the manner of speaking was exceedingly alluring to Ling's mind, perplexed as he had become through weighing and considering the various attitudes of the entire matter. To receive a certain and sufficient sum of money without his person being in any way mutilated would be a satisfactory, but as far as he had been able to observe an unapproachable, solution of the difficulty. In the mind of the amiable person with whom he was conversing, however, the accomplishment did not appear to be surrounded by unnatural obstacles, so that Ling was content to leave the entire design in his hands, after stating that he would again present himself on a certain occasion when it was asserted that the brother in question would be present.

So internally lightened did Ling feel after this inspiring conversation, and so confident of a speedy success had the obliging person's words made him become, that for the first time since his return to Canton he was able to take an intellectual interest in the pleasures of the city. Becoming aware that the celebrated play entitled 'The Precious Lamp of Spotted Butterfly Temple' was in process of being shown at the Tea Garden of Rainbow Lights and Voices, he purchased an entrance, and after passing several hours in this conscientious enjoyment, returned to his chamber, and passed a night untroubled by any manifestations of an unpleasant nature.

§ 12

Chang-ch'un, the brother of the one to whom Ling had applied in his determination, was confidently stated to be one of the richest persons in Canton. So great was the number of enterprises in which he had possessions, that he himself was unable to keep an account of them, and it was asserted that upon occasions he had run through the streets, crying aloud that such an undertaking had been the subject of most inferior and uninviting dreams and omens (a custom observed by those who wish a venture ill), whereas upon returning and consulting his written parchments, it became plain to him that he had indulged in a very objectionable exhibition, as he himself was the person most interested in the success of the matter. Far from discouraging him, however, such incidents tended to his advantage, as he could consistently point to them in proof of his unquestionable commercial honourableness, and in this way many persons of all classes, not only in Canton, or in the Province, but all over the Empire, would unhesitatingly entrust money to be placed in undertakings which he had purchased and was willing to describe as 'of much good.' A certain class of printed leaves – those in which Chang-ch'un did not insert purchased mentions of his forthcoming ventures or verses recording his virtues (in return for buying many examples of the printed leaf containing them) – took frequent occasion of reminding persons that Chang-ch'un owed the beginning of his prosperity to finding a written parchment connected with a mandarin of exalted rank and a low, caste attendant at the Ti-i tea-house among the paper heaps, which it was at that time his occupation to assort into various departments according to their quality and commercial value. Such printed leaves freely and unhesitatingly predicted that the day on which he would publicly lose face was incomparably nearer than that on which the Imperial army would receive its behind pay, and in a quaint and gravity-removing manner advised him to protect himself against an obscure but inevitable poverty by learning the accomplishment of chair-carrying – an occupation for which his talents and achievements fitted him in a high degree, they remarked.

In spite of these evilly intentioned remarks, and of illustrations representing him as being bowstrung for treacherous killing, being seized in the action of secretly conveying money from passers-by to himself and other similar annoying references to his private life, Chang-ch'un did not fail to prosper, and his undertakings succeeded to such an extent that without inquiry into the detail many persons were content to describe as 'gold-lined' anything to which he affixed his sign, and to hazard their savings for staking upon the ventures. In all other departments of life Chang was equally successful; his chief wife was the daughter of one who stood high in the Emperor's favour; his repast table was never unsupplied with sea-snails, rats' tongues, or delicacies, of an equally expensive nature, and it was confidently maintained that there was no official in Canton, not even putting aside the Taotai, who dare neglect to fondle Chang's hand if he publicly offered it to him for that purpose.

It was at the most illustrious point of his existence — at the time, indeed, when after purchasing without money the renowned and proficient charm-water Ho-Ko for a million taels, he had sold it again for ten — that Chang was informed by his brother of the circumstances connected with Ling. After becoming specially assured that the matter was indeed such as it was represented to be, Chang at once discerned that the venture was of too certain and profitable a nature to be put before those who entrusted their money to him in ordinary and doubtful cases. He accordingly called together certain persons whom he was desirous of obliging, and informing them privately and apart from business terms that the opportunity was one of exceptional attractiveness, he placed the facts before them. After displaying a number of diagrams bearing upon the matter, he proposed that they should form an enterprise to be called 'The Ling (After Death) Without Much Risk Assembly.' The manner of conducting this undertaking he explained to be as follows: The body of Ling, whenever the spirit left it, should become as theirs to be used for profit. For this benefit they would pay Ling fifty thousand taels when the understanding was definitely arrived at, five thousand taels each year until the matter ended, and when that period arrived another fifty thousand taels to persons depending upon him during his life. Having stated the figure business, Chang-ch'un put down his written papers, and causing his face to assume the look of irrepressible but dignified satisfaction which it was his custom to wear on most occasions, and especially when he had what appeared at first sight to be evil news to communicate to public assemblages of those who had entrusted money to his ventures, he proceeded to disclose the advantages of such a system. At the extreme, he said, the amount which they would be required to pay would be two hundred and fifty thousand taels; but this was in reality a very misleading view of the circumstance, as he would endeavour to show them. For one detail, he had allotted to Ling thirty years of existence, which was the extreme amount according to the calculations of those skilled in such prophecies; but, as they were all undoubtedly aware, persons of very expert intellects were known to enjoy a much shorter period of life than the gross and ordinary, and as Ling was clearly one of the former, by the fact of his contriving so ingenious a method of enriching himself, they might with reasonable foresight rely upon his departing when half the period had been attained; in that way seventy-five thousand taels would be restored to them, for every year represented a saving of five thousand. Another agreeable contemplation was that of the last sum, for by such a time they would have arrived at the most pleasurable part of the enterprise: a million taels' worth of pure gold would be displayed before them, and the question of the final fifty thousand could be disposed of by cutting off an arm or half a leg. Whether they adopted that course, or decided to increase their fortunes by exposing so exceptional and symmetrical a wonder to the public gaze in all the principal cities of the Empire, was a circumstance which would have to be examined within their minds when the time approached. In such a way the detail of purchase stood revealed as only fifty thousand taels in reality, a sum so despicably insignificant that he had internal pains at mentioning it to so wealthy a group of mandarins, and he had not yet made clear to them that each year they would receive gold to the amount of almost a thousand taels. This would be the result of Ling making smooth his surfaces, and it would enable them to know that the person in question actually existed, and to keep the circumstances before their intellects.

When Chang-ch'un had made the various facts clear to this extent, those who were assembled expressed their feelings as favourably turned towards the project, provided the tests to which Ling was to be put should prove encouraging, and a secure and intelligent understanding of things to be done and not to be done could be arrived at between them. To this end Ling was brought into the chamber, and fixing his thoughts steadfastly upon Mian, he permitted portions to be cut from various parts of his body without betraying any signs of ignoble agitation. No sooner had the pieces been separated and the virtue of Ling's existence passed from them than they changed colour and hardened, nor could the most delicate and searching trials to which they were exposed by a skilful worker in metals, who was obtained for the purpose, disclose any particular, however minute, in which they differed from the finest gold. The hair, the nails, and the teeth were similarly affected, and even Ling's blood dried into a fine gold powder. This detail of the trial being successfully completed, Ling subjected himself to intricate questionings on all matters connected with his religion and manner of conducting himself, both in public and privately, the history and behaviour of his ancestors, the various omens and remarkable sayings which had reference to his life and destiny, and the intentions which he then possessed regarding his future movements and habit of living. All the wise sayings and written and printed leaves which made any allusion to the existence and possibility of discovery of the wonderful gold fluid were closely examined, and found to be in agreement, whereupon those present made no further delay in admitting that the facts were indeed as they had been described, and indulged in a dignified stroking of each other's faces as an expression of pleasure and in proof of their satisfaction at taking part in so entrancing and remunerative an affair. At Chang's command many rare and expensive wines were then brought in, and partaken of without restraint by all persons, the repast being lightened by numerous well-considered and gravity-removing jests having reference to Ling and the unusual composition of his person. So amiably were the hours occupied that it was past the time of no light when Chang rose and read at full length the statement of things to be done and things not to be done, which was to be sealed by Ling for his part and the other persons who were present for theirs. It so happened, however, that at that period Ling's mind was filled with brilliant and versatile thoughts and images of Mian, and many-hued visions of the manner in which they would spend the entrancing future which was now before them, and in this way it chanced that he did not give any portion of his intellect to the reading, mistaking it, indeed, for a delicate and very ably-composed set of verses which Chang-ch'un was reciting as a formal blessing on parting. Nor was it until he was desired to affix his sign that Ling discovered his mistake, and being of too respectful and unobtrusive a disposition to require the matter to be repeated then, he carried out the obligation without in any particular understanding the written words to which he was agreeing.

As Ling walked through the streets to his chamber after leaving the house and company of Chang-ch'un, holding firmly among his garments the thin printed papers to the amount of fifty thousand taels which he had received, and repeatedly speaking to himself in terms of general and specific encouragement at the fortunate events of the past few days, he became aware that a person of mean and rapacious appearance, whom he had some memory of having observed within the residence he had but just left, was continually by his side. Not at first doubting that the circumstance resulted from a benevolent desire on the part of Chang-ch'un that he should be protected in his passage through the city, Ling affected not to observe the incident; but upon reaching his own door the person in question persistently endeavoured to pass in also. Forming a fresh judgment about the matter, Ling, who was very powerfully constructed, and whose natural instincts were enhanced in every degree by the potent fluid of which he had lately partaken, repeatedly threw him across the street until he became weary of the diversion. At length, however, the thought arose that one who patiently submitted to continually striking the opposite houses with his head must have something of importance to communicate, whereupon he courteously invited him to enter the apartment and un-weigh his mind.

'The facts of the case appear to have been somewhat inadequately represented,' said the stranger, bowing obse-quiously, 'for this unornamental person was assured by the benignant Chang-ch'un that the one whose shadow he was to become was of a mild and forbearing nature.'

'Such words are as the conversation of birds to me,' replied Ling, not conjecturing how the matter had fallen about. 'This person has just left the presence of the elegant and successful Chang-ch'un, and no word that he spoke gave indication of such a follower or such a service.'

'Then it is indeed certain that the various transactions have not been fully understood,' exclaimed the other, 'for the exact communication to this unseemly one was, "The valuable and enlightened Ling has heard and agreed to the different things to be done and not to be done, one phrase of which arranges for your continual presence, so that he will anticipate your attentions."'

At these words the truth became as daylight before Ling's eyes, and he perceived that the written paper to which he had affixed his sign contained the detail of such an office as that of the person before him. When too late, more than ever did he regret that he had not formed some pretext for causing the document to be read a second time, as in view of his immediate intentions such an arrange-ment as the one to which he had agreed had every appear-ance of becoming of an irksome and perplexing nature. Desiring to know the length of the attendant's commands, Ling asked him for a clear statement of his duties, feigning that he had missed that portion of the reading through a momentary attack of the giddy sickness. To this request the stranger, who explained that his name was Wang, instantly replied that his written and spoken orders were: never to permit more than an arm's length of space to separate them; to prevent, by whatever force was necessary for the purpose, all attempts at evading the things to be done and not to be done, and to ignore as of no interest all other circumstances. It seemed to Ling, in consequence, that little seclusion would be enjoyed unless an arrangement could be effected between Wang and himself; so to this end, after noticing the evident poverty and covetousness of the person in question, he made him an honourable offer of frequent rewards, provided a greater distance was allowed to come between them as soon as Si-chow was reached. On his side, Ling undertook not to break through the wording of the things to be done and not to be done, and to notify to Wang any movements upon which he meditated. In this reputable manner the obstacle was ingeniously removed, and the intelligent nature of the device was clearly proved by the fact that not only Ling but Wang also had in the future a much greater liberty of action than would have been possible if it had been necessary to observe the short-sighted and evidently hastily-thought-of condition which Chang-ch'un had endeavoured to impose.

§ 13

In spite of his natural desire to return to Mian as quickly as possible, Ling judged it expedient to give several days to the occupation of purchasing apparel of the richest kinds, weapons and armour in large quantities, jewels and ornaments of worked metals and other objects to indicate

his changed position. Nor did he neglect actions of a pious
and charitable nature, for almost his first care was to
arrange with the chief ones at the Temple of Benevolent
Intentions that each year, on the day corresponding to that
on which he drank the gold fluid, a sumptuous and well-
constructed coffin should be presented to the most deserving poor and aged person within that quarter of the city
in which he had resided. When these preparations were
completed, Ling set out with an extensive train of attendants; but riding on before, accompanied only by Wang, he
quickly reached Si-chow without adventure.

The meeting between Ling and Mian was affecting to
such an extent that the blind and the deaf attendants wept
openly without reproach, not withstanding the fact that
neither could become possessed of more than a half of the
occurrence. Eagerly the two reunited ones examined each
other's features to discover whether the separation had
brought about any change in the beloved and well-
remembered lines. Ling discovered upon Mian the
shadow of an anxious care at his absence, while the disappointments and trials which Ling had experienced in
Canton had left traces which were plainly visible to Mian's
penetrating gaze. In such an entrancing occupation the
time was to them without hours until a feeling of hunger
recalled them to lesser matters, when a variety of very
select foods and liquids were placed before them without
delay. After this elegant repast had been partaken of,
Mian, supporting herself upon Ling's shoulder, made a
request that he would disclose to her all the matters which
had come under his observation both within the city and
during his journey to and from that place. Upon this
encouragement, Ling proceeded to unfold his mind, not

withholding anything which appeared to be of interest, no matter how slight. When he had reached Canton without any perilous adventure, Mian breathed more freely; as he recorded the interview at the Office of War-like Deeds and Arrangements, she trembled at the in-sidious malignity of the evil person Li Keen. The con-versation with the wise reader of the future concerning the various states of such as be officially dead almost threw her into the rigid sickness, from which, however, the wonder-ful circumstance of the discovered properties of the gold fluid quickly recalled her. But to Ling's great astonish-ment no sooner had he made plain the exceptional advantages which he had derived from the circumstances, and the nature of the undertaking at which he had arrived with Chang-ch'un, than she became a prey to the most intolerable and unrestrained anguish.

'Oh, my devoted but excessively ill-advised lover,' she exclaimed wildly, and in tones which clearly indicated that she was inspired by every variety of affectionate emotion, 'has the unendurable position in which you and all your household will be placed by the degrading commercial schemes and instincts of the mercenary-souled person Chang-ch'un occupied no place in your generally well-regulated intellect? Inevitably will those who drink our almond tea, in order to have an opportunity of judging the value of the appointments of the house, pass the jesting remark that while the Lings assuredly have "a dead per-son's bones in the secret chamber," at the present they will not have one in the family graveyard by reason of the death of Ling himself. Better to lose a thousand limbs during life than the entire person after death; nor would your adoring Mian hesitate to clasp proudly to her organ of affection the veriest trunk that had parted with all its attributes in a noble and sacrificing endeavour to preserve at least some dignified proportions to embellish the Ancestral Temple and to receive the worship of posterity.'

'Alas!' replied Ling, with extravagant humiliation, 'it is indeed true; and this person is degraded beyond the common lot of those who break images and commit thefts from sacred places. The side of the transaction which is at present engaging our attention never occurred to this superficial individual until now.'

'Wise and incomparable one,' said Mian, in no degree able to restrain the fountains of bitter water which clouded her delicate and expressive eyes, 'in spite of this person's biting and ungracious words do not, she makes a formal petition, doubt the deathless strength of her affection. Cheerfully, in order to avert the matter in question, or even to save her lover the anguish of unavailing and soul-eating remorse, would she consign herself to a badly constructed and slow-consuming fire or expose her body to various undignified tortures. Happy are those even to whom is left a little ash to be placed in a precious urn and diligently guarded, for it, in any event, truly represents all that is left of the once living person, whereas after an honourable and spotless existence my illustrious but unthinking lord will be blended with a variety of baser substances and passed from hand to hand, his immaculate organs serving to reward murderers for their deeds, and to tempt the weak and vicious to all manner of unmentionable crimes.'

So overcome was Ling by the distressing nature of the oversight he had permitted that he could find no words with which to comfort Mian, who, after some moments, continued:

'There are even worse visions of degradation which occur to this person. By chance, that which was once the noble-minded Ling may be disposed of, not to the Imperial Treasury, for converting into pieces of exchange, but to some undiscriminating worker in metals who will fashion out of his beautiful and symmetrical stomach an elegant food-dish, so that from the ultimate developments of the circumstance may arise the fact that his own descendants, instead of worshipping him, use his internal organs for this doubtful if not absolutely unclean purpose, and thereby suffer numerous well-merited afflictions, to the end that the finally despised Ling and this discredited person, instead of founding a vigorous and prolific generation, become the parents of a line of feeble-minded and physically depressed lepers.'

'Oh, my peacock-eyed one!' exclaimed Ling, in immeasurable distress, 'so proficient an exhibition of virtuous grief crushes this misguided person completely to the ground. Rather would he uncomplainingly lose his pigtail than —'

'Such a course,' said a discordant voice, as the unpresentable person Wang stepped forth from behind a hanging curtain, where, indeed, he had stood concealed during the entire conversation, 'is especially forbidden by the twenty-third detail of the things to be done and not to be done.'

'What new adversity is this?' cried Mian, pressing to Ling with a still closer embrace. 'Having disposed of your incomparable body after death, surely an adequate amount of liberty and seclusion remains to us during life.'

'Nevertheless,' interposed the dog-like Wang, 'the refined person in question must not attempt to lose or to dispose of his striking and invaluable pigtail; for by such an action he would be breaking through his spoken and written word whereby he undertook to be ruled by the things to be done and not to be done; and he would also be robbing the ingenious-minded Chang-ch'un.'

'Alas!' lamented the unhappy Ling, 'that which appeared to be the end of all this persons' troubles is obviously simply the commencement of a new and more extensive variety. Understand, O conscientious but exceedingly inopportune Wang, that the words which passed from this person's mouth did not indicate a fixed determination, but merely served to show the unfeigned depth of his emotion. Be content that he has no intention of evading the definite principles of the things to be done and not to be done, and in the meantime honour this commonplace establishment by retiring to the hot and ill-ventilated chamber, and there partaking of a suitable repast which shall be prepared without delay.'

When Wang had departed, which he did with somewhat unseemly haste, Ling made an end of recording his narrative, which Mian's grief had interrupted. In this way he explained to her the reason of Wang's presence, and assured her that by reason of the arrangement he had made with that person, his near existence would not be so unsupportable to them as might at first appear to be the case.

While they were still conversing together, and endeavouring to divert their minds from the objectionable facts which had recently come within their notice, an attendant entered and disclosed that the train of servants and merchandise which Ling had preceded on the journey was arriving. At this fresh example of her lover's consistent thought for her, Mian almost forgot her recent agitation and eagerly lending herself to the entrancing occupation of unfolding and displaying the various objects, her brow finally lost the last trace of sadness. Greatly beyond the imaginings of anticipation were the expensive articles with which Ling proudly surrounded her; and in examining and learning the cost of the set jewels and worked metals, the ornamental garments for both persons, the wood and paper appointments for the house — even incenses, perfumes, spices and rare viands had not been forgotten — the day was quickly and profitably spent.

When the hour of sunset arrived, Ling, having learned that certain preparations which he had commanded were fully carried out, took Mian by the hand and led her into the chief apartment of the house, where were assembled all the followers and attendants, even down to the illiterate and superfluous Wang. In the centre of the room upon a table of the finest ebony stood a vessel of burning incense, some dishes of the most highly esteemed fruit, and an abundance of old and very sweet wine. Before these emblems Ling and Mian placed themselves in an attitude of deep humiliation, and formally expressed their gratitude to the Chief Deity for having called them into existence, to the cultivated earth for supplying them with the means of sustaining life, to the Emperor for providing the numerous safeguards by which their persons were protected at all times, and to their parents for educating them. This adequate ceremony being completed, Ling explicitly desired all those present to observe the fact that the two persons in question were, by that act and from that time, made as one being, and the bond between them incapable of severance.

When the ruling night-lantern came out from among the clouds, Ling and Mian became possessed of a great desire to go forth with pressed hands and look again on the forest paths and glades in which they had spent many hours of exceptional happiness before Ling's journey to Canton. Leaving the attendants to continue the feasting and drum-beating in a completely unrestrained manner, they therefore passed out unperceived, and wandering among the trees, presently stood on the banks of the Heng-Kiang.

'Oh, my beloved!' exclaimed Mian, gazing at the brilliant and unruffled water, 'greatly would this person esteem a short river journey, such as we often enjoyed together in the days when you were recovering.'

Ling, to whom the expressed desires of Mian were as the word of the Emperor, instantly prepared the small and ornamental junk which was fastened near for this purpose, and was about to step in, when a presumptuous and highly objectionable hand restrained him.

'Behold,' remarked a voice which Ling had some difficulty in ascribing to any known person, so greatly had it changed from its usual tone, 'behold how the immature and altogether too-inferior Ling observes his spoken and written assertions!'

At this low-conditioned speech, Ling drew his well-tempered sword without further thought, in spite of the restraining arms of Mian, but at the sight of the utterly incapable person Wang, who stood near smiling meaninglessly and waving his arms with a continuous and backward motion, he again replaced it.

'Such remarks can be left to fall unheeded from the lips of one who bears every indication of being steeped in rice spirit,' he said with unprovoked dignity.

'It will be the plain duty of this expert and uncorruptible person to furnish the unnecessary but, nevertheless, very severe and self-opinionated Chang-ch'un with a written account of how the traitorous and deceptive Ling has endeavoured to break through the thirty-fourth vessel of the liquids to be consumed and not to be consumed,' continued Wang with increased deliberation and an entire absence of attention to Ling's action and speech, 'and how by this refined person's unfailing civility and resourceful strategy he has been frustrated.'

'Perchance,' said Ling, after examining his thoughts for a short space, and reflecting that the list of things to be done and not to be done was to him as a blank leaf, 'there may even be some small portion of that which is accurate in his statement. In what manner,' he continued, addressing the really unendurable person, who was by this time preparing to pass the night in the cool swamp by the river's edge, 'does this one endanger any detail of the written and sealed parchment by such an action?'

'Inasmuch,' replied Wang, pausing in the process of removing his outer garments, 'as the seventy-ninth — the intricate name given to it escapes this person's tongue at the moment — but the ninety-seventh — experLingknowswhamean — provides that any person, with or without, attempting or not avoiding to travel by sea, lake, or river, or to place himself in such a position as he may reasonably and intelligently be drowned in salt water, fresh water, or — or honourable rice spirit, shall be guilty of, and suffer — complete loss of memory.' With these words the immoderate and contemptible person sank down in a very profound slumber.

'Alas!' said Ling, turning to Mian, who stood near,

D

unable to retire even had she desired, by reason of the extreme agitation into which the incident had thrown her delicate mind and body, 'how intensely aggravating a circumstance that we are compelled to entertain so dissolute a one by reason of this person's preoccupation when the matter was rea. Nevertheless, it is not unlikely that the detail he spoke c. was such as he insisted, to the extent of making it a thing not to be done to journey in any manner by water. It shall be an early endeavour of this person to get these restraining details equitably amended; but in the meantime we will retrace our footsteps through the wood, and the enraptured Ling will make a well-thought-out attempt to lighten the passage by a recital of his recently composed verses on the subject of "Exile from the Loved One; or, Farewell and Return."'

§ 14

'My beloved lord!' said Mian sadly, on a morning after many days had passed since the return of Ling, 'have you not every possession for which the heart of a wise person searches? Yet the dark mark is scarcely ever absent from your symmetrical brow. If she who stands before you, and is henceforth an integral part of your organization, has failed you in any particular, no matter how unimportant, explain the matter to her, and the amendment will be a speedy and a joyful task.'

It was indeed true that Ling's mind was troubled, but the fault did not lie with Mian, as the person in question was fully aware, for before her eyes as before those of Ling the unevadable compact which had been entered into with Chang-ch'un was ever present, insidiously planting bitterness within even the most select and accomplished delights.

Nor with increasing time did the obstinate and intrusive person Wang become more dignified in his behaviour; on the contrary, he freely made use of his position to indulge in every variety of abandonment, and almost each day he prevented, by reason of his knowledge of the things to be done and not to be done, some refined and permissible entertainment upon which Ling and Mian had determined. Ling had despatched many communications upon this subject to Chang-ch'un, praying also that some expert way out of the annoyance of the lesser and more unimportant things not to be done should be arrived at, but the time when he might reasonably expect an answer to these written papers had not yet arrived.

It was about this period that intelligence was brought to Ling from the villages on the road to Pekin, how Li Keen, having secretly ascertained that his Yamên was standing and his goods uninjured, had determined to return, and was indeed at that hour within a hundred li of Si-chow. Furthermore, he had repeatedly been understood to pronounce clearly that he considered Ling to be the head and beginning of all his inconveniences, and to declare that the first act of justice which he should accomplish on his return would be to submit the person in question to the most unbearable tortures, and then cause him to lose his head publicly as an outrager of the settled state of things and an enemy of those who loved tranquillity. Not doubting that Li Keen would endeavour to gain an advantage by treachery if the chance presented itself, Ling determined to go forth to meet him, and without delay settle the entire disturbance in one well-chosen and fatally destructive encounter. To this end, rather than disturb the placid mind of Mian, to whom the thought of the engagement would be weighted with many disquieting fears, he gave out that he was going upon an expedition to surprise and capture certain fish of a very delicate flavour, and, attended by only two persons, he set forth in the early part of the day.

Some hours later, owing to an ill-considered remark on the part of the deaf attendant, to whom the matter had been explained in an imperfect light, Mian became possessed of the true facts of the case, and immediately all the pleasure of existence went from her. She despaired of ever again beholding Ling in an ordinary state, and mournfully reproached herself for the bitter words which had risen to her lips when the circumstance of his condition and the arrangement with Chang-ch'un first became known to her. After spending an interval in a polished lament at the manner in which things were inevitably tending, the thought occurred to Mian whether by any means in her power she could influence the course and settled method of affairs. In this situation the memory of the person Wang, and the fact that on several occasions he had made himself objectionable when Ling had proposed to place himself in such a position that he incurred some very remote chance of death by drowning or by fire, recurred to her. Subduing the natural and pure-minded repulsion which she invariably experienced at the mere thought of so debased an individual, she sought for him, and discovering him in the act of constructing cardboard figures of men and animals, which it was his custom to dispose skilfully in little-frequented paths for the purpose of enjoying the sudden terror of those who passed by, she quickly put the matter before him, urging him, by some means, to prevent the encounter, which might assuredly cost the life of the one whom he had so often previously obstructed from incurring the slightest risk.

'By no means,' exclaimed Wang, when he at length understood the full meaning of the project; 'it would be a most unpresentable action for this commonplace person to interfere in so honourable an undertaking. Had the priceless body of the intrepid Ling been in any danger of disappearing, as, for example, by drowning or being consumed in fire, the nature of the circumstance would have been different. As the matter exists, however, there is every appearance that the far-seeing Chang-ch'un will soon reap the deserved reward of his somewhat speculative enterprise, and to that end this person will immediately procure a wooden barrier and the services of four robust carriers, and proceed to the scene of the conflict.'

Deprived of even this hope of preventing the encounter, Mian betook herself in extreme dejection to the secret room of the magician, which had been unopened since the day when the two attendants had searched for substances to apply to their master, and there she diligently examined every object in the remote chance of discovering something which might prove of value in averting the matter in question.

Not anticipating that the true reason of his journey would become known to Mian, Ling continued on his way without haste, and passing through Si-chow before the sun had risen, entered upon the great road to Pekin. At a convenient distance from the town he came to a favourable piece of ground where he decided to await the arrival of Li Keen, spending the time profitably in polishing his already brilliant sword, and making observations upon the nature of the spot and the condition of the surrounding omens, on which the success of his expedition would largely depend.

As the sun reached the highest point in the open sky the sound of an approaching company could be plainly heard; but at the moment when the chair of the Mandarin appeared within the sight of those who waited, the great luminary, upon which all portents depend directly or indirectly, changed to the colour of new-drawn blood and began to sink towards the earth. Without any misgivings, therefore, Ling disposed his two attendants in the wood, with instructions to step forth and aid him if he should be attacked by overwhelming numbers, while he himself remained in the way. As the chair approached, the Mandarin observed a person standing alone, and thinking that it was one who, hearing of his return, had come out of the town to honour him, he commanded the bearers to pause. Thereupon, stepping up to the opening, Ling struck the deceptive and incapable Li Keen on the cheek, at the same time crying in a full voice, 'Come forth, O traitorous and two-stomached Mandarin! for this person is very desirous of assisting you in the fulfilment of your boastful words. Here is a most irreproachable sword which will serve excellently to cut off this person's undignified head; here is a waist-cord which can be tightened round his breast, thereby producing excruciating pains over the entire body.'

At the knowledge of who the one before him was, and when he heard the words which unhesitatingly announced Ling's fixed purpose, Li Keen first urged the carriers to fall upon Ling and slay him, and then, perceiving that such a course was exceedingly distasteful to their natural tendencies, to take up the chair and save him by flight. But Ling in the meantime engaged their attention, and fully explained to them the treacherous and unworthy conduct of Li Keen, showing them how his death would be a just retribution for his ill-spent life, and promising them each a considerable reward in addition to their arranged payment when the matter in question had been accomplished. Becoming convinced of the justice of Ling's cause, they turned upon Li Keen, insisting that he should at once attempt to carry out the ill-judged threats against Ling, of which they were consistent witnesses, and announcing that, if he failed to do so, they would certainly bear him themselves to a not far distant well of stagnant water, and there gain the approbation of the good spirits by freeing the land of so unnatural a monster.

Seeing only a dishonourable death on either side, Li Keen drew his sword, and made use of every artifice of which he had knowledge in order to disarm Ling or to take him at a disadvantage. In this he was unsuccessful, for Ling, who was by nature a very expert sword-user, struck him repeatedly, until he at length fell in an expiring condition, remarking with his last words that he had indeed been a narrow-minded and extortionate person during his life, and that his death was an enlightened act of celestial accuracy.

Directing Wang and his four hired persons, who had in the meantime arrived, to give the body of the Mandarin an honourable burial in the deep of the wood, Ling rewarded and dismissed the chair-bearers, and without delay proceeded to Si-chow, where he charitably distributed the goods and possessions of Li Keen among the poor of the town. Having in this able and conscientious manner completely proved the misleading nature of the disgraceful statements which the Mandarin had spread abroad concerning him, Ling turned his footsteps towards Mian, whose entrancing joy at his safe return was judged by both persons to be a sufficient reward for the mental distress with which their separation had been accompanied.

§ 15

After the departure of Ling from Canton, the commercial affairs of Chang-ch'un began, from a secret and undetectable cause, to assume an ill-regulated condition. No venture which he undertook maintained a profitable attitude, so that many persons who in former times had been content to display the printed papers setting forth his name and virtues in an easily seen position in their receiving-rooms, now placed themselves daily before his house in order to accuse him of using their taels in ways which they themselves had not sufficiently understood, and for the purpose of warning passers-by against his inducements. It was in vain that Chang proposed new undertakings, each of an infallibly more prosperous nature than those before; the persons who had hitherto supported him were all entrusting their money to one named Pung Soo, who required millions where Chang had been content with thousands, and who persistently insisted on greeting the sacred Emperor as an equal.

In this unenviable state Chang's mind continually returned to thoughts of Ling, whose lifeless body would so opportunely serve to dispel the embarrassing perplexities of existence which were settling thickly about him. Urged forward by a variety of circumstances which placed him in an entirely different spirit from the honourable bearing which he had formerly maintained, he now closely examined all the papers connected with the matter, to discover whether he might not be able to effect his purpose with an outward exhibition of law forms. While engaged in this degrading occupation, a detail came to his notice which caused him to become very amiably disposed and confident of success. Proceeding with the matter, he caused a well-supported report to be spread about that Ling was suffering from a wasting sickness, which, without in any measure shortening his life, would cause him to return to the size and weight of a newly-born child, and being by these means enabled to secure the entire matter of 'The Ling (After Death) Without Much Risk Assembly' at a very small outlay, he did so, and then, calling together a company of those who hire themselves out for purposes of violence, journeyed to Si-chow.

Ling and Mian were seated together at a table in the great room, examining a vessel of some clear liquid, when Chang-ch'un entered with his armed ones, in direct opposition to the general laws of ordinary conduct and the rulings of hospitality. At the sight, which plainly indicated a threatened display of violence, Ling seized his renowned sword, which was never far distant from him, and prepared to carry out his spoken vow, that 'any person overstepping a certain mark on the floor should assuredly fall.'

'Put away your undoubtedly competent weapon, O Ling,' said Chang, who was desirous that the matter should be arranged if possible without any loss to himself, 'for such a course can be honourably adopted when it is taken into consideration that we are as twenty to one, and have, moreover, the appearance of being inspired by law forms.'

'There are certain matters of allowed justice which over-rule all other law forms,' replied Ling, taking a surer hold of his sword-grasp. 'Explain, for your part, O

obviously double-dealing Chang-ch'un, from whom this
person only recently parted on terms of equality and
courtesy, why you come not with an agreeable face and a
peaceful following, but with a countenance which indicates both violence and terror, and accompanied by many
whom this person recognizes as the most outcast and
degraded from the narrow and evil-smelling ways of
Canton?'

'In spite of your blustering words,' said Chang, with
some attempt at an exhibition of dignity, 'this person is
endowed by every right, and comes only for the obtaining,
by the help of this expert and proficient gathering, should
such a length become necessary, of his just claims. Understand that in the time since the venture was arranged this
person has become possessed of all the property of "The
Ling (After Death) Without Much Risk Assembly," and
thereby he is competent to act fully in the matter. It has
now come within his attention that the one Ling to whom
the particulars refer is officially dead, and as the written
and sealed document clearly undertook that the person's
body was to be delivered up for whatever use the Assembly
decided whenever death should possess it, this person has
now come for the honourable carrying out of the undertaking.'

At these words the true nature of the hidden contrivance
into which he had fallen descended upon Ling like a heavy
and unavoidable thunderbolt. Nevertheless, being by
nature and by reason of his late exploits, fearless of death
except for the sake of the loved one by his side, he betrayed
no sign of discreditable emotion at the discovery.

'In such a case,' he replied, with an appearance of
entirely disregarding the danger of the position, 'the com-

plete parchment must of necessity be overthrown; for if this person is now officially dead, he was equally so at the time of sealing, and arrangements entered into by dead persons have no actual existence.'

'That is a matter which has never been efficiently decided,' admitted Chang-ch'un, with no appearance of being thrown into a state of confusion at the suggestion, 'and doubtless the case in question can by various means be brought in the end before the Court of Final Settlement at Pekin, where it may indeed be judged in the manner you assert. But as such a process must infallibly consume the wealth of a province and the years of an ordinary lifetime, and as it is this person's unmoved intention to carry out his own view of the undertaking without delay, such speculations are not matters of profound interest.'

Upon this Chang gave certain instructions to his followers, who thereupon prepared to advance. Perceiving that the last detail of the affair had been arrived at, Ling threw back his hanging garment, and was on the point of rushing forward to meet them, when Mian, who had maintained a possessed and reliant attitude throughout, pushed towards him the vessel of pure and sparkling liquid with which they had been engaged when so presumptuously broken in upon, at the same time speaking to him certain words in an outside language. A new and Heaven-sent confidence immediately took possession of Ling, and striking his sword against the wall with such irresistible proficiency that the entire chamber trembled and the feeble-minded assassins shrank back in unrestrained terror, he leapt upon the table, grasping in one hand the open vessel.

'Behold the end, O most uninventive and slow-witted

Chang-ch'un!' he cried in a dreadful and awe-compelling voice. 'As a reward of your faithless and traitorous behaviour, learn how such avaricious-minded incompetence turns and fastens itself upon the vitals of those who beget it. In spite of many things which were not of a graceful nature towards him, this person has unassumingly maintained his part of the undertaking, and would have followed such a course conscientiously to the last. As it is, when he has made an end of speaking, the body which you are already covetously estimating in taels will in no way be distinguishable from that of the meanest and most ordinary maker of commercial ventures in Canton. For, behold! the fluid which he holds in his hand, and which it is his fixed intention to drain to the last drop, is in truth nothing but a secret and exceedingly powerful counteractor against the virtues of the gold drug; and though but a single particle passed his lips, and the swords of your brilliant and versatile murderers met the next moment in his breast, the body which fell at your feet would be meet for worms rather than for the melting-pot.'

It was indeed such a substance as Ling represented it to be, Mian having discovered it during her very systematic examination of the dead magician's inner room. Its composition and distillation had involved that self-opinionated person in many years of arduous toil, for with a somewhat unintelligent lack of foresight he had obstinately determined to perfect the antidote before he turned his attention to the drug itself. Had the matter been more ingeniously arranged, he would undoubtedly have enjoyed an earlier triumph and an affluent and respected old age.

At Ling's earnest words and prepared attitude an instant conviction of the truth of his assertions took possession of

Chang. Therefore, seeing nothing but immediate and unevadable ruin at the next step, he called out in a loud and imploring voice that he should desist, and no harm would come upon him. To this Ling consented, first insisting that the followers should be dismissed without delay, and Chang alone remain to have conversation on the matter. By this just act the lower parts of Canton were greatly purified, for the persons in question being driven forth into the woods, mostly perished by encounters with wild animals, or at the hands of the enraged villagers, to whom Ling had by this time become greatly endeared.

When the usual state had been restored, Ling made clear to Chang the altered nature of the conditions to which he would alone agree. 'It is a noble-minded and magnanimous proposal on your part, and one to which this misguided person had no claim,' admitted Chang, as he affixed his seal to the written undertaking and committed the former parchment to be consumed by fire. By this arrangement it was agreed that Ling should receive only one-half of the yearly payment which had formerly been promised, and that no sum of taels should become due to those depending upon him at his death. In return for these valuable allowances, there were to exist no details of things to be done and not to be done, Ling merely giving an honourable promise to observe the matter in a just spirit, while — most esteemed of all — only a portion of his body was to pass to Chang when the end arrived, the upper part remaining to embellish the family altar and receive the veneration of posterity.

. . . .

As the great sky-lantern rose above the trees and the time of no-noise fell upon the woods, a flower-laden pleasure-junk moved away from its restraining cords, and, without any sense of motion, gently bore Ling and Mian between the sweet-smelling banks of the Heng-Kiang. Presently Mian drew from beneath her flowing garment an instrument of stringed wood, and touching it with a quick but delicate stroke, like the flight and pausing of a butterfly, told in well-balanced words a refined narrative of two illustrious and noble-looking persons, and how, after many disagreeable evils and unendurable separations, they entered upon a destined state of earthly prosperity and celestial favour. When she made an end of the verses, Ling turned the junk's head by one well-directed stroke of the paddle, and prepared by using similar means to return to the place of mooring.

'Indeed,' he remarked, ceasing for a moment to continue this skilful occupation, 'the words which you have just spoken might, without injustice, be applied to the two persons who are now conversing together. For after suffering misfortunes and wrongs beyond an appropriate portion, they have now reached that period of existence when a tranquil and contemplative future is assured to them. In this manner is the sage and matured utterance of the inspired philosopher Nien-tsu again proved: that the life of every person is largely composed of two varieties of circumstances which together build up his existence — the Good and the Evil.'

THE END OF THE STORY OF LING

§ 16

When Kai Lung, the story-teller, made an end of speaking, he was immediately greeted with a variety of delicate and pleasing remarks, all persons who had witnessed the matter, down even to the lowest type of Miaotze, who by reason of their obscure circumstances had been unable to understand the meaning of a word that had been spoken, maintaining that Kai Lung's accomplishment of continuing for upwards of three hours without a pause had afforded an entertainment of a very high and refined order. While these polished sayings were being composed, together with many others of a similar nature, Lin Yi suddenly leapt to his feet with a variety of highly objectionable remarks concerning the ancestors of all those who were present, and declaring that the story of Ling was merely a well-considered stratagem to cause them to forget the expedition which they had determined upon, for by that time it should have been completely carried out. It was undoubtedly a fact that the hour spoken of for the undertaking had long passed, Lin Yi having completely overlooked the speed of time in his benevolent anxiety that the polite and valorous Ling should in the end attain to a high and remunerative destiny.

In spite of Kai Lung's consistent denials of any treachery, he could not but be aware that the incident tended greatly to his disadvantage in the eyes of those whom he had a fixed desire to conciliate, nor did his well-intentioned offer that he would without hesitation repeat the display for a like number of hours effect his amiable purpose. How the complication would finally have been determined without interruption is a matter merely of imagination, for at that moment an outpost, who had been engaged in guarding the secrecy of the expedition, threw himself into the enclosure in a torn and breathless condition, having run through the forest many li in a winding direction for the explicit purpose of warning Lin Yi that his intentions had become known, and that he and his followers would undoubtedly be surprised and overcome if they left the camp.

At this intimation of the eminent service which Kai Lung had rendered them, the nature of their faces towards him at once changed completely, those who only a moment before had been demanding his death particularly hailing him as their inspired and unobtrusive protector, and in all probability, indeed, a virtuous and benignant spirit in disguise.

Bending under the weight of offerings which Lin Yi and his followers pressed upon him, together with many clearly set out desires for his future prosperity, and assured of their unalterable protection on all future occasions, Kai Lung again turned his face towards the lanterns of Knei Yang. Far down the side of the mountain they followed his footsteps, now by a rolling stone, now by a snapping branch of yellow pine. Once again they heard his voice, cheerfully repeating to himself: 'Among the highest virtues of a pure existence –' But beyond that point the gentle forest breath bore him away.

CHAPTER TWO

THE STORY OF YUNG CHANG

*

NARRATED BY KAI LUNG, IN THE OPEN SPACE OF
THE TEA-SHOP OF THE CELESTIAL PRINCIPLES,
AT WU-WHEI

'Ho, illustrious passers-by!' said Kai Lung, the story-teller, as he spread out his embroidered mat under the mulberry-tree. 'It is indeed unlikely that you would condescend to stop and listen to the foolish words of such an insignificant and altogether deformed person as myself. Nevertheless, if you will but retard your elegant foot-steps for a few moments, this exceedingly unprepossessing individual will endeavour to entertain you with the recital of the adventures of the noble Yung Chang, as recorded by the celebrated Pe-ku-hi.'

Thus adjured, the more leisurely minded drew near to hear the history of Yung Chang. There was Sing You the fruit-seller, and Li Ton-ti the wood-carver; Hi Seng left his clients to cry in vain for water; and Wang Yu, the idle pipe-maker, closed his shop of 'The Fountain of Beauty,' and hung on the shutter the gilt dragon to keep away customers in his absence. These, together with a few more shopkeepers and a dozen or so loafers, constituted a respectable audience by the time Kai Lung was ready.

'It would be more seemly if this ill-conditioned person who is now addressing such a distinguished assembly were to reward his fine and noble-looking hearers for their trouble,' apologized the story-teller. 'But, as the Book of Verses says, "The meaner the slave, the greater the lord"; and it is, therefore, not unlikely that this majestic concourse will reward the despicable efforts of their servant by handfuls of coins till the air appears as though filled with swarms of locusts in the season of much heat. In particular, there is among this august crowd of mandarins one Wang Yu, who has departed on three previous occasions without bestowing the reward of a single cash. If the feeble and covetous-minded Wang Yu will place in this very ordinary bowl the price of one of his exceedingly ill-made pipes, this unworthy person will proceed.'

'Vast chasms can be filled, but the heart of man never,' quoted the pipe-maker in retort. 'Oh, most incapable of story-tellers, have you not on two separate occasions slept beneath my utterly inadequate roof without payment?'

But he, nevertheless, deposited three cash in the bowl, and drew nearer among the front row of the listeners.

'It was during the reign of the enlightened Emperor Tsing Nung,' began Kai Lung, without further introduction, 'that there lived at a village near Honan a wealthy and avaricious maker of idols, named Ti Hung. So skilful had he become in the making of clay idols that his fame had spread for many li around, and idol sellers from all the neighbouring villages, and even from the towns, came to him for their stock. No other idol-maker between Honan and Nankin employed so many clay-gatherers or so many modellers; yet, with all his riches, his avarice increased till at length he employed men whom he called "agents" and "travellers," who went from house to house selling his idols and extolling his virtues in verses composed by the most illustrious poets of the day. He did this in order that he might turn into his own pocket the full price of the idols, grudging those who would otherwise have sold them

the few cash which they would make. Owing to this he
had many enemies, and his army of travellers made him
still more; for they were more rapacious than the scorpion,
and more obstinate than the ox. Indeed, there is still the
proverb, "With honey it is possible to soften the heart of
the he-goat; but a blow from an iron cleaver is taken as
a mark of welcome by an agent of Ti Hung." So that
people barred the doors at their approach, and even hung
out signs of death and mourning.

'Now, among all his travellers there was none more
successful, more abandoned, and more valuable to Ti
Hung than Li Ting. So depraved was Li Ting that he
was never known to visit the tombs of his ancestors; indeed, it was said that he had been heard to mock their
venerable memories, and that he had jestingly offered to
sell them to anyone who should chance to be without
ancestors of his own. This objectionable person would call
at the houses of the most illustrious mandarins, and would
command the slaves to carry to their masters his tablets,
on which were inscribed his name and his virtues. Reaching their presence, he would salute them with the greeting
of an equal, "How is your stomach?" and then proceed
to exhibit samples of his wares, greatly overrating their
value. "Behold!" he would exclaim, "is not this elegantly
moulded idol worthy of the place of honour in this
sumptuous mansion which my presence defiles to such an
extent that twelve basins of rose water will not remove the
stain? Are not its eyes more delicate than the most select
of almonds? and is not its stomach rounder than the
cupolas upon the high temple at Pekin? Yet, in spite of
its perfections, it is not worthy of the acceptance of so
distinguished a mandarin, and therefore I will accept in

return the quarter-tael, which, indeed, is less than my illustrious master gives for the clay alone."

'In this manner Li Ting disposed of many idols at high rates, and thereby endeared himself so much to the avaricious heart of Ti Hung that he promised him his beautiful daughter Ning in marriage.

'Ning was indeed very lovely. Her eyelashes were like the finest willow twigs that grow in the marshes by the Yang-tse-Kiang; her cheeks were fairer than poppies; and when she bathed in the Hoang Ho, her body seemed transparent. Her brow was finer than the most polished jade; while she seemed to walk, like a winged bird, without weight, her hair floating in a cloud. Indeed, she was the most beautiful creature that has ever existed.'

'Now may you grow thin and shrivel up like a fallen lemon; but it is false!' cried Wang Yu, starting up suddenly and unexpectedly. 'At Chee Chou, at the shop of "The Heaven-sent Sugar-cane," there lives a beautiful and virtuous girl who is more than all that. Her eyes are like the inside circles on the peacock's feathers: her teeth are finer than the scales on the Sacred Dragon; her —'

'If it is the wish of this illustriously endowed gathering that this exceedingly illiterate paper tiger should occupy their august moments with a description of the deformities of the very ordinary young person at Chee Chou,' said Kai Lung imperturbably, 'then the remainder of the history of the noble-minded Yung Chang can remain until an evil fate has overtaken Wang Yu, as it assuredly will shortly.'

'A fair wind raises no storm,' said Wang Yu sulkily; and Kai Lung continued:

'Such loveliness could not escape the evil eye of Li Ting,

and accordingly, as he grew in favour with Ti Hung, he obtained his consent to the drawing up of the marriage contracts. More than this, he had already sent to Ning two bracelets of the finest gold, tied together with a scarlet thread, as a betrothal present. But, as the proverb says, "The good bee will not touch the faded flower," and Ning, although compelled by the second of the Five Great Principles to respect her father, was unable to regard the marriage with anything but abhorrence. Perhaps this was not altogether the fault of Li Ting, for on the evening of the day on which she had received his present, she walked in the rice fields, and sitting down at the foot of a funereal cypress, whose highest branches pierced the Middle Air, she cried aloud:

' "I cannot control my bitterness. Of what use is it that I should be called the 'White Pigeon among Golden Lilies,' if my beauty is but for the hog-like eyes of the exceedingly objectionable Li Ting? Ah, Yung Chang, my unfortunate lover! what evil spirit pursues you that you cannot pass your examination for the second degree? My noble-minded but ambitious boy, why were you not content with an agricultural or even a manufacturing career and happiness? By aspiring to a literary degree, you have placed a barrier wider than the Whang Hai between us."

' "As the earth seems small to the soaring swallow, so shall insuperable obstacles be overcome by the heart worn smooth with a fixed purpose," said a voice beside her, and Yung Chang stepped from behind the cypress-tree, where he had been waiting for Ning. "O one more symmetrical than the chrysanthemum," he continued, "I shall yet, with the aid of my ancestors, pass the second degree, and even obtain a position of high trust in the public office at Pekin."

'"And in the meantime," pouted Ning, "I shall have partaken of the wedding-cake of the utterly unpresentable Li Ting." And she exhibited the bracelets which she had that day received.

'"Alas!" said Yung Chang, "there are times when one is tempted to doubt even the most efficacious and violent means. I had hoped that by this time Li Ting would have come to a sudden and most unseemly end; for I have drawn up and affixed in the most conspicuous places notifications of his character, similar to the one here."

'Ning turned, and beheld fastened to the trunk of the cypress an exceedingly elegantly written and composed notice, which Yung read to her as follows: –

'"BEWARE OF INCURRING DEATH FROM STARVATION

'"Let the distinguished inhabitants of this district observe the exceedingly ungraceful walk and bearing of the low person who calls himself Li Ting. Truthfully, it is that of a dog in the act of being dragged to the river because his sores and diseases render him objectionable in the house of his master. So will this hunchbacked person be dragged to the place of execution, and be bowstrung, to the great relief of all who respect the five senses: A Respectful Physiognomy, Passionless Reflection, Soft Speech, Acute Hearing, Piercing Sight.

'"He hopes to attain to the Red Button and the Peacock's Feather; but the right hand of the Deity itches, and Li Ting will assuredly be removed suddenly."

'"Li Ting must certainly be in league with the evil forces if he can withstand so powerful a weapon," said Ning admiringly, when her lover had finished reading.

"Even now he is starting on a journey, nor will he return till the first day of the month when the sparrows go to the sea and are changed into oysters. Perhaps the fate will overtake him while he is away. If not –"

' "If not," said Yung, taking up her words as she paused, "then I have yet another hope. A moment ago you were regretting my choice of a literary career. Learn, then, the value of knowledge. By its aid (assisted, indeed, by the spirits of my ancestors) I have discovered a new and strange thing, for which I can find no word. By using this new system of reckoning, your illustrious but exceedingly narrow-minded and miserly father would be able to make five taels where he now makes one. Would he not, in consideration for this, consent to receive me as a son-in-law, and dismiss the inelegant and unworthy Li Ting?"

' "In the unlikely event of your being able to convince my illustrious parent of what you say, it would assuredly be so," replied Ning. "But in what way could you do so? My sublime and charitable father already employs all the means in his power to reap the full reward of his sacred industry. His 'solid household gods' are in reality mere shells of clay: higher-priced images are correspondingly constructed, and his clay-gatherers and modellers are all paid on a 'profit-sharing system.' Nay, further, it is beyond likelihood that he should wish for more purchasers, for so great is his fame that those who come to buy have sometimes to wait for days in consequence of those before them; for my exceedingly methodical sire entrusts none with the receiving of money, and the exchanges are therefore made slowly. Frequently an unnaturally devout person will require as many as a hundred idols, and so the greater part of the day will be passed."

' "In what way?" inquired Yung tremulously.

' "Why, in order that the countings may not get mixed, of course it is necessary that when he has paid for one idol he should carry it to a place aside, and then return and pay for the second, carrying it to the first, and in such a manner to the end. In this way the sun sinks behind the mountains."

' "But," said Yung, his voice thick with his great discovery, "if he could pay for the entire quantity at once, then it would take but a hundredth part of the time, and so more idols could be sold."

' "How could this be done?" inquired Ning wonderingly. "Surely it is impossible to conjecture the value of many idols."

' "To the unlearned it would indeed be impossible," replied Yung proudly, "but by the aid of my literary researches I have been enabled to discover a process by which such results would be not a matter of conjecture, but of certainty. These figures I have committed to tablets, which I am prepared to give to your mercenary and slow-witted father in return for your incomparable hand, a share of the profits, and the dismissal of the uninventive and morally threadbare Li Ting."

' "When the earth-worm boasts of his elegant wings, the eagle can afford to be silent," said a harsh voice behind them; and turning hastily they beheld Li Ting, who had come upon them unawares. "Oh, most insignificant of tablet-spoilers," he continued, "it is very evident that much over-study has softened your usually well-educated brains. Were it not that you are obviously mentally afflicted, I should unhesitatingly persuade my beautiful and refined sword to introduce you to the spirits of your ignoble ancestors. As it is, I will merely cut off your nose and your left ear, so that people may not say that the Dragon of the Earth sleep and wickedness goes unpunished."

'Both had already drawn their swords, and very soon the blows were so hard and swift that, in the dusk of the evening, it seemed as though the air were filled with innumerable and many-coloured fireworks. Each was a practised swordsman, and there was no advantage gained on either side, when Ning, who had fled on the appearance of Li Ting, reappeared, urging on her father, whose usually leisurely footsteps were quickened by the dread that the duel must result in certain loss to himself, either of a valuable servant, or of the discovery which Ning had briefly explained to him, and of which he at once saw the value.

' "Oh, most distinguished and expert persons," he exclaimed breathlessly, as soon as he was within hearing distance, "do not trouble to give so marvellous an exhibition for the benefit of this unworthy individual, who is the only observer of your illustrious dexterity! Indeed, your honourable condescension so fills this illiterate person with shame that his hearing is thereby preternaturally sharpened, and he can plainly distinguish many voices from beyond the Hoang Ho, crying for the Heaven-sent representative of the degraded Ti Hung to bring them more idols. Bend, therefore, your refined footsteps in the direction of Poo Chow, O Li Ting, and leave me to make myself objectionable to this exceptional young man with my intolerable commonplaces."

' "The shadow falls in such a direction as the sun wills," said Li Ting, as he replaced his sword and departed.

' "Yung Chang," said the merchant, "I am informed that you have made a discovery that would be of great value to me, as it undoubtedly would if it is all that you say. Let us discuss the matter without ceremony. Can you prove to me that your system possesses the merit you claim for it? If so, then the matter of arrangement will be easy."

' "I am convinced of the absolute certainty and accuracy of the discovery," replied Yung Chang. "It is not as though it were an ordinary matter of human intelligence, for this was discovered to me as I was worshipping at the tomb of my ancestors. The method is regulated by a system of squares, triangles, and cubes. But as the practical proof might be long, and as I hesitate to keep your adorable daughter out in the damp night air, may I not call at your inimitable dwelling in the morning, when we can go into the matter thoroughly?"

'I will not weary this intelligent gathering, each member of which doubtless knows all the books on mathematics off by heart, with a recital of the means by which Yung Chang proved to Ti Hung the accuracy of his tables and the value of his discovery of the multiplication table, which till then had been undreamt of,' continued the story-teller. 'It is sufficient to know that he did so, and that Ti Hung agreed to his terms, only stipulating that Li Ting should not be made aware of his dismissal until he had returned and given in his accounts. The share of the profits that Yung was to receive was cut down very low by Ti Hung, but the young man did not mind that, as he would live with his father-in-law for the future.

'With the introduction of this new system, the business increased like a river at flood-time. All rivals were left far behind, and Ti Hung put out this sign:

' "NO WAITING HERE!

' "Good-morning! Have you worshipped one of Ti Hung's refined ninety-nine cash idols?

' "Let the purchasers of ill-constructed idols at other establishments, where they have grown old and venerable while waiting for the all-thumb proprietors to count up to ten, come to the shop of Ti Hung and regain their lost youth. Our ninety-nine cash idols are worth a tael a set. We do not, however, claim that they will do everything. The ninety-nine cash idols of Ti Hung will not, for example, purify linen, but even the most contented and frozen-brained person cannot be happy till he possesses one. What is happiness? The exceedingly well-educated Philosopher defines it as the accomplishment of all our desires. Every one desires one of Ti Hung's ninety-nine cash idols, therefore get one; but be sure that it is Ti Hung's.

' "Have you a bad idol? If so, dismiss it, and get one of Ti Hung's ninety-nine cash specimens.

' "Why does your idol look old sooner than your neighbour's? Because yours is not one of Ti Hung's ninety-nine cash marvels.

' "They bring all delights to the old and the young,
    The elegant idols supplied by Ti Hung.

' "N.B. – The 'Great Sacrifice' idol, forty-five cash; delivered, carriage free, in quantities of not less than twelve, at any temple, on the evening before the sacrifice."

'It was about this time that Li Ting returned. His journey had been more than usually successful, and he was well satisfied in consequence. It was not until he had made

123

out his accounts and handed in his money that Ti Hung informed him of his agreement with Yung-Chang.

' "Oh, most treacherous and excessively unpopular Ti Hung," exclaimed Li Ting, in a terrible voice, "this is the return you make for all my entrancing efforts in your service, then? It is in this way that you reward my exceedingly unconscientious recommendations of your very inferior and unendurable clay idols, with their goggle eyes and concave stomachs! Before I go, however, I request to be inspired to make the following remark – that I confidently predict your ruin. And now this low and undignified person will finally shake the elegant dust of your distinguished house from his thoroughly inadequate feet, and proceed to offer his incapable services to the rival establishment over the way.'

' "The machinations of such an evilly disposed person as Li Ting will certainly be exceedingly subtle," said Ti Hung to his son-in-law when the traveller had departed. "I must counteract his omens. Herewith I wish to pro-phesy that henceforth I shall enjoy an unbroken run of good fortune. I have spoken, and assuredly I shall not eat my words."

'As the time went on, it seemed as though Ti Hung had indeed spoken truly. The ease and celerity with which he transacted his business brought him customers and dealers from more remote regions than ever, for they could spend days on the journey and still save time. The army of clay-gatherers and modellers grew larger and larger, and the work-sheds stretched almost down to the river's edge. Only one thing troubled Ti Hung, and that was the uncongenial disposition of his son-in-law, for Yung took no further interest in the industry to which his discovery had given so great an impetus, but resolutely set to work again to pass his examination for the second degree.

' "It is an exceedingly distinguished and honourable thing to have failed thirty-five times, and still to be undiscouraged," admitted Ti Hung; "but I cannot cleanse my throat from bitterness when I consider that my noble and lucrative business must pass into the hands of strangers, perhaps even into the possession of the unendurable Li Ting."

'But it had been appointed that this degrading thing should not happen, however, and it was indeed fortunate that Yung did not abandon his literary pursuits; for after some time it became very apparent to Ti Hung that there was something radically wrong with his business. It was not that his custom was falling off in any way; indeed, it had lately increased in a manner that was phenomenal, and when the merchant came to look into the matter, he found to his atonishment that the least order he had received in the past week had been for a hundred idols. All the sales had been large, and yet Ti Hung found himself most unaccountably deficient in taels. He was puzzled and alarmed, and for the next few days he looked into the business closely. Then it was that the reason was revealed, both for the falling off in the receipts and for the increase in the orders. The calculations of the unfortunate Yung Chang were correct up to a hundred, but at that number he had made a gigantic error – which however, he was never able to detect and rectify – with the result that all transactions above that point worked out at a considerable loss to the seller. It was in vain that the panic-stricken and infuriated Ti Hung goaded his miserable son-in-law to correct the mistake; it was equally in vain that he tried

to stem the current of his enormous commercial popularity.
He had competed for public favour, and he had won it,
and every day his business increased till ruin grasped him
by the pigtail. Then came an order from one firm at Pekin
for five millions of the ninety-nine cash idols, and at that
Ti Hung put up his shutters, and sat down in the dust.

' "Behold!" he exclaimed, "in the course of a lifetime
there are many very disagreeable evils that may overtake
a person. He may offend the Sacred Dragon, and be in
consequence reduced to a fine dry powder; or he may
incur the displeasure of the benevolent and pure-minded
Emperor, and he condemned to death by roasting; he may
also be troubled by demons or by the disturbed spirits of his
ancestors, or be struck by thunderbolts. Indeed, there are
numerous annoyances, but they all become as Heaven-
sent blessings in comparison to a self-opinionated and more
than ordinarily weak-minded son-in-law. Of what avail
is it that I have habitually sold one idol for the value of a
hundred? The very objectionable man in possession sits
in my delectable summer-house, and the unavoidable legal
documents settle around me like a flock of pigeons. It is
indeed necessary that I should declare myself to be in
voluntary liquidation, and make an assignment of my book
debts for the benefit of my creditors. Having accomplished
this, I will proceed to the well-constructed tomb of my
illustrious ancestors, and having kow-towed at their incomparable shrines, I will put an end to my distinguished
troubles with this exceedingly well-polished sword."

' "The wise man can adapt himself to circumstances as
water takes the shape of the vase that contains it," said the
well-known voice of Li Ting. "Let not the lion and the
tiger fight at the bidding of the jackal. By combining our

forces all may be well with you yet. Assist me to dispose of the entirely superfluous Yung Chang and to marry the elegant and symmetrical Ning, and in return I will allot to you a portion of my not inconsiderable income."

' "However high the tree, the leaves fall to the ground, and your hour has come at last, O detestable Li Ting!" said Yung, who had heard the speakers and crept upon them unperceived. "As for my distinguished and immaculate father-in-law, doubtless the heat has affected his indefatigable brains, or he would not have listened to your contemptible suggestion. For yourself, draw!"

'Both swords flashed, but before a blow could be sttuck the spirits of his ancestors hurled Li Ting lifeless to the ground, to avenge the memories that their unworthy descendant had so often reviled.

' "So perish all the enemies of Yung Chang," said the victor. "And now, my venerated but exceedingly short-sighted father-in-law, learn how narrowly you have escaped making yourself exceedingly objectionable to yourself. I have just received intelligence from Pekin that I have passed the second degree, and have in consequence been appointed to a remunerative position under the Government. This will enable us to live in comfort, if not in affluence, and the rest of your engaging days can be peacefully spent in flying kites." '

CHAPTER THREE
THE PROBATION OF SEN HENG

★

RELATED BY KAI LUNG, AT WU-WHEI, AS A REBUKE TO
WANG YU AND CERTAIN OTHERS WHO HAD QUESTIONED
THE PRACTICAL VALUE OF HIS STORIES

'IT is an undoubted fact that this person has not realized
the direct remunerative advantage which he confidently
anticipated,' remarked the idle and discontented pipe-
maker Wang Yu, as, with a few other persons of similar
inclination, he sat in the shade of the great mulberry-tree
at Wu-whei, waiting for the evil influence of certain
very mysterious sounds, which had lately been heard, to
pass away before he resumed his occupation. 'When the
seemingly proficient and trustworthy Kai Lung first made
it his practice to journey to Wu-whei, and narrate to us the
doings of persons of all classes of life,' he continued, 'it
seemed to this one that by closely following the recital of
how mandarins obtained their high position, and exceptionally rich persons their wealth, he must, in the end,
inevitably be rendered competent to follow in their
illustrious footsteps. Yet in how entirely contrary a direction has the whole course of events tended! In spite of the
honourable intention which involved a frequent absence
from his place of commerce, those who journeyed thither
with the set purpose of possessing one of his justly famed
opium pipes so perversely regarded the matter that, after
two or three fruitless visits, they deliberately turned their
footsteps towards the workshop of the inelegant Ming-yo,
whose pipes are confessedly greatly inferior to those produced by the person who is now speaking. Nevertheless,

the rapacious Kai Lung, to whose influence the falling off in custom was thus directly attributable, persistently declined to bear any share whatever in the loss which his profession caused, and, indeed, regarded the circumstances from so grasping and narrow-minded a point of observation that he would not even go to the length of suffering this much-persecuted one to join the circle of his hearers without on every occasion making the customary offering. In this manner a well-intentioned pursuit of riches has insidiously led this person within measurable distance of the bolted dungeon for those who do not meet their just debts, while the only distinction likely to result from his assiduous study of the customs and methods of those high in power is that of being publicly bow-strung as a warning to others. Manifestly the pointed finger of the unreliable Kai Lung is a very treacherous guide.'

'It is related,' said a dispassionate voice behind them, 'that a person of limited intelligence, on being assured that he would certainly one day enjoy an adequate competence if he closely followed the industrious habits of the thrifty bee, spent the greater part of his life in anointing his thighs with the yellow powder which he laboriously collected from the flowers of the field. It is not so recorded; but doubtless the nameless one in question was by profession a maker of opium pipes, for this person has observed from time to time how that occupation, above all others, tends to degrade the mental faculties, and to debase its followers to a lower position than that of the beasts of labour. Learn therefrom, O superficial Wang Yu, that wisdom lies in an intelligent perception of great principles, and not in a slavish imitation of details which are, for the most part, beyond your simple and insufficient understanding.'

'Such may, indeed, be the case, Kai Lung,' replied Wang Yu sullenly — for it was the story-teller in question who had approached unperceived, and who now stood before them — 'but it is none the less a fact that, on the last occasion when this misguided person joined the attending circle at your uplifted voice, a mandarin of the third degree chanced to pass through Wu-whei, and halted at the doorstep of "The Fountain of Beauty," fully intending to entrust this one with the designing and fashioning of a pipe of exceptional elaborateness. This matter, by his absence, has now passed from him, and to-day, through listening to the narrative of how the accomplished Yuin-Pel doubled his fortune, he is the poorer by many taels.'

'Yet to-morrow, when the name of the Mandarin of the third degree appears in the list of persons who have transferred their entire property to those who are nearly related to them in order to avoid it being seized to satisfy the just claims made against them,' replied Kai Lung, 'you will be able to regard yourself the richer by so many taels.'

At these words, which recalled to the minds of all who were present the not uncommon manner of behaving observed by those of exalted rank, who freely engaged persons to supply them with costly articles without in any way regarding the price to be paid, Wang Yu was silent.

'Nevertheless,' exclaimed a thin voice from the edge of the group which surrounded Kai Lung, 'it in nowise follows that the stories are in themselves excellent, or of such a nature that the hearing of their recital will profit a person. Wang Yu may be satisfied with empty words, but there are others present who were studying deep matters when Wang Yu was learning the art of walking. If Kai

Lung's stories are of such remunerative benefit as the person in question claims, how does it chance that Kai Lung himself, who is assuredly the best acquainted with them, stands before us in mean apparel, and on all occasions confessing an unassumed poverty?'

'It is Yan-hi Pung,' went from mouth to mouth among the bystanders – 'Yan-hi Pung, who traces on paper the words of chants and historical tales, and sells them to such as can afford to buy. And although his motive in exposing the emptiness of Kai Lung's stories may not be Heaven-sent – inasmuch as Kai Lung provides us with such matter as he himself purveys, only at a much more moderate price – yet his words are well considered, and must, therefore, be regarded.'

'O Yan-hi Pung,' replied Kai Lung, hearing the name from those who stood about him, and moving towards the aged person, who stood meanwhile leaning upon his staff, and looking from side to side with quickly moving eyelids in a manner very offensive towards the story-teller, 'your just remark shows you to be a person of exceptional wisdom, even as your well-bowed legs prove you to be one of great bodily strength; for justice is ever obvious and wisdom hidden, and they who build structures for endurance discard the straight and upright and insist upon such an arch as you so symmetrically exemplify.'

Speaking in this conciliatory manner, Kai Lung came up to Yan-hi Pung, and taking between his fingers a disc of thick polished crystal, which the aged and short-sighted chant-writer used for the purpose of magnifying and bringing nearer the letters upon which he was engaged, and which hung around his neck by an embroidered cord, the story-teller held it aloft, crying aloud:

'Observe closely, and presently it will be revealed and made clear how the apparently very conflicting words of the wise Yan-hi Pung, and those of this unassuming but nevertheless conscientious person who is now addressing you, are, in reality, as one great truth.'

With this assurance Kai Lung moved the crystal somewhat, so that it engaged the sun's rays, and concentrated them upon the uncovered crown of the unsuspecting and still objectionably engaged person before him. Without a moment's pause, Yan-hi Pung leapt high into the air, repeatedly pressing his hand to the spot thus selected, and crying aloud:

'Evil dragons and thunderbolts! but the touch was as hot as a scar left by the uncut nail of the sublime Buddha!'

'Yet the crystal –' remarked Kai Lung composedly, passing it into the hands of those who stood near.

'Is as cool as the innermost leaves of the river-side sycamore,' they declared.

Kai Lung said nothing further, but raised both his hands above his head, as if demanding their judgment. Thereupon a loud shout went up on his behalf, for the greater part of them loved to see the manner in which he brushed aside those who would oppose him; and the sight of the aged person Yan-hi Pung leaping far into the air had caused them to become exceptionally amused, and, in consequence, very amiably disposed towards the one who had afforded them the entertainment.

'The story of Sen Heng,' began Kai Lung, when the discussion had terminated in the manner already recorded, 'concerns itself with one who possessed an unsuspecting and ingenuous nature, which ill-fitted him to take an ordinary part in the everyday affairs of life, no matter how engaging such a character rendered him among his friends and relations. Having at an early age been entrusted with a burden of rice and other produce from his father's fields to dispose of in the best possible manner at a neighbouring mart, and having completed the transaction in a manner extremely advantageous to those with whom he trafficked, but very intolerable to the one who had sent him, it at once became apparent that some other means of gaining a livelihood must be discovered for him.

' "Beyond all doubt," said his father, after considering the matter for a period, "it is a case in which one should be governed by the wise advice and example of the Mandarin Poo-chow."

' "Illustrious sire," exclaimed Sen Heng, who chanced to be present, "the illiterate person who stands before you is entirely unacquainted with the one to whom you have referred; nevertheless, he will, as you suggest, at once set forth, and journeying with all speed to the abode of the estimable Poo-chow, solicit his experience and advice."

' "Unless a more serious loss should be occasioned," replied the father coldly, "there is no necessity to adopt so extreme a course. The benevolent Mandarin in question existed at a remote period of the Thang dynasty, and the incident to which an allusion has been made arose in the following way: To the public court of the enlightened Poo-chow there came one day a youth of very inferior appearance and hesitating manner, who besought his explicit advice, saying: 'The degraded and unprepossessing being before you, O select and venerable Mandarin, is by nature and attainments a person of the utmost timidity and fearfulness. From this cause life itself has become a detestable observance in his eyes, for those who should be his companions of both sexes hold him in undisguised contempt, making various unendurable allusions to the colour and nature of his internal organs whenever he would endeavour to join them. Instruct him, therefore, the manner in which this cowardice may be removed, and no service in return will be esteemed too great.' 'There is a remedy,' replied the benevolent Mandarin, without any hesitation whatever, 'which if properly carried out is efficacious beyond the possibility of failure. Certain component parts of your body are lacking, and before the desired result can be obtained these must be supplied from without. Of all courageous things the tiger is the most fearless, and in consequence it combines all those ingredients which you require; furthermore, as the teeth of the tiger are the instruments with which it accomplishes its vengeful purpose, there reside the essential principles of its inimitable courage. Let the person who seeks instruction in the matter, therefore, do as follows: taking the teeth of a full-grown tiger as soon as it is slain, and before the essences have time to return into the body, he shall grind them to a powder, and mixing the powder with a portion of rice, consume it. After seven days he must repeat the observance, and yet again a third time, after another similar lapse. Let him, then, return for further guidance; for the present the matter interests this person no further.' At these words the youth departed, filled with a new and inspired hope; for the wisdom of the sagacious Poo-chow was a matter which did not admit of any doubt whatever, and he had spoken with well-defined certainty of the success of the experiment. Nevertheless, after several days industriously spent in endeavouring to obtain by purchase the teeth of a newly-slain tiger, the details of the undertaking began to assume a new and entirely unforeseen aspect; for those whom he approached as being the most likely to possess what he required either became very immoderately and disagreeably amused at the nature of the request, or regarded it as a new and ill-judged form of ridicule, which they prepared to avenge by blows and by base remarks of the most personal variety. At length it became unavoidably obvious to the youth that if he was to obtain the articles in question it would first be necessary that he should become adept in the art of slaying tigers, for in no other way were the required conditions likely to be present. Although the prospect was one which did not greatly tend to allure him, yet he did not regard it with the utterly incapable emotions which would have been present on an earlier occasion; for the habit of continually guarding himself from the onslaughts of those who received his inquiry in an attitude of narrow-minded distrust had inspired him with a new-found valour, while his amiable and unrestrained manner of life increased his bodily vigour in every degree. First perfecting himself in the use of the bow and arrow, therefore, he betook himself to a wild and very extensive forest, and there concealed himself among the upper foliage of a tall tree standing by the side of a pool of water. On the second night of his watch the youth perceived a large but somewhat ill-conditioned tiger approaching the pool for the purpose of quenching its thirst, whereupon he tremblingly fitted an arrow to his bow-string, and profiting by the instruction he had received, succeeded in piercing the creature to the heart. After fulfilling the observance laid upon him by the discriminating Poo-chow, the youth determined to remain in the forest, and sustain himself upon such food as fell to his weapons, until the time arrived when he should carry out the rite for the last time. At the end of seven days, so subtle had he become in all kinds of hunting, and so strengthened by the meat and herbs upon which he existed, that he disdained to avail himself of the shelter of a tree, but standing openly by the side of the water, he engaged the attention of the first tiger which came to drink, and discharged arrow after arrow into its body with unfailing power and precision. So entrancing, indeed, had the pursuit become that the next seven days lengthened out into the apparent period of as many moons, in such a leisurely manner did they rise and fall. On the appointed day, without waiting for the evening to arrive, the youth set out with the first appearance of light, and penetrated into the most inaccessible jungles, crying aloud words of taunt-laden challenge to all the beasts therein, and accusing the ancestors of their race of every imaginable variety of evil behaviour. Yet so great had become the renown of the one who stood forth, and so widely had the warning voice been passed from tree to tree, preparing all who dwelt in the forest against his anger, that not even the fiercest replied openly, though low growls and mutterings proceeded from every cave within a bowshot's distance around. Wearying quickly of such feeble and timorous demonstrations, the youth rushed into the cave from which the loudest murmurs proceeded, and there discovered a tiger of unnatural size, surrounded by the bones of innumerable ones whom it had devoured; for from time to time its ravages became so great and unbearable, that armies were raised in the neighbouring villages and sent to destroy it, but more than a few stragglers never returned. Plainly recognizing that a just and inevitable vengeance had overtaken it, the tiger made only a very inferior exhibition of resistance, and the youth, having first stunned it with a blow of his closed hand, seized it by the middle, and repeatedly dashed its head against the rocky sides of its retreat. He then performed for the third time the ceremony enjoined by the Mandarin, and having cast upon the cringing and despicable forms concealed in the surrounding woods and caves a look of dignified and ineffable contempt, set out upon his homeward journey, and in the space of three days' time reached the town of the versatile Poo-chow. 'Behold,' exclaimed that person, when, lifting up his eyes, he saw the youth approaching laden with the skins of the tigers and other spoils, 'now at least the youths and maidens of your native village will no longer withdraw themselves from the company of so undoubtedly heroic a person.' 'Illustrious Mandarin,' replied the other, casting both his weapons and his trophies before his inspired adviser's feet, 'what has this person to do with the little ones of either sex? Give him rather the foremost place in your ever-victorious company of bowmen, so that he may repay in part the undoubted debt under which he henceforth exists.' This proposal found favour with the pure-minded Poo-chow, so that in course of time the unassuming youth who had come supplicating his advice became the valiant commander of his army, and the one eventually chosen to present plighting gifts to his only daughter."

'When the father had completed the narrative of how the faint-hearted youth became in the end a courageous and resourceful leader of bowmen, Sen looked up, and not in any degree understanding the purpose of the story, or why it had been set forth before him, exclaimed:

' "Undoubtedly the counsel of the graceful and intelligent Mandarin Poo-chow was of inestimable service in the case recorded, and this person would gladly adopt it as his guide for the future, on the chance of it leading to a similar honourable career; but alas! there are no tigers to be found throughout this Province."

' "It is a loss which those who are engaged in commerce in the city of Hankow strive to supply adequately," replied his father, who had an assured feeling that it would be of no avail to endeavour to show Sen that the story which he had just related was one setting forth a definite precept rather than fixing an exact manner of behaviour. "For that reason," he continued, "this person has concluded an arrangement by which you will journey to that place, and there enter into the house of commerce of an expert and conscientious vendor of moving contrivances. Among so rapacious and keen-witted a class of persons as they of Hankow, it is exceedingly unlikely that your amiable disposition will involve any individual one in an unavoidable serious loss, and even should such an unforeseen event come to pass, there will, at least, be the undeniable satisfaction of the thought that the unfortunate occurrence will in no way affect the prosperity of those to whom you are bound by the natural ties of affection."

' "Benevolent and virtuous-minded father," replied Sen gently, but speaking with an inspired conviction; "from his earliest infancy this unassuming one has been instructed in an inviolable regard for the Five General Principles of Fidelity to the Emperor, Respect for Parents, Harmony between Husband and Wife, Agreement among Brothers, and Constancy in Friendship. It will be entirely unnecessary to inform so pious-minded a person as the one now being addressed that no evil can attend the footsteps of an individual who courteously observes these enactments."

' "Without doubt it is so arranged by the protecting Deities," replied the father; "yet it is an exceedingly desirable thing for those who are responsible in the matter that the footsteps to which reference has been made should not linger in the neighbourhood of this village, but should, with all possible speed, turn in the direction of Hankow."

'In this manner it came to pass that Sen Heng set forth on the following day, and coming without delay to the great and powerful city of Hankow, sought out the house of commerce known as "The Pure Gilt Dragon of Exceptional Symmetry," where the versatile King-y-Yang engaged in the entrancing occupation of contriving moving figures, and other devices of an ingenious and mirth-provoking character, which he entrusted into the hands of numerous persons to sell throughout the Province. From this cause, although enjoying a very agreeable recompense from the sale of the objects, the greatly perturbed King-y-Yang suffered continual internal misgivings; for the habit of behaving of those whom he appointed to go forth in the manner described was such that he could not entirely dismiss from his mind an assured conviction that the details were not invariably as they were represented to be. Frequently would one return in a very deficient and unpresentable condition of garment, asserting that on his return, while passing through a lonely and unprotected district, he had been assailed by an armed band of robbers, and despoiled of all he possessed. Another would claim to have been made the sport of evil spirits, who led him astray by means of false signs in the forest, and finally destroyed his entire burden of commodities, accompanying the unworthy act by loud cries of triumph, and remarks of an insulting nature concerning King-y-Yang; for the honourable character and charitable actions of the person in question had made him very objectionable to that class of beings. Others continually accounted for the absence of the required number of taels by declaring that at a certain point of their journey they were made the object of marks of amiable condescension on the part of a high and dignified public official, who, on learning in whose service they were, immediately professed an intimate personal friendship with the estimable King-y-Yang, and, out of a feeling of gratified respect for him, took away all such contrivances as remained undisposed of, promising to arrange the payment with the refined King-y-Yang himself when they should next meet. For these reasons King-y-Yang was especially desirous of obtaining one whose spoken word could be received, upon all points, as an assured fact, and it was, therefore, with an emotion of internal lightness that he confidently heard from those who were acquainted with the person that Sen Heng was, by nature and endowments, utterly incapable of representing matters of even the most insignificant degree to be otherwise than what they really were.

'Filled with an acute anxiety to discover what amount of success would be accorded to his latest contrivance, King-y-Yang led Sen Heng to a secluded chamber, and there instructed him in the method of selling certain apparently very ingeniously constructed ducks, which would have the appearance of swimming about on the surface of an open vessel of water, at the same time uttering loud and ever-increasing cries, after the manner of their kind. With ill-restrained admiration at the skilful nature of the deception, King-y-Yang pointed out that the ducks which were to be disposed of, and upon which a seemingly very low price was fixed, did not, in reality, possess any of these accomplishments, but would, on the contrary, if placed in water, at once sink to the bottom in a most incapable manner; it being part of Sen's duty to exhibit only a specially prepared creature which was restrained upon the surface by means of hidden cords, and, while bending over it, to simulate the cries as agreed upon. After satisfying himself that Sen could perform these movements competently, King-y-Yang sent him forth, particularly charging him that he should not return without a sum of money which fully represented the entire number of ducks entrusted to him, or an adequate number of unsold ducks to compensate for the deficiency.

'At the end of seven days Sen returned to King-y-Yang, and although entirely without money, even to the extent of being unable to provide himself with the merest necessities of a frugal existence, he honourably returned the full number of ducks with which he had set out. It then became evident that although Sen had diligently perfected himself in the sounds and movements which King-y-Yang had contrived, he had not fully understood that they were to be executed stealthily, but had, in consequence, manifested the accomplishment openly, not unreasonably supposing that such an exhibition would be an additional inducement to those who appeared to be well-disposed towards the purchase. From this cause it came about that although large crowds were attracted by Sen's manner of conducting the enterprise, none actually engaged to purchase even the least expensively valued of the ducks, although several publicly complimented Sen on his exceptional proficiency, and repeatedly urged him to louder and more frequent cries, suggesting that by such means possible buyers might be attracted to the spot from remote and inaccessible villages in the neighbourhood.

'When King-y-Yang learned how the venture had been carried out, he became most intolerably self-opinionated in his expressions towards Sen's mental attainments and the manner of his bringing up. It was entirely in vain that the one referred to pointed out in a tone of persuasive and courteous restraint that he had not, down to the most minute particulars, transgressed either the general or the specific obligations of the Five General Principles, and that, therefore, he was blameless, and even worthy of commendation for the manner in which he had acted. With an inelegant absence of all refined feeling, King-y-Yang most incapably declined to discuss the various aspects of the controversy in an amiable manner, asserting, indeed, that for the consideration of as many brass cash as Sen had mentioned principles he would cause him to be thrown into prison as a person of unnatural ineptitude. Then, without rewarding Sen for the time spent in his service, or even inviting him to partake of food and wine, the insufferable deviser of very indifferent animated contrivances again sent him out, this time into the streets of Hankow with a number of delicately inlaid boxes, remarking in a tone of voice which plainly indicated an exactly contrary desire that he would be filled with an overwhelming satisfaction if Sen could discover any excuse for returning a second time without disposing of anything. This remark Sen's ingenuous nature led him to regard as a definite fact, so that when a passer-by, who tarried to examine the boxes, chanced to remark that the colours might have been arranged to greater advantage, in which case he would certainly have purchased at least one of the articles, Sen hastened back, although in a distant part of the city, to inform King-y-Yang of the suggestion, adding that he himself had been favourably impressed with the improvement which would be effected by such an alteration.

'The nature of King-y-Yang's emotion when Sen again presented himself before him – and when by repeatedly applied tests on various parts of his body he understood that he was neither the victim of malicious demons, nor wandering in an insensible condition in the Middle Air, but that the cause of the return was such as had been plainly stated – was of so mixed and benumbing a variety, that for a considerable space of time he was quite unable to express himself in any way, either by words or by signs. By the time these attributes returned there had formed itself within King-y-Yang's mind a design of most contemptible malignity, which seemed to present to his enfeebled intellect a scheme by which Sen would be adequately punished, and finally disposed of without causing him any further trouble in the matter. For this purpose he concealed the real condition of his sentiments towards Sen, and warmly expressed himself in terms of delicate flattery regarding that one's sumptuous and unfailing taste in the matter of the blending of the colours. Without doubt, he continued, such an alteration as the one proposed would greatly increase the attractiveness of the inlaid boxes, and the matter should be engaged upon without delay. In the meantime, however, not to waste the immediate services of so discriminating and persevering a servant, he would entrust Sen with a mission of exceptional importance, which would certainly tend greatly to his remunerative benefit. In the district of Yun, in the north-western part of the Province, said the crafty and treacherous King-y-

Yang, a particular kind of insect was greatly esteemed on account of the beneficent influence which it exercised over the rice plants, causing them to mature earlier, and to attain a greater size than ever happened in its absence. In recent years this creature had rarely been seen in the neighbourhood of Yun, and, in consequence, the earth-tillers throughout that country had been brought into a most disconcerting state of poverty, and would, inevitably, be prepared to exchange whatever they still possessed for even a few of the insects, in order that they might liberate them to increase, and so entirely reverse the objectionable state of things. Speaking in this manner, King-y-Yang entrusted to Sen a carefully prepared box containing a score of the insects, obtained at a great cost from a country beyond the Bitter Water, and after giving him further directions concerning the journey, and enjoining the utmost secrecy about the valuable contents of the box, he sent him forth.

'The discreet and sagacious will already have understood the nature of King-y-Yang's intolerable artifice; but, for the benefit of the amiable and unsuspecting, it is necessary to make it clear that the words which he had spoken bore no sort of resemblance to affairs as they really existed. The district around Yun was indeed involved in a most unprepossessing destitution, but this had been caused, not by the absence of any rare and auspicious insect, but by the presence of vast hordes of locusts, which had overwhelmed and devoured the entire face of the country. It so chanced that among the recently constructed devices at "The Pure Gilt Dragon of Exceptional Symmetry" were a number of elegant representations of rice fields and fruit gardens so skilfully fashioned that they deceived even the creatures,

and attracted, among other living things, all the locusts in
Hankow into that place of commerce. It was a number of
these insects that King-y-Yang vindictively placed in the
box which he instructed Sen to carry to Yun, well knowing that the reception which would be accorded to anyone
who appeared there on such a mission would be of so fatally
destructive a kind that the consideration of his return need
not engage a single conjecture.

'Entirely tranquil in intellect – for the possibility of
King-y-Yang's intention being in any way other than what
he had represented it to be did not arise within Sen's
ingenuous mind – the person in question cheerfully set
forth on his long but unavoidable march towards the region
of Yun. As he journeyed along the way, the nature of his
meditation brought before him the events which had taken
place since his arrival at Hankow; and, for the first time, it
was brought within his understanding that the story of the
youth and the three tigers, which his father had related to
him, was in the likeness to a proverb, by which counsel and
warning is conveyed in a graceful and inoffensive manner.
Readily applying the fable to his own condition, he could
not doubt but that the first two animals to be overthrown
were represented by the two undertakings which he had
already conscientiously performed in the matter of the
mechanical ducks and the inlaid boxes, and the conviction
that he was even then engaged on the third and last trial
filled him with an intelligent gladness so unobtrusive and
refined that he could express his entrancing emotions in no
other way than by lifting up his voice and uttering the far-
reaching cries which he had used on the first of the occasions just referred to.

'In this manner the first part of the journey passed

away with engaging celerity. Anxious as Sen undoubtedly
was to complete the third task, and approach the details
which, in his own case, would correspond with the command of the bowmen and the marriage with the Mandarin's daughter of the person in the story, the noontide
heat compelled him to rest in the shade by the wayside for a
lengthy period each day. During one of these pauses it
occurred to his versatile mind that the time which was
otherwise uselessly expended might be well disposed of in
endeavouring to increase the value and condition of the
creatures under his care by instructing them in the per-
formance of some simple accomplishments, such as might
not be too laborious for their feeble and immature understanding. In this he was more successful than he had
imagined could possibly have been the case, for the discriminating insects, from the first, had every appearance of
recognizing that Sen was inspired by a sincere regard for
their ultimate benefit, and was not merely using them
for his own advancement. So assiduously did they devote
themselves to their allotted tasks, that in a very short space
of time there was no detail in connection with their own
simple domestic arrangements that was not understood and
daily carried out by an appointed band. Entranced at this
intelligent manner of conducting themselves, Sen industriously applied his time to the more congenial task of
instructing them in the refined arts, and presently he had
the enchanting satisfaction of witnessing a number of the
most cultivated faultlessly and unhesitatingly perform a
portion of the well-known gravity-removing play entitled
"The Benevolent Omen of White Dragon Tea Garden;
or, Three Times a Mandarin." Not even content with
this elevating display, Sen ingeniously contrived, from

various objects which he discovered at different points by the wayside, an effective and lifelike representation of a war-junk, for which he trained a crew, who, at an agreed signal, would take up their appointed places and go through the required movements, both of sailing and of discharging the guns, in reliable and efficient manner.

'As Sen was one day educating the least competent of the insects, in the simpler parts of banner-carriers, gong-beaters, and the like, to their more graceful and versatile companions, he lifted up his eyes and beheld, standing by his side, a person of very elaborately embroidered apparel and commanding personality, who had all the appearance of one who had been observing his movements for some space of time. Calling up within his remembrance the warning which he had received from King-y-Yang, Sen was preparing to restore the creatures to their closed box, when the stranger, in a loud and dignified voice, commanded him to refrain, adding:

' "There is, resting at a spot within the immediate neighbourhood, a person of illustrious name and ancestry, who would doubtless be gratified to witness the diverting actions of which this one has recently been a spectator. As the reward of a tael cannot be unwelcome to a person of your inferior appearance and unpresentable garments, take up your box without delay, and follow the one who is now before you."

'With these words the richly clad stranger led the way through a narrow woodland path, closely followed by Sen, to whom the attraction of the promised reward – a larger sum, indeed, than he had ever possessed – was sufficiently alluring to make him determined that the other should not, for the briefest possible moment, pass beyond his sight.

'Not to withhold that which Sen was entirely ignorant of until a later period, it is now revealed that the person in question was the official Provider of Diversions and Pleasurable Occupations to the sacred and illimitable Emperor, who was then engaged in making an unusually extensive march through the eight Provinces surrounding his Capital — for the acute and well-educated will not need to be reminded that Nankin occupied that position at the time now engaged with. Until his providential discovery of Sen, the distinguished Provider had been immersed in a most unenviable condition of despair, for his enlightened but exceedingly perverse-minded master had, of late, declined to be in any way amused, or even interested, by the simple and unpretentious entertainment which could be obtained in so inaccessible a region. The well-intentioned efforts of the followers of the Court, who engagingly endeavoured to divert the Imperial mind by performing certain feats which they remembered to have witnessed on previous occasions, but which, until the necessity arose, they had never essayed, were entirely without result of a beneficial order. Even the accomplished Provider's one attainment — that of striking together both the hands and the feet thrice simultaneously, while leaping into the air, and at the same time producing a sound not unlike that emitted by a large and vigorous bee when held captive in the fold of a robe, an action which never failed to throw the illustrious Emperor into a most uncontrollable state of amusement when performed within the Imperial Palace — now only drew from him the unsympathetic, if not actually offensive, remark that the attitude and the noise bore a remarked resemblance to those produced by a person when being bowstrung, adding, with unprepossessing significance, that of the two entertainments he had an unevadable conviction that the bowstringing would be the more acceptable and gravity-removing.

'When Sen beheld the size and the silk-hung magnificence of the camp into which his guide led him, he was filled with astonishment, and at the same time recognized that he had acted in an injudicious and hasty manner by so readily accepting the offer of a tael; whereas, if he had been in possession of the true facts of the case, as they now appeared, he would certainly have endeavoured to obtain double that amount before consenting. As he was hesitating in a most uncongenial state of uncertainty, and debating within himself whether the matter might not even yet be arranged in a more advantageous manner, he was suddenly led forward into the most striking and ornamental of the tents, and commanded to engage the attention of the one in whose presence he found himself, without delay.

'From the first moment when the inimitable creatures began, at Sen's spoken word, to go through the ordinary details of their domestic affairs, there was no sort of doubt as to the nature of the success with which their well-trained exertions would be received. The dark shadows instantly forsook the enraptured Emperor's select brow, and from time to time he expressed himself in words of most unrestrained and intimate encouragement. So exuberant became the overjoyed Provider's emotion at having at length succeeded in obtaining the services of one who was able to recall his Imperial master's unclouded countenance, that he came forward in a most unpresentable state of haste, and rose into the air uncommanded, for the display of his usually not unwelcome acquirement. This he would doubtless have executed competently had not Sen, who stood immediately behind him, suddenly and unexpectedly raised his voice in a very vigorous and proficient duck cry, thereby causing the one before him to endeavour to turn round in alarm, while yet in the air — an intermingled state of movements of both the body and the mind that caused him to abandon his original intention in a manner which removed the gravity of the Emperor to an even more pronounced degree than had been effected by the diverting attitudes of the insects.

'When the gratified Emperor had beheld every portion of the tasks which Sen had instilled into the minds of the insects, down even to the minutest detail, he called the well-satisfied Provider before him, and addressing him in a voice which might be designed to betray either sternness or an amiable indulgence said:

' "You, O Shan-se, are reported to be a person of no particular intellect or discernment, and, for this reason, these ones who are speaking have a desire to know how the matter will present itself in your eyes. Which is it the more commendable and honourable for a person to train to a condition of unfailing excellence, human beings of confessed intelligence or insects of a low and degraded standard?"

'To this remark the discriminating Shan-se made no reply, being, indeed, undecided in his mind whether such a course was expected of him. On several previous occasions the somewhat introspective Emperor had addressed himself to persons in what they judged to be the form of a question, as one might say, "How blue is the unapproachable air canopy, and how delicately imagined the colour of the clouds!" yet when they had expressed their deliberate opinion on the subjects referred to, stating the exact degree of blueness, and the like, the nature of their reception ever afterwards was such that, for the future, persons endeavoured to determine exactly the intention of the Emperor's mind before declaring themselves in words. Being exceedingly doubtful on this occasion, therefore, the very cautious Shan-se adopted the more prudent and uncompromising attitude, and smiling acquiescently, he raised both his hands with a self-deprecatory movement.

' "Alas!" exclaimed the Emperor, in a tone which plainly indicated that the evasive Shan-se had adopted a course which did not commend itself, "how unendurable a condition of affairs is it for a person of acute mental perception to be annoyed by the inopportune behaviour of one who is only fit to mix on terms of equality with beggars and low-caste street cleaners –"

' "Such a condition of affairs is indeed most offensively unbearable, illustrious Being," remarked Shan-se, who clearly perceived that his former silence had not been productive of a delicate state of feeling towards himself.

' "It has frequently been said," continued the courteous and pure-minded Emperor, only signifying his refined displeasure at Shan-se's really ill-considered observation by so arranging his position that the person in question no longer enjoyed the sublime distinction of gazing upon his beneficent face, "that titles and offices have been accorded, from time to time, without any regard for the fitting qualifications of those to whom they were presented. The truth that such a state of things does occasionally exist has been brought before our eyes during the past few days by the abandoned and inefficient behaviour of one who will henceforth be a marked official; yet it has always been our endeavour to reward expert and unassuming merit, whenever it is discovered. As we were setting forth, when we were interrupted in a most obstinate and superfluous manner, the one who can guide and cultivate the minds of unthinking, and not infrequently obstinate and rapacious, insects would certainly enjoy an even greater measure of success if entrusted with the discriminating intellects of human beings. For this reason it appears that no more fitting person could be found to occupy the important and well-rewarded position of Chief Arranger of the Competitive Examinations than the one before us — provided his opinions and manner of expressing himself are such as commend themselves to us. To satisfy us on this point let Sen Heng now stand forth and declare his beliefs."

'On this invitation Sen advanced the requisite number of paces, and not in any degree understanding what was required of him, determined that the occasion was one when he might fittingly declare the Five General Principles, which were ever present in his mind. "Unquestioning Fidelity to the Sacred Emperor —" he began, when the person in question signified that the trial was over.

' " After so competent and inspired an expression as that which has just been uttered, which, if rightly considered, includes all lesser things, it is unnecessary to say more," he declared affably. "The appointment which has already been specified is now declared to be legally conferred. The evening will be devoted to a repetition of the entrancing manœuvres performed by the insects, to be followed by a feast and music in honour of the recognized worth and position of the accomplished Sen Heng. There is really no necessity for the apparently over-fatigued Shan-se to attend the festival."

'In such a manner was the foundation of Sen's ultimate prosperity established, by which he came in the process of time to occupy a very high place in public esteem. Yet, being a person of honourable-minded conscientiousness, he did not hesitate, when questioned by those who made pilgrimages to him for the purpose of learning by what means he had risen to so remunerative a position, to ascribe his success, not entirely to his own intelligent perception of persons and events, but, in part also, to a never-failing regard for the dictates of the Five General Principles, and a discriminating subservience to the inspired wisdom of the venerable Poo-chow, as conveyed to him in the story of the faint-hearted youth and the three tigers. This story Sen furthermore caused to be inscribed in letters of gold, and displayed in a prominent position in his native village, where it has since doubtless been the means of instructing and advancing countless observant ones who have not been too insufferable to be guided by the experience of those who have gone before.'

CHAPTER FOUR

THE EXPERIMENT OF THE MANDARIN CHAN HUNG

*

RELATED BY KAI LUNG AT SHAN TZU, ON THE OCCASION OF HIS RECEIVING A VERY UNEXPECTED REWARD

'THERE are certainly many occasions when the principles of the Mandarin Chan Hung appear to find practical favour in the eyes of those who form this usually uncomplaining person's audiences at Shan Tzu,' remarked Kai Lung, with patient resignation, as he took up his collecting-bowl and transferred the few brass coins which it held to a concealed place among his garments. 'Has the village lately suffered from a visit of one of those persons who come armed with authority to remove by force or stratagem such goods as bear names other than those possessed by their holders? or is it, indeed — as they of Wu-whei confidently assert — that when the Day of Vows arrives the people of Shan Tzu, with one accord, undertake to deny themselves in the matter of gifts and free offerings, in spite of every conflicting impulse?'

'They of Wu-whei!' exclaimed a self-opinionated bystander, who had by some means obtained an inferior public office, and who was, in consequence, enable to be present on all occasions without contributing any offering. 'Well is that village named "The Refuge of Unworthiness," for its dwellers do little but rob and ill-treat strangers, and spread evil and lying reports concerning better endowed ones than themselves.'

'Such a condition of affairs may exist,' replied Kai Lung

without any indication of concern either one way or the other; 'yet it is an undeniable fact that they reward this commonplace story-teller's too often under-estimated efforts in a manner which betrays them either to be of noble birth, or very desirous of putting to shame their less prosperous neighbouring places.'

'Such exhibitions of uncalled-for lavishness are merely the signs of an ill-regulated and inordinate vanity,' remarked a Mandarin of the eighth grade, who chanced to be passing, and who stopped to listen to Kai Lung's words. 'Nevertheless, it is not fitting that a collection of decaying hovels which Wu-whei assuredly is, should, in however small a detail, appear to rise above Shan Tzu, so that if the versatile and unassuming Kai Lung will again honour this assembly by allowing his well-constructed bowl to pass freely to and fro, this obscure and otherwise entirely superfluous individual will make it his especial care that the brass of Wu-whei shall be answered with solid copper, and its debased pewter with doubly refined silver.'

With these encouraging words the very opportune Mandarin of the eighth grade himself followed the story-teller's collecting-bowl, observing closely what each person contributed, so that, although he gave nothing from his own store, Kai Lung had never before received so honourable an amount.

'O illustrious Kai Lung,' exclaimed a very industrious and ill-clad herb-gatherer, who, in spite of his poverty, could not refrain from mingling with the listeners whenever the story-teller appeared in Shan Tzu, 'a single piece of brass money is to this person more than a block of solid gold to many of Wu-whei; yet he has twice made the customary offering, once freely, once because a courteous and pure-minded individual who possesses certain written papers of his connected with the repayment of some few taels walked behind the bowl and engaged his eyes with an unmistakable and very significant glance. This fact emboldens him to make the following petition: that in place of the not altogether unknown story of Yung Chang which had been announced, the proficient and nimble-minded Kai Lung will entice our attention with the history of the Mandarin Chan Hung, to which reference has already been made.'

'The occasion is undoubtedly one which calls for recognition to an unusual degree,' replied Kai Lung with extreme affability. 'To that end this person will accordingly narrate the story which has been suggested, notwithstanding the fact that it has been specially prepared for the ears of the sublime Emperor, who is at this moment awaiting this unseemly one's arrival in Pekin with every mark of ill-restrained impatience, tempered only by his expectation of being the first to hear the story of the well-meaning but somewhat premature Chan Hung.

'The Mandarin in question lived during the reign of the accomplished Emperor Tsint-Sin, his Yamên being at Fow Hou, in the Province of Shan-Tung, of which place he was consequently the chief official. In his conscientious desire to administer a pure and beneficent rule, he not infrequently made himself a very prominent object for public disregard, especially by his attempts to introduce untried things, when from time to time such matters arose within his mind and seemed to promise agreeable and remunerative results. In this manner it came about that the streets of Fow Hou were covered with large flat stones, to the great inconvenience of those persons who had, from a very remote period, been in the habit of passing the night on the soft clay which at all seasons of the year afforded a pleasant and efficient resting-place. Nevertheless, in certain matters his engaging efforts were attended by an obvious success. Having noticed that misfortunes and losses are much less keenly felt when they immediately follow in the steps of an earlier evil, the benevolent and humane-minded Chan Hung devised an ingenious method of lightening the burden of a necessary taxation by arranging that those persons who were the most heavily involved should be made the victims of an attack and robbery on the night before the matter became due. By this thoughtful expedient the unpleasant duty of parting from so many taels was almost imperceptibly led up to, and when, after the lapse of some slight period, the first sums of money were secretly returned, with a written proverb appropriate to the occasion, the public rejoicing of those who, had the matter been left to its natural course, would still have been filling the air with bitter and unendurable lamentations plainly testified to the inspired wisdom of the enlightened Mandarin.

'The well-merited success of this amiable expedient caused the Mandarin Chan Hung every variety of intelligent emotion, and no day passed without him devoting a portion of his time to the labour of discovering other advantages of a similar nature. Engrossed in deep and very sublime thought of this order, he chanced on a certain day to be journeying through Fow Hou, when he met a person of irregular intellect, who made an uncertain livelihood by following the unassuming and charitably disposed from place to place, chanting in a loud voice set verses recording their virtues, which he composed in their honour. On account of his undoubted infirmities this person was permitted a greater freedom of speech with those above him than would have been the case had his condition been merely ordinary; so that when Chan Hung observed him becoming very grossly amused on his approach, to such an extent, indeed, that he neglected to perform any of the fitting acts of obeisance, the wise and noble-minded Mandarin did not in any degree suffer his complacency to be affected, but, drawing near, addressed him in a calm and dignified manner.

' "Why, O Ming-hi," he said, "do you permit your gravity to be removed to such an exaggerated degree at the sight of this in no way striking or exceptional person? and why, indeed, do you stand in so unbecoming an attitude in the presence of one who, in spite of his depraved inferiority, is unquestionably your official superior, and could, without any hesitation, condemn you to the tortures or even to bowstringing on the spot?"

' "Mandarin," exclaimed Ming-hi, stepping up to Chan Hung, and, without any hesitation, pressing the gilt button which adorned the official's body garment, accompanying the action by a continuous muffled noise which suggested the repeated striking of a hidden bell, "you wonder that this person stands erect on your approach, neither rolling his lowered head repeatedly from side to side, nor tracing circles in the dust of Fow Hou with his submissive stomach? Know, then, the meaning of the proverb, 'Distrust an inordinate appearance of servility. The estimable person who retires from your presence walking backwards may adopt that deferential manner in order to keep concealed the long double-edged knife with which he had hoped to slay you.' The excessive amusement that seized this offensive person when he beheld your well-defined figure in the distance arose from his perception of your internal satisfaction, which is, indeed, unmistakably reflected in your symmetrical countenance. For, O Mandarin, in spite of your honourable endeavours to turn things which are devious into a straight line, the matters upon which you engage your versatile intellect — little as you suspect the fact — are as grains of the finest Foochow sand in comparison with that which escapes your attention."

' "Strange are your words, O Ming-hi, and dark to this person your meaning," replied Chan Hung, whose feelings were evenly balanced between a desire to know what thing he had neglected and a fear that his dignity might suffer if he were observed to remain long conversing with a person of Ming-hi's low mental attainments. "Without delay, and with an entire absence of lengthy and ornamental forms of speech, express the omission to which you have made reference; for this person has an uneasy inside emotion that you are merely endeavouring to engage his attention to the end that you may make an unseemly and irrelevant reply, and thereby involve him in an undeserved ridicule."

' "Such a device would be the pastime of one of immature years, and could have no place in this person's habit of conduct," replied Ming-hi, with every appearance of a fixed sincerity. "Moreover, the matter is one which touches his own welfare closely, and expressed in the fashion which the proficient Mandarin has commanded, may be set forth as follows: By a wise and all-knowing divine system, it is arranged that certain honourable occupations, which by their nature cannot become remunerative to any marked degree, shall be singled out for special marks of reverence, so that those who engage therein may be compensated in dignity for what they must inevitably lack in taels. By this refined dispensation the literary occupations, which are in general the highroads to the Establishment of Public Support and Uniform Apparel, are held in the highest veneration. Agriculture, from which it is possible to wrest a competency, follows in esteem; while the various branches of commerce, leading as they do to vast possessions and the attendant luxury, are very justly deprived of all the attributes of dignity and respect. Yet observe, O justice-loving Mandarin, how unbecomingly this ingenious system of universal compensation has been debased at the instance of grasping and avaricious ones. Dignity, riches and ease now go hand in hand, and the highest rewarded in all matters are also the most esteemed; whereas, if the discriminating provision of those who have gone before and so arranged it was observed, the direct contrary would be the case."

' "It is a state of things which is somewhat difficult to imagine in general matters of life, in spite of the fair-seemingness of your words," said the Mandarin thoughtfully; "nor can this rather obtuse and slow-witted person fully grasp the practical application of the system on the edge of the moment. In what manner would it operate in the case of ordinary persons, for example?"

' "There should be a fixed and settled arrangement that the low-minded and degrading occupations — such as that of following charitable persons from place to place, chanting verses composed in their honour, that of misleading travellers who inquire the way, so that they fall into the hands of robbers, and the like callings — should be the most highly rewarded to the end that those who are engaged therein may obtain some solace for the loss of dignity they experience, and the mean intellectual position which they are compelled to maintain. By this device they would be enabled to possess certain advantages and degrees of comfort which at present are utterly beyond their grasp, so that in the end they would escape being entirely debased. To turn to the other foot, those who are now high in position, and engaged in professions which enjoy the confidence of all persons, have that which in itself is sufficient to insure contentment. Furthermore, the most proficient and engaging in every department, mean or high-minded, have certain attributes of respect among those beneath them, so that they might justly be content with the lowest reward in whatever calling they professed, the least skilful and most left-handed being compensated for the mental anguish which they must undoubtedly suffer by receiving the greatest number of taels."

'"Such a scheme would, as far as the matter has been expressed, appear to possess all the claims of respect, and to be, indeed, what was originally intended by those who framed the essentials of existence," said Chan Hung, when he had for some space of time considered the details. "In one point, however, this person fails to perceive how the arrangement could be amiably conducted in Fow Hou. The one who is addressing you maintains, as a matter of right, a position of exceptional respect, nor, if he must express himself upon such a detail, are his excessively fatiguing duties entirely unremunerative. . . ."

'"In the case of the distinguished and unalterable Mandarin," exclaimed Ming-hi, with no appearance of hesitation, "the matter would of necessity be arranged otherwise.

Being from that time, as it were, the controller of the destinies and remunerations of all those in Fow Hou, he would, manifestly, be outside the working of the scheme; standing apart and regulating, like the person who turns the handle of the corn-mill, but does not suffer himself to be drawn between the stones, he could still maintain both his respect and his remuneration unaltered."

' "If the detail could honourably be regarded in such a light," said Chan Hung, "this person would, without delay, so rearrange matters in Fow Hou, and thereby create universal justice and an unceasing contentment within the minds of all."

' "Undoubtedly such a course could be justly followed," assented Ming-hi, "for in precisely that manner of working was the complete scheme revealed to this highly favoured person."

'Entirely wrapped up in thoughts concerning the inception and manner of operation of this project, Chan Hung began to retrace his steps towards the Yamên, failing to observe in his benevolent abstraction of mind that the unaffectedly depraved person Ming-hi was stretching out his feet towards him and indulging in every other form of low-minded and undignified contempt.

'Before he reached the door of his residence the Mandarin overtook one who occupied a high position of confidence and remuneration in the Department of Public Fireworks and Coloured Lights. Fully assured of this versatile person's enthusiasm on behalf of so humane and charitable a device, Chan Hung explained the entire matter to him without delay, and expressly desired that if there were any details which appeared capable of improvement, he would declare himself clearly regarding them.

' "Alas!" exclaimed the person with whom the Mandarin was conversing, speaking in so unfeignedly disturbed and terrified a voice that several who were passing by stopped in order to learn the full circumstance, "have this person's ears been made the object of some unnaturally light-minded demon's ill-disposed pastime, or does the usually well-balanced Chan Hung in reality contemplate so violent and un-Chinese an action? What but evil could arise from a single word of the change which he proposes to the extent of a full written book? The entire fixed nature of events would become reversed; persons would no longer be fully accountable to one another; and Fow Hou being thus thrown into a most unendurable state of confusion, the protecting Deities would doubtless withdraw their influence, and the entire region would soon be given over to the malicious guardianship of rapacious and evilly disposed spirits. Let this person entreat the almost invariably clear-sighted Chan Hung to return at once to his adequately equipped and sumptuous Yamên, and barring well the door of his inner chamber, so that it can only be opened from the outside, partake of several sleeping essences of unusual strength, after which he will awake in an undoubtedly refreshed state of mind, and in a condition toobserve matters with his accustomed diamond-like penetration."

' "By no means!" cried one of those who had stopped to learn the occasion of the incident — a very inferior maker of unserviceable imitation pigtails — "the devout and conscientious-minded Mandarin Chan Hung speaks as the inspired mouthpiece of the omnipotent Buddha, and must, for that reason, be obeyed in every detail. This person would unhesitatingly counsel the now invaluable Mandarin to proceed to his well-constructed residence without delay, and there calling together his entire staff of those who set down his spoken words, put the complete Heaven-sent plan into operation, and beyond recall, before he retires to his inner chamber."

'Upon this there arose a most inelegant display of un-dignified emotions on the part of the assembly which had by this time gathered together. While those who occupied honourable and remunerative positions very earnestly entreated the Mandarin to act in the manner which had been suggested by the first speaker, others – who had, in the meantime, made use of imagined figures, and thereby discovered that the proposed change would be greatly to their advantage – raised shouts of encouragement towards the proposal of the pigtail-maker, urging the noble Mandarin not to become small in the face towards the insignificant few who were ever opposed to enlightened reform, but to maintain an unflaccid upper lip, and carry the entire matter through to its destined end. In the course of this very unseemly tumult, which soon involved all persons present in hostile demonstrations towards each other, both the Mandarin and the official from the Fireworks and Coloured Light Department found an opportunity to pass away secretly, the former to consider well the various sides of the matter, towards which he became better disposed with every thought, the latter to find a purchaser of his appointment and leave Fow Hou before the likelihood of Chan Hung's scheme became generally known.

'At this point an earlier circumstance, which affected the future enrolling of events to no insignificant degree, must be made known, concerning as it does Lila, the fair and very accomplished daughter of Chan Hung. Possessing no son or heir to succeed him, the Mandarin exhibited towards

Lila a very unusual depth of affection, so marked, indeed, that when certain evil-minded ones endeavoured to encompass his degradation, on the plea of eccentricity of character, the written papers which they despatched to the high ones at Pekin contained no other accusation in support of the contention than that the individual in question regarded his daughter with an obvious pride and pleasure which no person of well-balanced intellect lavished on any but a son.

'It was his really conscientious desire to establish Lila's welfare above all things that had caused Chan Hung to become in some degree undecided when conversing with Ming-hi on the detail of the scheme; for, unaffected as the Mandarin himself would have been at the prospect of an honourable poverty, it was no part of his intention that the adorable and exceptionally refined Lila should be drawn into such an existence. That, indeed, had been the essential of his reply on a certain and not far removed occasion, when two persons of widely differing positions had each made a formal request that he might be allowed to present marriage-pledging gifts to the very desirable Lila. Maintaining an enlightened openness of mind upon the subject, the Mandarin had replied that nothing but the merit and undoubted suitableness of a person would affect him in such a decision. As it was ordained by the wise and unchanging Deities that merit should always be fittingly rewarded, he went on to express himself, and as the most suitable person was obviously the one who could the most agreeably provide for her, the two circumstances inevitably tended to the decision that the one chosen should be the person who could amass the greatest number of taels. To this end he instructed them both to present themselves at the end of a year, bringing with them the entire profits of their under-takings between the two periods.

'This deliberate pronouncement affected the two persons in question in an entirely opposite manner, for one of them was little removed from a condition of incessant and most uninviting poverty, while the other was the very highly rewarded picture-maker Pe-tsing. Both to this latter person, and to the other one, Lee Sing, the ultimate conclusion of the matter did not seem to be a question of any conjecture therefore, and, in consequence, the one became most offensively self-confident, and the other leaden-minded to an equal degree, neither remember-ing the unswerving wisdom of the proverb, "Wait! all men are but as the black, horn-cased beetles which overrun the inferior cooking-rooms of the city, and even at this moment the heavily shod and unerring foot of Buddha may be lifted."

'Lee Sing was, by profession, one of those who hunt and ensnare the brilliantly coloured winged insects which are to be found in various parts of the Empire in great variety and abundance, it being his duty to send a certain number every year to Pekin to contribute to the amusement of the dignified Emperor. In spite of the not too intelligent nature of the occupation, Lee Sing took an honourable pride in all matters connected with it. He disdained, with well-expressed contempt, to avail himself of the stealthy and somewhat deceptive methods employed by others engaged in a similar manner of life. In this way he had, from necessity, acquired agility to an exceptional degree, so that he could leap far into the air, and while in that position select from a passing band of insects any which he might desire. This useful accomplishment was, in a measure, the direct means of bringing together the person in question and the engaging Lila; for on a certain occasion, when Lee Sing was passing through the streets of Fow Hou, he heard a great outcry, and beheld persons of all ranks running towards him, pointing at the same time in an upward direction. Turning his gaze in the manner indicated, Lee beheld, with every variety of astonishment, a powerful and unnaturally large bird of prey, carrying in its talons the lovely and now insensible Lila, to whom it had been attracted by the magnificence of her raiment. The rapacious and evilly inspired creature was already above the highest dwelling-houses when Lee first beheld it, and was plainly directing its course towards the inaccessible mountain crags beyond the city walls. Nevertheless, Lee resolved upon an inspired effort, and without any hesitation bounded towards it with such well-directed proficiency, that if he had not stretched forth his hand on passing he would inevitably have been carried far above the desired object. In this manner he succeeded in dragging the repulsive and completely disconcerted monster to the ground, where its graceful and unassuming prisoner was released, and the presumptuous bird itself torn to pieces amid continuous shouts of a most respectful and engaging description in honour of Lee and of his versatile attainment.

'In consequence of this incident the grateful Lila would often deliberately leave the society of the rich and well-endowed in order to accompany Lee on his journeys in pursuit of exceptionally precious winged insects. Regarding his unusual ability as the undoubted cause of her existence at that moment, she took an all-absorbing pride in such displays, and would utter loud and frequent exclamations of triumph when Lee leaped out from behind some rock, where he had lain concealed, and with unfailing regularity secured the object of his adroit movement. In this manner a state of feeling which was by no means favourable to the aspiring picture-maker Pe-tsing had long existed between the two persons; but when Lee Sing put the matter in the form of an explicit petition before Chan Hung (to which adequate reference has already been made), the nature of the decision then arrived at seemed to clothe the realization of their virtuous and estimable desires with an air of extreme improbability.

' "Oh, Lee," exclaimed the greatly disappointed maiden when her lover had explained to her the nature of the arrangement – for in her unassuming admiration of the noble qualities of Lee she had anticipated that Chan Hung would at once have received him with ceremonious embraces and assurances of his permanent affection – "how unendurable a state of things is this in which we have become involved! Far removed from this one's anticipation was the thought of becoming inalienably associated with that outrageous person Pe-tsing, or of entering upon an existence which will necessitate a feigned admiration of his really unpresentable efforts. Yet in such a manner must the entire circumstance complete its course unless some ingenious method of evading it can be discovered in the meantime. Alas, my beloved one! the occupation of ensnaring winged insects is indeed an alluring one, but, as far as this person has observed, it is also exceedingly unproductive of taels. Could not some more expeditious means of enriching yourself be discovered? Frequently has the unnoticed but nevertheless very attentive Lila heard her father and the round-bodied ones who visit him speak of exploits which seem to consist of assuming the shapes of certain wild animals, and in that guise appearing from time to time at the place of exchange within the city walls. As this form of entertainment is undoubtedly very remunerative in its results, could not the versatile and ready-witted Lee conceal himself within the skin of a bear, or some other untamed beast, and in this garb, joining them unperceived, play an appointed part and receive a just share of the reward?"

' "The result of such an enterprise might, if the matter chanced to take an unforeseen development, prove of a very doubtful nature," replied Lee Sing, to whom, indeed, the proposed venture appeared in a somewhat undignified light, although, with refined consideration, he withheld such a thought from Lila, who had proposed it for him, and also confessed that her usually immaculate father had taken part in such an exhibition. "Nevertheless, do not permit the dark shadow of an inward cloud to reflect itself upon your almost invariably amiable countenance, for this person has become possessed of a valuable internal suggestion which, although he has hitherto neglected, being content with a small but assured competency, would doubtless bring together a serviceable number of taels if rightly utilized."

' "Greatly does this person fear that the valuable internal suggestion of Lee Sing will weigh but lightly in the commercial balance against the very rapidly executed pictures of Pe-tsing," said Lila, who had not fully recalled from her mind a disturbing emotion that Lee would have been well advised to have availed himself of her ingenious and well-thought-out suggestion. "But of what does the matter consist?"

' "It is the best explained by a recital of the circumstances leading up to it," said Lee. "Upon an occasion when this person was passing through the streets of Fow Hou, there gathered around him a company of those who had, on previous occasions, beheld his exceptional powers of hurling himself through the air in an upward direction, praying that he would again delight their senses by a similar spectacle. Not being unwilling to afford those estimable persons the amusement they desired, this one, without any elaborate show of affected hesitancy, put himself into the necessary position, and would without doubt have risen uninterruptedly almost into the Middle Air, had he not, in making the preparatory movements, placed his left foot upon an over-ripe wampee which lay unperceived on the ground. In consequence of this really blameworthy want of caution the entire manner and direction of this short-sighted individual's movements underwent a sudden and complete change, so that to those who stood around it appeared as though he were making a well-directed endeavour to penetrate through the upper surface of the earth. This unexpected display had the effect of removing the gravity of even the most aged and severe-minded persons present, and for the space of some moments the behaviour and positions of those who stood around were such that they were quite unable to render any assistance, greatly as they doubtless wished to do so. Being in this manner allowed a period for inward reflection of a very concentrated order, it arose within this one's mind that at every similar occurrence which he had witnessed, those who observed the event had been seized in a like fashion, being very excessively amused. The fact was made even more undoubted by the manner of behaving of an exceedingly stout and round-faced person, who had not been present from the beginning, but who was affected to a most incredible extent when the details, as they had occurred, were made plain to him, he declaring, with many references to the Sacred Dragon and the Seven Walled Temple at Pekin, that he would willingly have contributed a specified number of taels rather than have missed the diversion. When at length this person reached his own chamber, he diligently applied himself to the task of carrying into practical effect the suggestion which had arisen in his mind. By an arrangement of transparent glasses and reflecting surfaces – which, were it not for a well-defined natural modesty, he would certainly be tempted to describe as highly ingenious – he ultimately succeeded in bringing about the effect he desired."

'With these words Lee put into Lila's hands an object which closely resembled the contrivances by which those who are not sufficiently powerful to obtain positions near the raised platform, in the Halls of Celestial Harmony, are nevertheless enabled to observe the complexions and attire of all around them. Regulating it by means of a hidden spring, he requested her to follow closely the actions of a heavily burdened passer-by who was at that moment some little distance beyond them. Scarcely had Lila raised the glass to her eyes than she became irresistibly amused to a most infectious degree, greatly to the satisfaction of Lee, who therein beheld the realization of his hopes. Not for the briefest space of time would she permit the object to pass from her, but directed it at every person who came within her sight, with frequent and unfeigned exclamations of wonder and delight.

'"How pleasant and fascinating a device is this!"

exclaimed Lila at length. "By what means is so diverting and gravity-removing a result obtained?"

' "Further than that it is the concentration of much labour of continually trying with glasses and reflecting surfaces, this person is totally unable to explain it," replied Lee. "The chief thing, however, is that at whatever moving object it is directed — no matter whether a person so observed is being carried in a chair, riding upon an animal, or merely walking — at a certain point he has every appearance of being unexpectedly hurled to the ground in a most violent and mirth-provoking manner. Would not the stout and round-faced one, who would cheerfully have contributed a certain number of taels to see this person manifest a similar exhibition, unhesitatingly lay out that sum to secure the means of so gratifying his emotions whenever he felt the desire, even with the revered persons of the most dignified ones in the Empire? Is there, indeed, a single person between The Wall and the Bitter Waters on the South who is so devoid of ambition that he would miss the opportunity of subjecting, as it were, perhaps even the sacred Emperor himself to the exceptional feat?"

' "The temptation to possess one would inevitably prove overwhelming to any person of ordinary intelligence," admitted Lila. "Yet in spite of this one's unassumed admiration for the contrivance, internal doubts regarding the ultimate happiness of the two persons who are now discussing the matter again attack her. She recollects, somewhat dimly, an almost forgotten but nevertheless very unassailable proverb, which declares that more contentment of mind can assuredly be obtained from the unexpected discovery of a tael among the folds of a discarded garment than could, in the most favourable circumstances, ensue from the well-thought-out construction of a new and hitherto unknown device. Furthermore, although the span of a year may seem unaccountably protracted when persons who reciprocate engaging sentiments are parted, yet when the acceptance or refusal of Pe-tsing's undesirable pledging-gifts hangs upon the accomplishment of a remote and not very probable object within that period, it becomes as a breath of wind passing through an autumn forest."

'Since the day when Lila and Lee had sat together side by side, and conversed in this unrestrained and irreproachable manner, the great sky-lantern had many times been obscured for a period. Only an insignificant portion of the year remained, yet the affairs of Lee Sing were in no more prosperous a condition than before, nor had he found an opportunity to set aside any store of taels. Each day the unsupportable Pe-tsing became more and more obtrusive and self-conceited, even to the extent of throwing far into the air coins of insignificant value whenever he chanced to pass Lee in the street, at the same time urging him to leap after them and thereby secure at least one or two pieces of money against the day of calculating. In a similar but entirely opposite fashion, Lila and Lee experienced the acutest pangs of an ever-growing despair, until their only form of greeting consisted in gazing into each other's eyes with a soul-benumbing expression of self-reproach.

'Yet at this very time, when even the natural and unalterable powers seemed to be conspiring against the success of Lee's modest and inoffensive hopes, an event was taking place which was shortly to reverse the entire settled arangement of persons and affairs, and involve Fow Hou in a very inextricable state of uncertainty. For, not to make a pretence of concealing a matter which has been

173

already in part revealed, the Mandarin Chan Hung had by this time determined to act in the manner which Ming-hi had suggested; so that on a certain morning Lee Sing was visited by two persons, bearing between them a very weighty sack of taels, who also conveyed to him the fact that a like amount would be deposited within his door at the end of each succeeding seven days. Although Lee's occupation had in the past been very meagrely rewarded, either by taels or by honour, the circumstance which resulted in his now receiving so excessively large a sum is not made clear until the detail of Ming-hi's scheme is closely examined. The matter then becomes plain, for it had been suggested by that person that the most proficient in any occupation should be rewarded to a certain extent, and the least proficient to another stated extent, the original amounts being reversed. When those engaged by Chan Hung to draw up the various rates came to the profession of ensnaring winged insects, however, they discovered that Lee Sing was the only one of that description in Fow Hou, so that it became necessary in consequence to allot him a double portion, one amount as the most proficient, and a much larger amount as the least proficient.

'It is unnecessary now to follow the not altogether satisfactory condition of affairs which began to exist in Fow Hou as soon as the scheme was put into operation. The full written papers dealing with the matter are in the Hall of Public Reference at Pekin, and can be seen by any person on the payment of a few taels to every one connected with the establishment. Those who found their possessions reduced thereby completely overlooked the obvious justice of the arrangement, and immediately began to take most severe measures to have the order put aside; while those who suddenly and unexpectedly found themselves raised to positions of affluence tended to the same end by conducting themselves in a most incapable and undiscriminating manner. And during the entire period that this state of things existed in Fow Hou the really contemptible Minghi continually followed Chan Hung about from place to place, spreading out his feet towards him, and allowing himself to become openly amused to a most unseemly extent.

'Chief among those who sought to have the original manner of rewarding persons again established was the picture-maker, Pe-tsing, who now found himself in a condition of most abject poverty, so unbearable, indeed, that he frequently went by night, carrying a lantern, in the hope that he might discover some of the small pieces of money which he had been accustomed to throw into the air on meeting Lee Sing. To his pangs of hunger was added the fear that he would certainly lose Lila, so that from day to day he redoubled his efforts, and in the end, by using false statements and other artifices of a questionable nature, the party which he led was successful in obtaining the degradation of Chan Hung and his dismissal from office, together with an entire reversal of all his plans and enactments.

'On the last day of the year which Chan Hung had appointed as the period of test for his daughter's suitors, the person in question was seated in a chamber of his new abode — a residence of unassuming appearance but undoubted comfort — surrounded by Lila and Lee, when the hanging curtains were suddenly flung aside, and Pe-tsing, followed by two persons of low rank bearing sacks of money, appeared among them.

' "Chan Hung," he said at length, "in the past events arose which compelled this person to place himself against you in your official position. Nevertheless, he has always maintained towards you personally an unchanging affection, and understanding full well that you are one of those who maintain their spoken word in spite of all happenings, he has now come to exhibit the taels which he has collected together, and to claim the fuifilment of your deliberate promise."

'With these words the commonplace picture-maker poured forth the contents of the sacks, and stood looking at Lila in a most confident and unprepossessing manner.

' "Pe-tsing," replied Chan Hung, rising from his couch and speaking in so severe and impressive a voice that the two servants of Pe-tsing at once fled in great apprehension, "this person has also found it necessary, in his official position, to oppose you; but here the similarity ends, for, on his part, he has never felt towards you the remotest degree of affection. Nevertheless, he is always desirous, as you say, that persons should regard their spoken word, and as you seem to hold a promise from the Chief Mandarin of Fow Hou regarding marriage-gifts towards his daughter, he would advise you to go at once to that person. A misunderstanding has evidently arisen, for the one whom you are addressing is merely Chan Hung, and the words spoken by the Mandarin have no sort of interest for him — indeed, he understands that all that person's acts have been reversed, so that he fails to see how anyone at all can regard you and your claim in other than a gravity-removing light. Furthermore, the maiden in question is now definitely and irretrievably pledged to this faithful and successful one by my side, who, as you will doubtless be gracefully overjoyed to learn, has recently disposed of a most ingenious and diverting contrivance for an enormous number of taels, so many, indeed, that both the immediate and the far-distant futures of all the persons who are here before you are now in no sort of doubt whatever."

'At these words the three persons whom he had interrupted again turned their attention to the matter before them; but as Pe-tsing walked away, he observed, though he failed to understand the meaning, that they all raised certain objects to their eyes, and at once became amused to a most striking and uncontrollable degree.'

CHAPTER FIVE

THE CONFESSION OF KAI LUNG

*

RELATED BY HIMSELF AT WU-WHEI WHEN OTHER MATTER
FAILED HIM

As Kai Lung, the story-teller, unrolled his mat and selected with grave deliberation the spot under the mulberry-tree which would the longest remain sheltered from the sun's rays, his impassive eye wandered round the thin circle of listeners who had been drawn together by his uplifted voice with a glance which, had it expressed his actual thoughts, would have betrayed a keen desire that the assembly should be composed of strangers rather than of his most consistent patrons, to whom his stock of tales was indeed becoming embarrassingly familiar. Nevertheless, when he began there was nothing in his voice but a trace of insufficiently restrained triumph, such as might be fitly assumed by one who has discovered and makes known for the first time a story by the renowned historian Lo Châ.

'The adventures of the enlightened and nobly born Yuin-Pel –'

'Have already thrice been narrated within Wu-whei by the versatile but exceedingly uninventive Kai Lung,' remarked Wang Yu placidly. 'Indeed, has there not come to be a saying by which an exceptionally frugal host's rice, having undoubtedly seen the inside of the pot many times, is now known in this town as Kai-Pel?'

'Alas!' exclaimed Kai Lung, 'well was this person warned of Wu-whei at the previous village, as a place of desolation and excessively bad taste, whose inhabitants, led by an evil-minded maker of very commonplace pipes, named Wang Yu, are unable to discriminate in all matters not connected with the cooking of food and the evasion of just debts. They at Shan Tzu hung on to my cloak as I strove to leave them, praying that I would again entrance their ears with what they termed the melodious word-music of this person's inimitable version of the inspired story of Yuin-Pel.'

'Truly the story of Yuin-Pel is in itself excellent,' interposed the conciliatory Hi Seng; 'and Kai Lung's accomplishment of having three times repeated it here without deviating in the particular of a single word from the first recital stamps him as a story-teller of no ordinary degree. Yet the saying "Although it is desirable to lose persistently when playing at squares and circles with the broad-minded and sagacious Emperor, it is none the less a fact that the observance of this etiquette deprives the intellectual diversion of much of its interest for both players," is no less true to-day than when the all-knowing H'sou uttered it.'

'They well said – they of Shan Tzu – that the people of Wu-whei were intolerably ignorant and of low descent,' continued Kai Lung, without heeding the interruption; 'that although invariably of a timorous nature, even to the extent of retiring to the woods on the approach of those who select bowmen for the Imperial army, all they require in a story is that it shall be garnished with deeds of bloodshed and violence to the exclusion of the higher qualities of well-imagined metaphors and literary style which alone constitute true excellence.'

'Yet it has been said,' suggested Hi Seng, 'that the inimitable Kai Lung can so mould a narrative in the telling

that all the emotions are conveyed therein without unduly
disturbing the intellects of the hearers.'

'O amiable Hi Seng,' replied Kai Lung with extreme
affability, 'doubtless you are the most expert of water-
carriers, and on a hot and dusty day, when the insatiable
desire of all persons is towards a draught of unusual length
without much regard to its composition, the sight of your
goatskins is indeed a welcome omen; yet when in the
season of Cold White Rains you chance to meet the
belated chair-carrier who has been reluctantly persuaded
into conveying persons beyond the limit of the city, the
solitary official watchman who knows that his chief is not
at hand, or a returning band of those who make a practice
of remaining in the long narrow rooms until they are
driven forth at a certain gong-stroke, can you supply them
with the smallest portion of that invigorating rice spirit
for which alone they crave? From this simple and homely
illustration, specially conceived to meet the requirements
of your stunted and meagre understanding, learn not to
expect both grace and thorns from the willow-tree.
Nevertheless, your very immature remarks on the art of
story-telling are in no degree more foolish than those
frequently uttered by persons who make a living by such a
practice; in proof of which this person will relate to the
select and discriminating company now assembled an
entirely new and unrecorded story — that, indeed, of the
unworthy but frequently highly rewarded Kai Lung
himself.'

'The story of Kai Lung!' exclaimed Wang Yu. 'Why
not the story of Ting, the sightless beggar, who has sat
all his life outside the Temple of Miraculous Cures? Who
is Kai Lung, that *he* should have a story? Is he not known

to us all here? Is not his speech that of this Province, his food mean, his arms and legs unshaven? Does he carry a sword or wear silk raiment? Frequently have we seen him fatigued with journeying; many times has he arrived destitute of money; nor, on those occasions when a newly appointed and unnecessarily officious mandarin has commanded him to betake himself elsewhere and struck him with a rod has Kai Lung caused the stick to turn into a deadly serpent and destroy its master, as did the just and dignified Lu Fei. How, then, can Kai Lung have a story that is not also the story of Wang Yu and Hi Seng, and all others here?'

'Indeed, if the refined and enlightened Wang Yu so decides, it must assuredly be true,' said Kai Lung patiently; 'yet (since even trifles serve to dispel the darker thoughts of existence) would not the history of so small a matter as an opium pipe chain his intelligent consideration? such a pipe, for example, as this person beheld only to-day exposed for sale, the bowl composed of the finest red clay, delicately baked and fashioned, the long bamboo stem smoother than the sacred tooth of the divine Buddha, the spreading support patiently and cunningly carved with scenes representing the Seven Joys, and the Tenth Hell of unbelievers.'

'Ah!' exclaimed Wang Yu eagerly, 'it is indeed as you say, a mandarin among masterpieces. That pipe, O most unobserving Kai Lung, is the work of this retiring and superficial person who is now addressing you, and, though the fact evidently escaped your all-seeing glance, the place where it is exposed is none other than his shop of "The Fountain of Beauty," which you have on many occasions endowed with your honourable presence.'

'Doubtless the carving is the work of the accomplished Wang Yu, and the fitting together,' replied Kai Lung; 'but the materials for so refined and ornamental a production must of necessity have been brought many thousand li; the clay perhaps from the renowned beds of Honan, the wood from Pekin, and the bamboo from one of the great forests of the North.'

'For what reason?' said Wang Yu proudly. 'At this person's very door is a pit of red clay, purer and infinitely more regular than any to be found at Honan; the hard wood of Wu-whei is extolled among carvers throughout the Empire, while no bamboo is straighter or more smooth than that which grows in the neighbouring woods.'

'O most inconsistent Wang Yu!' cried the story-teller, 'assuredly a very commendable local pride has dimmed your usually penetrating eyesight. Is not the clay pit of which you speak that in which you fashioned exceedingly unsymmetrical imitations of rat-pies in your childhood? How, then, can it be equal to those of Honan, which you have never even seen? In the dark glades of these woods have you not chased the gorgeous butterfly, and, in later years, the no less gaily attired maidens of Wu-whei in the entrancing game of Kiss in the Circle? Have not the bamboo-trees to which you have referred provided you with the ideal material wherewith to roof over those cunningly constructed pits into which it has ever been the chief delight of the young and audacious to lure dignified and unnaturally stout mandarins? All these things you have seen and used ever since your mother made a successful offering to the Goddess Kum-Fa. How, then, can they be even equal to the products of remote Honan and fabulous Pekin? Assuredly the generally veracious Wang

Yu speaks this time with closed eyes and will, upon mature reflection, eat his words.'

The silence was broken by a very aged man who arose from among the bystanders.

'Behold the length of this person's pigtail,' he exclaimed, 'the whiteness of his moustaches and the venerable appearance of his beard! There is no more aged person present — if, indeed, there be such a one in all the Province. It accordingly devolves upon him to speak in this matter, which shall be as follows: The noble-minded and proficient Kai Lung shall relate the story as he has proposed, and the garrulous Wang Yu shall twice contribute to Kai Lung's bowl when it is passed round, once for himself and once for this person, in order that he may learn either to be more discreet or more proficient in the art of aptly replying.'

'The events which it is this person's presumptuous intention to describe to this large-hearted and providentially indulgent gathering,' began Kai Lung, when his audience had become settled, and the wooden bowl had passed to and fro among them, 'did not occupy many years, although they were of a nature which made them of far more importance than all the remainder of his existence, thereby supporting the sage discernment of the philosopher Wenweng, who first made the observation that man is greatly inferior to the meanest fly, inasmuch as that creature, although granted only a day's span of life, contrives during that period to fulfil all the allotted functions of existence.

'Unutterably to the astonishment and dismay of this person and all those connected with him (for several of the most expensive readers of the future to be found in the

Empire had declared that his life would be marked by great events, his career a source of continual wonder, and his death a misfortune to those who had dealings with him) his efforts to take a degree at the public literary competitions were not attended with any adequate success. In view of the very plainly expressed advice of his father it therefore became desirable that this person should turn his attention to some other method of regaining the esteem of those upon whom he was dependent for all the necessaries of existence. Not having the means wherewith to engage in any form of commerce, and being entirely ignorant of all matters save the now useless details of attempting to pass public examinations, he reluctantly decided that he was destined to become one of those who imagine and write out stories and similar devices for printed leaves and books.

'This determination was favourably received, and upon learning it, this person's dignified father took him aside, and with many assurances of regard presented to him a written sentence, which, he said, would be of incomparable value to one engaged in a literary career, and should in fact, without any particular qualifications, insure an honourable competency. He himself, he added, with what at the time appeared to this one as an unnecessary regard for detail, having taken a very high degree, and being in consequence appointed to a distinguished and remunerative position under the Board of Fines and Tortures, had never made any use of it.

'The written sentence, indeed, was all that it had been pronounced. It had been composed by a remote ancestor, who had spent his entire life in crystallizing all his knowledge and experience into a few written lines, which as a result became correspondingly precious. It defined in a very original and profound manner several undisputable principles, and was so engagingly subtle in its manner of expression that the most superficial person was irresistibly thrown into a deep inward contemplation upon reading it. When it was complete, the person who had contrived this ingenious masterpiece, discovering by means of omens that he still had ten years to live, devoted each remaining year to the task of reducing the sentence by one word without in any way altering its meaning. This unapproachable example of conciseness found such favour in the eyes of those who issued printed leaves that as fast as this person could inscribe stories containing it they were eagerly purchased; and had it not been for a very incapable want of foresight on this narrow-minded individual's part, doubtless it would still be affording him an agreeable and permanent means of living.

'Unquestionably the enlightened Wen-weng was well acquainted with the subject when he exclaimed, "Better a frugal dish of olives flavoured with honey than the most sumptuously devised puppy-pie of which the greater portion is sent forth in silver-lined boxes and partaken of by others." At that time, however, this versatile saying — which so gracefully conveys the truth of the undeniable fact that what a person possesses is sufficient if he restrain his mind from desiring aught else — would have been lightly treated by this self-conceited story-teller, even if his immature faculties had enabled him fully to understand the import of so profound and well-digested a remark.

'At that time Tiao Ts'un was undoubtedly the most beautiful maiden in all Pekin. So frequently were verses describing her habits and appearance affixed in the most prominent places of the city, that many persons obtained an honourable livelihood by frequenting those spots and disposing of the sacks of written papers which they collected to merchants who engaged in that commerce. Owing to the fame attained by his written sentence, this really very much inferior being had many opportunities of meeting the incomparable maiden Tiao at flower-feasts, melon-seed assemblies, and those gatherings where persons of both sexes exhibit themselves in revolving attitudes, and are permitted to embrace openly without reproach; whereupon he became so subservient to her charms and virtues that he lost no opportunity of making himself utterly unendurable to any who might chance to speak to, or even gaze upon, this Heaven-sent creature.

'So successful was this person in his endeavour to meet the sublime Tiao and to gain her conscientious esteem that all emotions of prudence forsook him, or it would soon have become apparent even to his enfeebled understanding that such consistent good-fortune could only be the work of unforgiving and malignant spirits whose ill-will he had in some way earned, and who were luring him on in order that they might accomplish his destruction. That object was achieved on a certain evening when this person stood alone with Tiao upon an eminence overlooking the city and watched the great sky-lantern rise from behind the hills. Under these delicate and ennobling influences he gave speech to many very ornamental and refined thoughts which arose within his mind concerning the graceful brilliance of the light which was cast all around, yet notwithstanding which a still more exceptional and brilliant light was shining in his own internal organs by reason of the nearness of an even purer and more engaging orb. There was no need, this person felt, to hide even his most inside thoughts from the dignified and sympathetic being at his side, so without hesitation he spoke – in what he believes even now must have been a very decorative manner – of the many thousand persons who were then wrapped in sleep, of the constantly changing lights which appeared in the city beneath, and of the vastness which everywhere lay around.

' "O Kai Lung," exclaimed the lovely Tiao, when this person had made an end of speaking, "how expertly and in what a proficient manner do you express yourself, uttering even the sentiments which this person has felt inwardly, but for which she has no words. Why, indeed, do you not inscribe them in a book?"

'Under her elevating influence it had already occurred to this illiterate individual that it would be a more dignified and, perhaps, even a more profitable course for him to write out and dispose of, to those who print such matters, the versatile and high-minded expressions which now continually formed his thoughts, rather than be dependent upon the concise sentence for which, indeed, he was indebted to the wisdom of a remote ancestor. Tiao's spoken word fully settled his determination, so that without delay he set himself to the task of composing a story which should omit the usual sentence, but should contain instead a large number of his most graceful and diamond-like thoughts. So engrossed did this near-sighted and superficial person become in the task (which daily seemed to increase rather than lessen as new and still more sublime images arose within his mind) that many months passed before the matter was complete. In the end, instead of a story, it had assumed the proportions of an important and many-volumed book; while Tiao had in the meantime accepted the wedding gifts of an objectionable and excessively round-bodied individual, who had amassed an inconceivable number of taels by inducing persons to take part in what at first sight appeared to be an ingenious but very easy competition connected with the order in which certain horses should arrive at a given and clearly defined spot. By that time, however, this unduly sanguine story-teller had become completely entranced in his work, and merely regarded Tiao Ts'un as a Heaven-sent but no longer necessary incentive to his success. With every hope, therefore, he went forth to dispose of his written leaves, confident of finding some very wealthy person who would be in a condition to pay him the correct value of the work.

'At the end of two years this somewhat disillusionized but still undaunted person chanced to hear of a benevolent and unassuming body of men who made a habit of issuing works in which they discerned merit, but which, nevertheless, others were unanimous in describing as "of no good." Here this person was received with gracious effusion, and being in a position to impress those with whom he was dealing with his undoubted knowledge of the subject, he finally succeeded in making a very advantageous arrangement by which he was to pay one-half of the number of taels expended in producing the work, and to receive in return all the profits which should result from the undertaking. Those who were concerned in the matter were so engagingly impressed with the incomparable literary merit displayed in the production that they counselled a great number of copies being made ready in order, as they said, that this person should not lose by there being any delay when once the accomplishment became the one topic of conversation in tea-houses and yamêns. From this cause it came about that the matter of taels to be expended was much greater than had been anticipated at the beginning, so that when the day arrived on which the volumes were to be sent forth this person found that almost his last piece of money had disappeared.

'Alas! how small a share has a person in the work of controlling his own destiny. Had only the necessarily penurious and now almost degraded Kai Lung been born a brief span before the great writer Lo Kuan Chang, his name would have been received with every mark of esteem from one end of the Empire to the other, while taels and honourable decorations would have been showered upon him. For the truth, which could no longer be concealed, revealed the fact that this inopportune individual possessed a mind framed in such a manner that his thoughts had already been the thoughts of the inspired Lo Kuan, who, as this person would not be so presumptuous as to inform this ornamental and well-informed gathering, was the most ingenious and versatile-minded composer of written words that this Empire – and therefore the entire world – has seen, as, indeed, his honourable title of "The Many-hued Mandarin Duck of the Yang-tse" plainly indicates.

'Although this self-opinionated person had frequently been greatly surprised himself during the writing of his long work by the brilliance and many-sidedness of the thoughts and metaphors which arose in his mind without conscious effort, it was not until the appearance of the printed leaves which make a custom of warning persons against being persuaded into buying certain books, that he definitely understood how all these things had been fully expressed many dynasties ago by the all-knowing Lo Kuan Chang, and formed, indeed, the great national standard of unapproachable excellence. Unfortunately, this person had been so deeply engrossed all his life in literary pursuits that he had never found an opportunity to glance at the works in question, or he would have escaped the embarrassing position in which he now found himself.

'It was with a hopeless sense of illness of ease that this unhappy one reached the day on which the printed leaves already alluded to would make known their deliberate opinion of his writing, the extremity of his hope being that some would at least credit him with honourable motives, and perhaps a knowledge that if the inspired Lo Kuan Chang had never been born the entire matter might have been brought to a very different conclusion. Alas! only one among the many printed leaves which made reference to the venture contained any words of friendship or encouragement. This benevolent exception was sent forth from a city in the extreme Northern Province of the Empire, and contained many inspiring though delicately guarded messages of hope for the one to whom they gracefully alluded as "this undoubtedly youthful but nevertheless distinctly promising writer of books." While admitting that altogether they found the production undeniably tedious, they claimed to have discovered indications of an obvious talent, and therefore they unhesitatingly counselled the person in question to take courage at the prospect of a moderate competency which was certainly within his grasp if he restrained his somewhat over-ambitious im-

THE CONFESSION OF KAI LUNG

pulses and closely observed the simple subjects and manner of expression of their own Chang Chow, whose "Lines to a Wayside Chrysanthemum," "Mongolians who Have," and several other composed pieces, they then set forth. Although it became plain that the writer of this amiably devised notice was, like this incapable person, entirely un-acquainted with the masterpieces of Lo Kuan Chang, yet the indisputable fact remained that, entirely on its merit, the work had been greeted with undoubted enthusiasm, so that after purchasing many examples of the refined printed leaf containing it, this person sat far into the night continually reading over the one unprejudiced and dis-criminating expression.

'All the other printed leaves displayed a complete absence of good taste in dealing with the matter. One boldly asserted that the entire circumstance was the out-come of a foolish jest or wager on the part of a person who possessed a million taels; another predicted that it was a cunning and elaborately thought-out method of gaining the attention of the people on the part of certain persons who claimed to vend a reliable and fragrantly scented cleansing substance. The *Valley of Hoang Rose Leaves and Sweetness* hoped, in a spirit of no sincerity, that the ingenious Kai Lung would not rest on his tea-leaves, but would soon send forth an equally entertaining amended example of the "Sayings of Confucius" and other sacred works, while the *Pure Essence of the Seven Days' Happen-ings* merely printed side by side similar portions from the two books under the large inscription, "IS THERE REALLY ANY NEED FOR US TO EXPRESS OURSELVES MORE CLEARLY?"

'The disappointment both as regards public esteem and

taels — for, after the manner in which the work had been received by those who advise on such productions, not a single example was purchased — threw this ill-destined individual into a condition of most unendurable depression, from which he was only aroused by a remarkable example of the unfailing wisdom of the proverb which says, "Before hastening to secure a possible reward of five taels by dragging an unobservant person away from a falling building examine well his features lest you find, when too late, that it is one to whom you are indebted for double that amount." Disappointed in the hope of securing large gains from the sale of his great work, this person now turned his attention again to his former means of living, only to find, however, that the discredit in which he had become involved even attached itself to his concise sentence; for in place of the remunerative and honourable manner in which it was formerly received, it was now regarded on all hands with open suspicion. Instead of meekly kow-towing to an evidently pre-arranged doom the last misfortune aroused this usually resigned story-teller to an ungovernable frenzy. Regarding the accomplished but at the same time exceedingly over-productive Lo Kuan Chang as the beginning of all his evils, he took a solemn oath to do everything in his power to discredit his illustrious memory, as a mark of disapproval that he had not been content to inscribe on paper only half of his brilliant thoughts, leaving the other half for the benefit of this hard-striving and equally well-endowed individual, in which case there would have been a sufficiency of taels and of fame for both.

'For a very considerable space of time this person could conceive no method by which he might attain his object.

At length, however, as a result of very keen and subtle intellectual searching, and many well-selected sacrifices, it was conveyed by means of a dream that one very ingenious yet simple way was possible. The renowned and universally admired writings of the distinguished Lo Kuan for the most part take their action within a few dynasties of their creator's own time: all that remained for this inventive person to accomplish, therefore, was to trace out the entire matter, making the words and speeches to proceed from the mouths of those who existed in still earlier periods. By this crafty method it would at once appear as though the not-too-original Lo Kuan had been indebted to one who came before him for all his most subtle thoughts, and, in consequence, his tomb would become dishonoured and his memory execrated. Without any delay this person cheerfully set himself to the somewhat laborious task before him. Lo Kuan's well-known exclamation of the Emperor Tsing on the battlefield of Shih-ho, "A sedan-chair! a sedan-chair! This person will unhesitatingly exchange his entire and well-regulated Empire for such an article," was attributed to an Emperor who lived several thousand years before the treacherous and unpopular Tsing. The new matter of a no less frequently quoted portion ran: "O nobly intentioned but nevertheless exceedingly morose Tung-shin, the object before you is your distinguished and evilly-disposed-of father's honourably-inspired demon," the change of a name effecting whatever alteration was necessary; while the delicately imagined speech beginning "The person who becomes amused at matters resulting from double-edged knives has assuredly never felt the effect of a well-directed blow himself" was taken from the mouth of one

THE WALLET OF KAI LUNG

person and placed in that of one of his remote ancestors.
In such a manner, without in any great degree altering the
matter of Lo Kuan's works, all the scenes and persons
introduced were transferred to much earlier dynasties than
those affected by the incomparable writer himself, the final
effect being to give an air of extreme unoriginality to his
really undoubtedly genuine conceptions.

'Satisfied with his accomplishment, and followed by a
hired person of low class bearing the writings, which, by
nature of the research necessary in fixing the various dates
and places so that even the wary should be deceived, had
occupied the greater part of a year, this now fully confident story-teller — unmindful of the well-tried excellence
of the inspired saying, "Money is hundred-footed; upon
perceiving a tael lying apparently unobserved upon the
floor, do not lose the time necessary in stooping, but quickly
place your foot upon it, for one fails nothing in dignity
thereby; but should it be a gold piece, distrust all things,
and valuing dignity but as an empty name, cast your entire
body upon it" — went forth to complete his great task of
finally erasing from the mind and records of the Empire
the hitherto venerated name of Lo Kuan Chang. Entering the place of commerce of the one who seemed the most
favourable for the purpose, he placed the facts as they
would in future be represented before him, explained the
undoubted remunerative fame that would ensue to all
concerned in the enterprise of sending forth the printed
books in their new form, and, opening at a venture the
written leaves which he had brought with him, read out
the following words as an indication of the similarity of
the entire work:

'"*Whai-Keng.* Friends, Chinamen, labourers who are

engaged in agricultural pursuits, entrust to this person **your** acute and well-educated ears;

' "He has merely come to assist in depositing the body of Ko'ung in the Family Temple, not for the purpose of making remarks about him of a graceful and highly complimentary nature;

' "The unremunerative actions of which persons may have been guilty possess an exceedingly undesirable amount of endurance;

' "The successful and well-considered almost invariably are involved in a directly contrary course;

' "This person desires nothing more than a like fate to await Ko'ung."

'When this one had read so far, he paused in order to give the other an opportunity of breaking in and offering half his possessions to be allowed to share in the undertaking. As he remained unaccountably silent, however, an inelegant pause occurred which this person at length broke by desiring an expressed opinion on the matter.

' "O exceedingly painstaking, but nevertheless highly inopportune Kai Lung," he replied at length, while in his countenance this person read an expression of no-encouragement towards his venture, "all your entrancing efforts do undoubtedly appear to attract the undesirable attention of some spiteful and tyrannical demon. This closely written and elaborately devised work is in reality not worth the labour of a single stroke, nor is there in all Pekin a sender forth of printed leaves who would encourage any project connected with its issue."

' "But the importance of such a fact as that which would clearly show the hitherto venerated Lo Kuan Chang to be a person who passed off as his own the work of an earlier one!" cried this person in despair, well knowing that the deliberately expressed opinion of the one before him was a matter that would rule all others. "Consider the interest of the discovery."

'"The interest would not demand more than a few lines in the ordinary printed leaves," replied the other calmly. "Indeed, in a manner of speaking, it is entirely a detail of no consequence whether or not the sublime Lo Kuan ever existed. In reality his very commonplace name may have been simply Lung; his inspired work may have been written a score of dynasties before him by some other person, or they may have been composed by the enlightened Emperor of the period, who desired to conceal the fact, yet these matters would not for a moment engage the interest of any ordinary passer-by. Lo Kuan Chang is not a person in the ordinary expression; he is the embodiment of a distinguished and utterly unassailable national institution. The Heaven-sent works with which he is, by general consent, connected form the necessary unchangeable standard of literary excellence, and remain for ever above rivalry and above mistrust. For this reason the matter is plainly one which does not interest this person."

'In the course of a not uneventful existence this self-deprecatory person has suffered many reverses and disappointments. During his youth the high-minded Empress on one occasion stopped and openly complimented him on the dignified outline presented by his body in profile, and when he was relying upon this incident to secure him a very remunerative public office, a jealous and powerful Mandarin substituted a somewhat similar, though really very much inferior, person for him at the interview which the Empress had commanded. Frequently in matters of commerce which have appeared to promise very satisfactorily at the beginning this person has been induced to entrust sums of money to others, when he had hoped from the indications and the manner of speaking that the exact contrary would be the case; and in one instance he was released at a vast price from the torture dungeon in Canton — where he had been thrown by the subtle and unconscientious plots of one who could not relate stories in so accurate and unvarying a manner as himself — on the day before that on which all persons were freely set at liberty on account of exceptional public rejoicing. Yet in spite of these and many other very unendurable incidents, this impetuous and ill-starred being never felt so great a desire to retire to a solitary place and there disfigure himself permanently as a mark of his unfeigned internal displeasure, as on the occasion when he endured extreme poverty and great personal inconvenience for an entire year in order that he might take away face from the memory of a person who was so placed that no one expressed any interest in the matter.

'Since then this very ill-clad and really necessitous person has devoted himself to the honourable but exceedingly arduous and in general unremunerative occupation of story-telling. To this he would add nothing save that not unfrequently a nobly born and highly cultured audience is so entranced with his commonplace efforts to hold the attention, especially when a story not hitherto known has been related, that in order to afford it an opportunity of expressing its gratification, he has been requested to allow another offering to be made by all persons present at the conclusion of the entertainment.'

CHAPTER SIX

THE VENGEANCE OF TUNG FEL

*

For a period not to be measured by days or weeks the air of Ching-fow had been as unrestful as that of the locust plains beyond the Great Wall, for every speech which passed bore two faces, one fair to hear, as a greeting, but the other insidiously speaking behind a screen, of rebellion, violence, and the hope of overturning the fixed order of events. With those whom they did not mistrust of treachery persons spoke in low voices of definite plans, while at all times there might appear in prominent places of the city skilfully composed notices setting forth great wrongs and injustices towards which resignation and a lowly bearing were outwardly counselled, yet with the same words cunningly inflaming the minds, even of the patient, as no pouring out of passionate thoughts and undignified threatenings could have done. Among the people, unknown, unseen, and unsuspected, except to the proved ones to whom they desired to reveal themselves, moved the agents of the Three Societies. While to the many of Ching-fow nothing was desired or even thought of beyond the downfall of their own officials, and, chief of all, the execution of the evil-minded and depraved Mandarin Ping Siang, whose cruelties and extortions had made his name an object of wide and deserved loathing, the agents only regarded the city as a bright spot in the line of blood and fire which they were fanning into life from Pekin to Canton, and which would presently burst forth and involve the entire Empire.

Although it had of late become a plain fact, by reason of the manner of behaving of the people, that events of a

sudden and turbulent nature could not long be restrained,
yet outwardly there was no exhibition of violence, not even
to the length of resisting those whom Ping Siang sent
to enforce his unjust demands, chiefly because a well-
founded whisper had been sent round that nothing was to
be done until Tung Fel should arrive, which would not
be until the seventh day in the month of Winged Dragons.
To this all persons agreed, for the more aged among them,
who, by virtue of their years, were also the formers of
opinion on all matters, called up within their memories
certain events connected with the two persons in question
which appeared to give to Tung Fel the privilege of
expressing himself clearly when the matter of finally dealing with the malicious and self-willed Mandarin should
be engaged upon.

Among the mountains which enclose Ching-fow on the
southern side dwelt a jade-seeker, who also kept goats.
Although a young man and entirely without relations, he
had, by patient industry, contrived to collect together a
large flock of the best-formed and most prolific goats to be
found in the neighbourhood, all the money which he received in exchange for jade being quickly bartered again
for the finest animals which he could obtain. He was
dauntless in penetrating to the most inaccessible parts of the
mountains in search of the stone, unfailing in his skilful
care of the flock, in which he took much honourable pride,
and on all occasions discreet and unassumingly restrained
in his discourse and manner of life. Knowing this to be
his invariable practice, it was with emotions of an agreeable
curiosity that on the seventh day of the month of Winged
Dragons those persons who were passing from place to
place in the city beheld this young man, Yang Hu,

descending the mountain path with unmistakable signs of profound agitation, and an entire absence of prudent care. Following him closely to the inner square of the city, on the continually expressed plea that they themselves had business in that quarter, these persons observed Yang Hu take up a position of unendurable dejection as he gazed reproachfully at the figure of the all-knowing Buddha which surmounted the Temple where it was his custom to sacrifice.

'Alas!' he exclaimed, lifting up his voice, when it became plain that a large number of people was assembled, awaiting his words, 'to what end does a person strive in this excessively evilly regulated district? Or is it that this obscure and ill-destined one alone is marked out as with a deep white cross for humiliation and ruin? Father, and Sacred Temple of Ancestral Virtues, wherein the meanest can repose their trust, he has none; while now, being more destitute than the beggar at the gate, the hope of honourable marriage and a robust family of sons is more remote than the chance of finding the miracle-working Crystal Image which marks the last footstep of the Pure One. Yesterday this person possessed no secret store of silver or gold, nor had he knowledge of any special amount of jade hidden among the mountains, but to his call there responded four score goats, the most select and majestic to be found in all the Province, of which, nevertheless, it was his yearly custom to sacrifice one, as those here can testify, and to offer another as a duty at the Yamên of Ping Siang, in neither case opening his eyes widely when the hour for selecting arrived. Yet in what an unseemly manner is his respectful piety and courteous loyalty rewarded! To-day, before this person went forth on his usual quest, there came those bearing outward signs of authority, armed, and exhibiting written papers by which they claimed, on the authority of Ping Siang, in accordance with a command from the high ones at Pekin, the whole of this person's flock, as a punishment and fine for his not contributing without warning to the Celebration of Kissing the Emperor's Face — the very obligation of such a matter being entirely unknown to him. Nevertheless, those who came drove off this person's entire wealth, the desperately won increase of a life full of great toil and uncomplainingly endured hardship, leaving him only his cave in the rocks, which even the most grasping of many-handed mandarins cannot remove, his cloak of skins, which no beggar would gratefully receive, and a bright and increasing light of deep hate scorching within his mind which nothing but the blood of the obdurate extortioner can efficiently quench. No protection of charms or heavily mailed bowmen shall avail him, for in his craving for just revenge this person will meet witchcraft with a Heaven-sent cause and oppose an unsleeping subtlety against strength. Therefore let not the innocent suffer through an insufficient understanding, O Divine One, but direct the hand of your faithful worshipper towards the heart that is proud in tyranny, and holds as empty words the clearly defined promise of an all-seeing justice.'

Scarcely had Yang Hu made an end of speaking before there happened an event which could be regarded in no other light than as a direct answer to his plainly expressed request for a definite sign. Upon the clear air, which had become unnaturally still at Yang Hu's words, as though to remove any chance of doubt that this indeed was the requested answer, came the loud beating of many very powerful brass gongs, indicating the approach of some person of undoubted importance. In a very brief period the procession reached the square, the gong-beaters being followed by persons carrying banners, bowmen in armour, others bearing various weapons and instruments of torture, slaves displaying innumerable changes of raiment to prove the rank and consequence of their master, umbrella carriers and fan wavers, and finally, preceded by incense burners and surrounded by servants who cleared away all obstructions by means of their formidable and heavily knotted lashes, the unworthy and deceitful Mandarin Ping Siang, who sat in a silk-hung and elaborately wrought chair, looking from side to side with gestures and expressions of contempt and ill-restrained cupidity.

At the sight of this powerful but unscrupulous person all those who were present fell upon their faces, leaving a broad space in their midst, except Yang Hu, who stepped back into the shadow of a doorway, being resolved that he would not prostrate himself before one whom Heaven had pointed out as the proper object of his just vengeance.

When the chair of Ping Siang could no longer be observed in the distance, and the sound of his gongs had died away, all the persons who had knelt at his approach rose to their feet, meeting each other's eyes with glances of assured and profound significance. At length there stepped forth an exceedingly aged man, who was generally believed to have the power of reading omens and forecasting futures, so that at his upraised hand all persons became silent.

'Behold!' he exclaimed, 'none can turn aside in doubt from the deliberately pointed finger of Buddha. Henceforth, in spite of the well-intentioned suggestions of those who would shield him under the plea of exacting orders from high ones at Pekin or extortions practised by slaves under him of which he is ignorant, there can no longer be any two voices concerning the guilty one. Yet what does the knowledge of the cormorant's cry avail the golden carp in the shallow waters of the Yuen-Kiang? A prickly mimosa is an adequate protection against a naked man armed only with a just cause, and a company of bowmen has been known to quench an entire city's Heaven-felt desire for retribution. This person, and doubtless others also, would have experienced a more heartfelt enthusiasm in the matter if the sublime and omnipotent Buddha had gone a step farther, and pointed out not only the one to be punished, but also the instrument by which the destiny could be prudently and effectively accomplished.'

From the mountain path which led to Yang Hu's cave came a voice, like an expressly devised reply to this speech. It was that of some person uttering the 'Chant of Rewards and Penalties':

' "How strong and unyielding is the mountain syca-
    more!

' "Its branches reach the Middle Air, and the eye of
    none can pierce its foliage;

' "It draws power and nourishment from all around, so
    that weeds alone may flourish under its shadow.

' "Robbers find safety within the hollow of its trunk;
    its branches hide vampires and all manner of evil
    things which prey upon the innocent;

' "The wild boar of the forest sharpens its tusks agains
    the bark, for it is harder than flint, and the axe of
    the woodsman turns back upon the striker.

' "Then cries the sycamore, 'Hail and rain have no
power against me, nor can the fiercest sun penetrate
beyond my outside fringe;

' " 'The man who impiously raises his hand against me
falls by his own stroke and weapon.

' " 'Can there be a greater or a more powerful than this
one? Assuredly, *I* am Buddha; let all things obey
me.'

' "Whereupon the weeds bow their heads, whispering
among themselves, 'The voice of the Tall One we
hear, but not that of Buddha. Indeed, it is doubtless as he says.'

' "In his musk-scented Heaven Buddha laughs, and not
deigning to raise his head from the lap of the
Phœnix Goddess, he thrusts forth a stone which lies
by his foot.

' "Saying, 'A god's present for a god. Take it carefully,
O presumptuous Little One, for it is hot to the
touch.'

' "The thunderbolt falls and the mighty tree is rent
in twain. 'They asked for my messenger,' said the
Pure One, turning again to repose."

'Lo *he comes*!'

With the last spoken word there came into the sight of
those who were collected together a person of stern yet
engaging appearance. His hands and face were the colour
of mulberry stain by long exposure to the sun, while his
eyes looked forth like two watch-fires outside a wolf-
haunted camp. His long pigtail was tangled with the
binding tendrils of the forest, and damp with the dew of an
open couch. His apparel was in no way striking or
brilliant, yet he strode with the dignity and air of a

high official, pushing before him a covered box upon wheels.

'It is Tung Fel!' cried many who stood there watching his approach, in tones which showed those who spoke to be inspired by a variety of impressive emotions. 'Undoubtedly this is the seventh day of the month of Winged Dragons, and, as he specifically stated would be the case, lo! he has come.'

Few were the words of greeting which Tung Fel accorded even to the most venerable of those who awaited him.

'This person has slept, partaken of fruit and herbs, and devoted an allotted time to inward contemplation,' he said briefly. 'Other and more weighty matters than the exchange of dignified compliments and the admiration of each other's profits remain to be accomplished. What, for example, is the significance of the written parchment which is displayed in so obtrusive a manner before our eyes? Bring it to this person without delay.'

At these words all those present followed Tung Fel's gaze with astonishment, for conspicuously displayed upon the wall of the Temple was a written notice which all joined in asserting had not been there the moment before, though no man had approached the spot. Nevertheless it was quickly brought to Tung Fel, who took it without any fear or hesitation and read aloud the words which it contained.

'TO THE CUSTOM-RESPECTING PERSONS OF CHING-FOW

'Truly the span of existence of any upon this earth is brief and not to be considered; therefore, O unfortunate dwellers of Ching-fow, let it not affect your digestions that your bodies are in peril of sudden and most excruciating tortures and your Family Temples in danger of humiliating disregard.

'Why do your thoughts follow the actions of the noble Mandarin Ping Siang so insidiously, and why after each unjust exaction do your eyes look redly towards the Yamên?

'Is he not the little finger of those at Pekin, obeying their commands and only carrying out the taxation which others have devised? Indeed, he himself has stated such to be the fact. If, therefore, a terrible and unforeseen fate overtook the usually cautious and well-armed Ping Siang, doubtless — perhaps after the lapse of some considerable time — another would be sent from Pekin for a like purpose and in this way, after a too-brief period of Heaven-sent rest and prosperity affairs would regulate themselves into almost as unendurable a condition as before.

'Therefore ponder these things well, O passer-by. Yesterday the only man-child of Huang the wood-carver was taken away to be sold into slavery by the emissaries of the most just Ping Siang (who would not have acted thus, we are assured, were it not for the insatiable ones at Pekin), as it had become plain that the very necessitous Huang had no other possession to contribute to the amount to be expended in coloured lights as a mark of public rejoicing on the occasion of the noonday of the sublime Emperor. The illiterate and prosaic-minded Huang, having in a most unseemly manner reviled and even assailed those who acted in the matter, has been effectively disposed of, and his wife now alternately laughs and shrieks in the Establishment of Irregular Intellects.

'For this reason, gazer, and because the matter touches

you more closely than, in your self-imagined security, you are prone to think, deal expediently with the time at your disposal. Look twice and lingeringly to-night upon the face of your first-born, and clasp the form of your favourite one in a closer embrace, for he by whose hand the blow is directed may already have cast devouring eyes upon their fairness, and to-morrow he may say to his armed men: "The time is come; bring her to me." '

'From the last sentence of the well-intentioned and un-doubtedly moderately framed notice this person will take two phrases,' remarked Tung Fel, folding the written paper and placing it among his garments, 'which shall serve him as the title of the life-like and accurately repre-sented play which it is his self-conceited intention now to disclose to this select and unprejudiced gathering. The scene represents an enlightened and well-merited justice overtaking an arrogant and intolerable being who — need this person add? — existed many dynasties ago, and the title is:

'THE TIME IS COME!

'BY WHOSE HAND?'

Delivering himself in this manner, Tung Fel drew back the hanging drapery which concealed the front of his large box, and disclosed to those who were gathered round, not, as they had expected, a passage from the 'Record of the Three Kingdoms,' or some other dramatic work of un-doubted merit, but an ingeniously constructed representa-tion of a scene outside the walls of their own Ching-fow On one side was a small but minutely accurate copy of a wood-burner's hut, which was known to all present, while behind stood out the distant but nevertheless unmistakable walls of the city. But it was the nearest part of the spectacle that first held the attention of the entranced beholders, for there disported themselves, in every variety of guileless and attractive attitude, a number of young and entirely unconcerned doves. Scarcely had the delighted onlookers fully observed the pleasing and effective scene, or uttered their expressions of polished satisfaction at the graceful and unassuming behaviour of the pretty creatures before them, than the view entirely changed, and, as if by magic, the massive and inelegant building of Ping Siang's Yamên was presented before them. As all gazed, astonished, the great door of the Yamên opened stealthily, and without a moment's pause a lean and ill-conditioned rat, of unnatural size and rapacity, dashed out and seized the most select and engaging of the unsuspecting prey in its hungry jaws. With the expiring cry of the innocent victim the entire box was immediately, and in the most unexpected manner, involved in a profound darkness, which cleared away as suddenly and revealed the forms of the despoiler and the victim lying dead by each other's side.

Tung Fel came forward to receive the well-selected compliments of all who had witnessed the entertainment. 'It may be objected,' he remarked, 'that the play is, in a manner of expressing one's self, incomplete; for it is unrevealed by whose hand the act of justice was accomplished. Yet in this detail is the accuracy of the representation justified, for though the time has come, the hand by which retribution is accorded shall never be observed.'

In such a manner did Tung Fel come to Ching-fow on the seventh day of the month of Winged Dragons, throwing aside all restraint, and no longer urging prudence or delay. Of all the throng which stood before him scarcely one was without a deep offence against Ping Siang, while those who had not as yet suffered feared what the morrow might display.

A wandering monk from the Island of Irredeemable Plagues was the first to step forth in response to Tung Fel's plainly understood suggestion.

'There is no necessity for this person to undertake further acts of benevolence,' he remarked, dropping the cloak from his shoulder and displaying the hundred and eight scars of extreme virtue; 'nor,' he continued, holding up the left hand, from which three fingers were burnt away, 'have greater endurances been neglected. Yet the matter before this distinguished gathering is one which merits the favourable consideration of all persons, and this one will in no manner turn away, recounting former actions, while he allows others to press forward towards the accomplishment of the just and divinely inspired act.'

With these words the devout and unassuming person in question inscribed his name upon a square piece of rice-paper, attesting his sincerity to the fixed purpose for which it was designed by dipping his thumb into the mixed blood of the slain animals and impressing this unalterable seal upon the paper also. He was followed by a seller of drugs and subtle medicines, whose entire stock had been seized and destroyed by order of Ping Siang, so that no one in Ching-fow might obtain poison for his destruction. Then came an overwhelming stream of persons, all of whom had received some severe and well-remembered injury at the hands of the malicious and vindictive Mandarin. All these followed a similar observance, inscribing their names and binding themselves by the Blood Oath. Last of all Yang Hu stepped up, partly from a natural modesty which restrained him from offering himself when so many more versatile persons of proved excellence were willing to engage in the matter, and partly because an ill-advised conflict was taking place within his mind as to whether the extreme course which was contemplated was the most expedient to pursue. At last, however, he plainly perceived that he could not honourably withhold himself from an affair that was in a measure the direct outcome of his own unendurable loss, so that without further hesitation he added his obscure name to the many illustrious ones already in Tung Fel's keeping.

When at length dark fell upon the city and the cries of the watchmen, warning all prudent ones to bar well their doors against robbers, as they themselves were withdrawing until the morrow, no longer rang through the narrow ways of Ching-fow, all those persons who had pledged themselves by name and seal went forth silently, and came together at the place whereof Tung Fel had secretly conveyed them knowledge. There Tung Fel, standing somewhat apart, placed all the folded papers in the form of a circle, and having performed over them certain observances designed to insure a just decision and to keep away evil influences, submitted the selection to the discriminating choice of the Sacred Flat and Round Sticks. Having in this manner secured the name of the appointed person who should carry out the act of justice and retribution, Tung Fel unfolded the paper, inscribed certain words upon it, and replaced it among the others.

'The moment before great deeds,' began Tung Fel,

stepping forward and addressing himself to the expectant ones who were gathered round, 'is not the time for light speech, nor, indeed, for sentences of dignified length, no matter how pleasantly turned to the ear they may be. Before this person stand many who are undoubtedly illustrious in various arts and virtues, yet one among them is pre-eminently marked out for distinction in that his name shall be handed down in imperishable history as that of a patriot of a pure-minded and uncompromising degree. With him there is no need of further speech, and to this end I have inscribed certain words upon his name-paper. To every one this person will now return the paper which has been entrusted to him, folded so that the nature of its contents shall be an unwritten leaf to all others. Nor shall the papers be unfolded by any until he is within his own chamber with barred doors, where all, save the one who shall find the message, shall remain, not venturing forth until daybreak. I, Tung Fel, have spoken, and assuredly I shall not eat my word, which is that a certain and most degrading death awaits any who transgress these commands.'

It was with the short and sudden breath of the cowering antelope, when the stealthy tread of the pitiless tiger approaches its lair, that Yang Hu opened his paper in the seclusion of his own cave; for his mind was darkened with an inspired inside emotion that he, the one doubting one among the eagerly proffering and destructively inclined multitude, would be chosen to accomplish the high aim for which, indeed, he felt exceptionally unworthy. The written sentence which he perceived immediately upon unfolding the paper, instructing him to appear again before Tung Fel at the hour of midnight, was, therefore, nothing but the echo and fulfilment of his own thoughts, and served in reality to impress his mind with calmer feelings of dignified unconcern than would have been the case had he not been chosen. Having neither possessions nor relations, the occupation of disposing of his goods and making ceremonious and affectionate leave-takings of his family, against the occurrence of any unforeseen disaster, engrossed no portion of Yang Hu's time. Yet there was one matter to which no reference has yet been made, but which now forces itself obtrusively upon the attention, which was in a large measure responsible for many of the most prominent actions of Yang Hu's life, and, indeed, in no small degree influenced his hesitation in offering himself before Tung Fel.

Not a bowshot distance from the place where the mountain path entered the outskirts of the city lived Hiya-ai-Shao with her parents, who were persons of assured position, though of no particular wealth. For a period not confined to a single year it had been the custom of Yang Hu to offer to this elegant and refined maiden all the rarest pieces of jade which he could discover, while the most symmetrical and remunerative she-goat in his flock enjoyed the honourable distinction of bearing her incomparable name. Towards the almond garden of Hiya's abode Yang Hu turned his footsteps upon leaving his cave, and standing there, concealed from all sides by the white and abundant flower-laden foliage, he uttered a sound which had long been an agreed signal between them. Presently a faint perfume of choo-lân spoke of her near approach, and without delay Hiya herself stood by his side.

'Well-endowed one,' said Yang Hu, when at length

they had gazed upon each other's features and made re-
newals of their protestations of mutual regard, 'the fixed
intentions of a person have often been fitly likened to the
seed of the tree-peony, so ineffectual are their efforts
among the winds of constantly changing circumstance.
The definite hope of this person had long pointed towards
a small but adequate habitation, surrounded by sweet-
smelling olive-trees and not far distant from the jade cliffs
and pastures which would afford a sufficient remuneration
and a means of living. This entrancing picture has been
blotted out for the time, and in its place this person finds
himself face to face with an arduous and dangerous undertaking, followed, perhaps, by hasty and immediate flight.
Yet if the adorable Hiya will prove the unchanging depths
of her constantly expressed intention by accompanying
him as far as the village of Hing, where suitable marriage
ceremonies can be observed without delay, the exile will in
reality be in the nature of a triumphal procession, and the
emotions with which this person has hitherto regarded the
entire circumstance will undergo a complete and highly
accomplished change.'

'Oh, Yang!' exclaimed the maiden, whose feelings at
hearing these words were in no way different from those of
her lover when he was on the point of opening the folded
paper upon which Tung Fel had written; 'what is the
nature of the mission upon which you are so impetuously
resolved? and why will it be followed by flight?'

'The nature of the undertaking cannot be revealed by
reason of a deliberately taken oath,' replied Yang Hu;
'and the reason of its possible consequence is a less important question to the two persons who are here conversing
together than of whether the amiable and graceful Hiya

is willing to carry out her often expressed desire for an opportunity of displaying the true depths of her emotions towards this one.'

'Alas!' said Hiya, 'the sentiments which this person expressed with irreproachable honourableness when the sun was high in the heavens and the probability of secretly leaving an undoubtedly well-appointed home was engagingly remote seem to have an entirely different significance when recalled by night in a damp orchard, and on the eve of their fulfilment. To deceive one's parents is an ignoble prospect; furthermore, it is often an exceedingly difficult undertaking. Let the matter be arranged in this way: that Yang leaves the ultimate details of the scheme to Hiya's expedient care, he proceeding without delay to Hing, or, even more desirable, to the further town of Liyunnan, and there awaiting her coming. By such means the risk of discovery and pursuit will be lessened, Yang will be able to set forth on his journey with greater speed, and this one will have an opportunity of getting together certain articles without which, indeed, she would be very inadequately equipped.'

In spite of his conscientious desire that Hiya should be by his side on the journey, together with an unendurable certainty that evil would arise from the course she had proposed, Yang was compelled by an innate feeling of respect to agree to her wishes, and in this manner the arrangement was definitely concluded. Thereupon Hiya, without delay, returned to the dwelling, remarking that otherwise her absence might be detected and the entire circumstance thereby discovered, leaving Yang Hu to continue his journey and again present himself before Tung Fel, as he had been instructed.

Tung Fel was engaged with brush and ink when Yang Hu entered. Round him were many written parchments, some venerable with age, and a variety of other matters, among which might be clearly perceived weapons, and devices for reading the future. He greeted Yang with many tokens of dignified respect, and with an evidently restrained emotion led him towards the light of a hanging lantern, where he gazed into his face for a considerable period with every indication of exceptional concern.

'Yang Hu,' he said at length, 'at such a moment many dark and searching thoughts may naturally arise in the mind concerning objects and reasons, omens, and the moving cycle of events. Yet in all these, out of a wisdom gained by deep endurance and a hardly-won experience beyond the common lot, this person would say, Be content. The hand of destiny, though it may at times appear to move in a devious manner, is ever approaching its appointed aim. To this end were you chosen.'

'The choice was openly made by wise and proficient omens,' replied Yang Hu, without any display of uncertainty of purpose, 'and this person is content.'

Tung Fel then administered to Yang the Oath of Buddha's Face and the One called the Unutterable (which may not be further described in written words), thereby binding his body and soul, and the souls and repose of all who had gone before him in direct line and all who should in a like manner follow after, to the accomplishment of the design. All spoken matter being thus complete between them, he gave him a mask with which he should pass unknown through the streets and into the presence of Ping Siang, a variety of weapons to use as the occasion arose, and a sign by which the attendants at the Yamên would admit him without further questioning.

As Yang Hu passed through the streets of Ching-fow, which were in a great measure deserted owing to the command of Tung Fel, he was aware of many mournful and foreboding sounds which accompanied him on all sides, while shadowy faces, bearing signs of intolerable anguish and despair, continually formed themselves out of the wind. By the time he reached the Yamên a tempest of exceptional violence was in progress, nor were other omens absent which tended to indicate that matters of a very unpropitious nature were about to take place.

At each successive door of the Yamên the attendant stepped back and covered his face, so that he should by no chance perceive who had come upon so destructive a mission, the instant Yang Hu uttered the sign with which Tung Fel had provided him. In this manner Yang quickly reached the door of the inner chamber upon which was inscribed: 'Let the person who comes with a doubtful countenance, unbidden, or meditating treachery, remember the curse and manner of death which attended Lai Kuen, who slew the one over him; so shall he turn and go forth in safety.' This unworthy safeguard at the hands of a person who passed his entire life in altering the fixed nature of justice, and who never went beyond his outer gate without an armed company of bowmen, inspired Yang Hu with so incautious a contempt, that without any hesitation he drew forth his brush and ink, and in a spirit of bitter significance added the words, ' "Come, let us eat together," said the wolf to the she-goat.'

Being now within a step of Ping Siang and the completion of his undertaking, Yang Hu drew tighter the cords of his mask, tested and proved his weapons, and then, without further delay, threw open the door before him and stepped into the chamber, barring the door quickly so that no person might leave or enter without his consent.

At this interruption and manner of behaving, which clearly indicated the nature of the errand upon which the person before him had come, Ping Siang rose from his couch and stretched out his hand towards a gong which lay beside him.

'All summonses for aid are now unavailing, Ping Siang,' exclaimed Yang, without in any measure using delicate or set phrases of speech; 'for, as you have doubtless informed yourself, the slaves of tyrants are the first to welcome the downfall of their lord.'

'The matter of your speech is as emptiness to this person,' replied the Mandarin, affecting with extreme difficulty an appearance of no-concern. 'In what manner has he fallen? And how will the depraved and self-willed person before him avoid the well-deserved tortures which certainly await him in the public square on the morrow, as the reward of his intolerable presumption?'

'O Mandarin,' cried Yang Hu, 'the fitness and occasion for such speeches as the one to which you have just given utterance lie as far behind you as the smoke of yesterday's sacrifice. With what manner of eyes have you frequently journeyed through Ching-fow of late, if the signs and omens there have not already warned you to prepare a coffin adequately designed to receive your well-proportioned body? Has not the pungent vapour of burning houses assailed your senses at every turn, or the salt tears from the eyes of forlorn ones dashed your peach-tea and spiced foods with bitterness?'

'Alas!' exclaimed Ping Siang, 'this person now certainly begins to perceive that many things which he has unthinkingly allowed would present a very unendurable face to others.'

'In such a manner has it appeared to all Ching-fow,' said Yang Hu; 'and the justice of your death has been universally admitted. Even should this one fail, there would be an innumerable company eager to take his place. Therefore, O Ping Siang, as the only favour which it is within this person's power to accord, select that which in your opinion is the most agreeable manner and weapon for your end.'

'It is truly said that at the Final Gate of the Two Ways the necessity for elegant and well-chosen sentences ends,' remarked Ping Siang, with a sigh, 'otherwise the manner of your address would be open to reproach. By your side this person perceives a long and apparently highly tempered sword, which, in his opinion, will serve the purpose efficiently. Having no remarks of an improving but nevertheless exceedingly tedious nature with which to imprint the occasion for the benefit of those who come after, his only request is that the blow shall be an unhesitating and sufficiently well-directed one.'

At these words Yang Hu threw back his cloak to grasp the sword-handle, when the Mandarin, with his eyes fixed on the naked arm, and evidently inspired by every manner of conflicting emotions, uttered a cry of unspeakable wonder and incomparable surprise.

'The Serpent!' he cried, in a voice from which all

evenness and control were absent. 'The Sacred Serpent of our Race! O mysterious one, who and whence are you?'

Engulfed in an all-absorbing doubt at the nature of events, Yang could only gaze at the form of the serpent which had been clearly impressed upon his arm from the earliest time of his remembrance, while Ping Siang, tearing the silk garment from his own arm and displaying thereon a similar form, continued:

'Behold the inevitable and unvarying birthmark of our race! So it was with this person's father and the ones before him; so it was with his treacherously stolen son; so i will be to the end of all time.'

Trembling beyond all power of restraint, Yang removed the mask which had hitherto concealed his face.

'Father or race has this person none,' he said, looking into Ping Siang's features with an all-engaging hope, tempered in a measure by a soul-benumbing dread; 'nor memory or tradition of an earlier state than when he herded goats and sought for jade in the southern mountains.'

'Nevertheless,' exclaimed the Mandarin, whose countenance was lightened with an interest and a benevolent emotion which had never been seen there before, 'beyond all possibility of doubting, you are this person's lost and greatly desired son, stolen away many years ago by the treacherous conduct of an unworthy woman, yet now happily and miraculously restored to cherish his declining years and perpetuate an honourable name and race.'

'Happily!' exclaimed Yang, with fervent indications of uncontrollable bitterness. 'Oh, my illustrious sire, at whose venerated feet this unworthy person now prostrates himself with well-merited marks of reverence and self-abasement, has the errand upon which an ignoble son entered — the very memory of which now causes him the acutest agony of the lost, but which nevertheless he is pledged to Tung Fel by the Unutterable Oath to perform — has this unnatural and eternally cursed thing escaped your versatile mind?'

'Tung Fel!' cried Ping Siang. 'Is, then, this blow also by the hand of that malicious and vindictive person? Oh, what a cycle of events and interchanging lines of destiny do your words disclose!'

'Who, then, is Tung Fel, my revered Father?' demanded Yang.

'It is a matter which must be made clear from the beginning,' replied Ping Siang. 'At one time this person and Tung Fel were, by nature and endowments, united in the most amiable bonds of an inseparable friendship. Presently Tung Fel signed the preliminary contract of a marriage with one who seemed to be endowed with every variety of enchanting and virtuous grace, but who was, nevertheless, as the unrolling of future events irresistibly discovered, a person of irregular character and undignified habits On the eve of the marriage ceremony this person was made known to her by the undoubtedly enraptured Tung Fel, whereupon he too fell into the snare of her engaging personality, and putting aside all thoughts of prudent restraint, made her more remunerative offers of marriage than Tung Fel could by any possible chance overbid. In such a manner — for after the nature of her kind riches were exceptionally attractive to her degraded imagination — she became this person's wife, and the mother of his only son. In spite of these great honours, however, the undoubted perversity of her nature made her an easy accomplice to the duplicity of Tung Fel, who, by means of various disguises, found frequent opportunity of uttering in her presence numerous well-thought-out suggestions specially designed to lead her imagination towards an existence in which this person had no adequate representation. Becoming at length terrified at the possibility of these unworthy emotions obtruding themselves upon this person's notice, the two in question fled together, taking with them the one who without any doubt is now before me. Despite the most assiduous search and very tempting and profitable offers of reward, no information of a reliable nature could be obtained, and at length this dispirited and completely changed person gave up the pursuit as unavailing. With his son and heir, upon whose future he had greatly hoped, all emotions of a generous and high-minded nature left him, and in a very short space of time he became the avaricious and deservedly unpopular individual against whose extortions the amiable and long-suffering ones of Ching-fow have for so many years protested mildly. The sudden and not altogether unexpected fate which is now on the point of reaching him is altogether too lenient to be entirely adequate.'

'Oh, my distinguished and really immaculate sire!' cried Yang Hu, in a voice which expressed the deepest feelings of contrition. 'No oaths or vows, however sacred, can induce this person to stretch forth his hand against the one who stands before him.'

'Nevertheless,' replied Ping Siang, speaking of the matter as though it were one which did not closely concern his own existence, 'to neglect the Unutterable Oath would inevitably involve not only the two persons who are now conversing together, but also those before and those who are to come after in direct line, in a much worse condition of affairs. That is a fate which this person would by no means permit to exist, for one of his chief desires has ever been to establish a strong and vigorous line, to which end, indeed, he was even now concluding a marriage arrangement with the beautiful and refined Hiya-ai-Shao, whom he had at length persuaded into accepting his betrothal tokens without reluctance.'

'Hiya-ai-Shao!' exclaimed Yang; 'she has accepted your silk-bound gifts?'

'The matter need not concern us now,' replied the Mandarin, not observing in his complicated emotions the manner in which the name of Hiya had affected Yang, revealing as it undoubtedly did the treachery of his beloved one. 'There only appears to be one honourable way in which the full circumstances can be arranged, and this person will in no measure endeavour to avoid it.'

Yang Hu looked at him inquiringly, and Ping Siang, crossing the room, opened an inlaid cabinet and drew from a hidden part a closed vessel in which gold-leaf floated in a sweet-scented oil.

'Such an end is neither ignoble nor painful,' he said in an unchanging voice; 'nor will this one in any way shrink from so easy and honourable a solution.'

'The affairs of the future do not exhibit themselves in delicately coloured hues to this person,' said Yang Hu; 'and he would, if the thing could be so arranged, cheerfully submit to a similar fate in order that a longer period of existence should be assured to one who has every variety of claim upon his affection.'

'The proposal is a graceful and conscientious one,' said

Ping Siang, 'and is, moreover, a gratifying omen for the future of our race, which must of necessity be left in your hands. But, for that reason itself, such a course cannot be pursued. Nevertheless, the events of the past few hours have been of so exceedingly prosperous and agreeable a nature that this short-sighted and frequently desponding person can now pass beyond with a tranquil countenance and every assurance of divine favour.'

With these words Ping Siang indicated that he was desirous of setting forth the Final Expression, and arranging the necessary matters upon the table beside him, he stretched forth his hands over Yang Hu, who placed himself in a suitable attitude of reverence and abasement.

'Yang Hu,' began the Mandarin, 'undoubted son, and, after the accomplishment of the intention which it is our fixed purpose to carry out, fitting representative of the person who is here before you, engrave well within your mind the various details upon which he now gives utterance. Regard the virtues; endeavour to pass an amiable and at the same time not unremunerative existence; and on all occasions sacrifice freely, to the end that the torments of those who have gone before may be made lighter, and that others may be induced in turn to perform a like benevolent charity for yourself. Having expressed himself upon these general subjects, this person now makes a last and respectfully considered desire, which it is his deliberate wish should be carried to the proper deities as his final expression of opinion: That Yang Hu may grow as supple as the dried juice of the bending-palm, and as straight as the most vigorous bamboo from the forests of the North. That he may increase beyond the prolificness of the white-

223

necked crow and cover the ground after the fashion of the binding grass. That in battle his sword may be as a vividly coloured and many-forked lightning flash, accompanied by thunderbolts as irresistible as Buddha's divine wrath; in peace his voice as resounding as the rolling of many powerful drums among the Khingan Mountains. That when the kindled fire of his existence returns to the great Mountain of Pure Flame the earth shall accept again its component parts, and in no way restrain the divine essence from journeying to its destined happiness. These words are Ping Siang's last expression of opinion before he passes beyond, given in the unvarying assurance that so sacred and important a petition will in no way be neglected.'

Having in this manner completed all the affairs which seemed to be of a necessary and urgent nature, and fixing his last glances upon Yang Hu with every variety of affectionate and estimable emotion, the Mandarin drank a sufficient quantity of the liquid, and placing himself upon a couch in an attitude of repose, passed in this dignified and unassuming manner into the Upper Air.

After the space of a few moments spent in arranging certain objects and in inward contemplation, Yang Hu crossed the chamber, still holding the half-filled vessel of gold-leaf in his hand, and drawing back the hanging silk, gazed over the silent streets of Ching-fow and towards the great sky-lantern above.

'Hiya is faithless,' he said at length in an unspeaking voice; 'this person's mother a bitter-tasting memory, his father a swiftly passing shadow that is now for ever lost.' His eyes rested upon the closed vessel in his hand. 'Gladly would –' his thoughts began, but with this unworthy image a·new impression formed itself within his mind. 'A clearly expressed wish was uttered,' he concluded, 'and Tung Fel still remains.' With this resolution he stepped back into the chamber and struck the gong loudly.

CHAPTER SEVEN

THE CAREER OF THE CHARITABLE QUEN-KI-TONG

★

FIRST PERIOD

The Public Official

'The motives which inspired the actions of the devout Quen-Ki-Tong have long been ill-reported,' said Kai Lung the story-teller, upon a certain occasion at Wu-whei, 'and, as a consequence, his illustrious memory has suffered somewhat. Even as the insignificant earth-worm may bring the precious and many-coloured jewel to the surface, so has it been permitted to this obscure and superficially educated one to discover the truth of the entire matter among the badly arranged and frequently really illegible documents preserved at the Hall of Public Reference at Pekin. Without fear of contradiction, therefore, he now sets forth the credible version.

'Quen-Ki-Tong was one who throughout his life had been compelled by the opposing force of circumstances to be content with what was offered rather than attain to that which he desired. Having been allowed to wander over the edge of an exceedingly steep crag, while still a child, by the aged and untrustworthy person who had the care of him, and yet suffering little hurt, he was carried back to the city in triumph by the one in question, who, to cover her neglect, declared amid many chants of exultation that as he slept a majestic winged form had snatched him from her arms and traced magical figures with his body on the ground in token of the distinguished sacred existence for which he was undoubtedly set apart. In such a manner he

226

became famed at a very early age for an unassuming mildness of character and an almost inspired piety of life, so that on every side frequent opportunity was given him for the display of these amiable qualities. Should it chance that an insufficient quantity of puppy-pie had been prepared for the family repast, the undesirable but necessary portion of old dried rat would inevitably be allotted to the uncomplaining Quen, doubtless accompanied by the engaging but unnecessary remark that he alone had a Heaven-sent intellect which was fixed upon more sublime images than even the best-constructed puppy-pie. Should the number of sedan-chairs not be sufficient to bear to the Exhibition of Kites all who were desirous of becoming entertained in such a fashion, inevitably would Quen be the one left behind, in order that he might have adequate leisure for dignified and pure-minded internal reflection.

'In this manner it came about that when a very wealthy but unnaturally avaricious and evil-tempered person who was connected with Quen's father in matters of commerce expressed his fixed determination that the most deserving and enlightened of his friend's sons should enter into a marriage agreement with his daughter, there was no manner of hesitation among those concerned, who admitted without any questioning between themselves that Quen was undeniably the one referred to.

'Though naturally not possessing an insignificant intellect, a continuous habit, together with a most irreproachable sense of filial duty, subdued within Quen's internal organs whatever reluctance he might otherwise have displayed in the matter, so that as courteously as was necessary he presented to the undoubtedly very ordinary and slow-witted maiden in question the gifts of irretrievable intention, and honourably carried out his spoken and written words towards her.

'For a period of years the circumstances of the various persons did not in any degree change, Quen in the meantime becoming more pure-souled and inward-seeing with each moon-change, after the manner of the sublime Lienti, who studied to maintain an unmoved endurance in all varieties of events by placing his body to a greater extent each day in a vessel of boiling liquid. Nevertheless, the good and charitable deities to whom Quen unceasingly sacrificed were not altogether unmindful of his virtues; for a son was born, and an evil disease which arose from a most undignified display of uncontrollable emotion on her part ended in his wife being deposited with becoming ceremony in the Family Temple.

'Upon a certain evening, when Quen sat in his inner chamber deliberating upon the really beneficent yet somewhat inexplicable arrangement of the all-seeing ones to whom he was very amiably disposed in consequence of the unwonted tranquillity which he now enjoyed, yet who, it appeared to him, could have set out the entire matter in a much more satisfactory way from the beginning, he was made aware by the unexpected beating of many gongs, and by other signs of refined and deferential welcome, that a person of exalted rank was approaching his residence. While he was still hesitating in his uncertainty regarding the most courteous and delicate form of self-abasement with which to honour so important a visitor – whether to rush forth and allow the chair-carriers to pass over his prostrate form, to make a pretence of being a low-caste slave, and in that guise doing menial service, or to conceal himself beneath a massive and overhanging table until his guest should have availed himself of the opportunity to examine at his leisure whatever the room contained — the person in question stood before him. In every detail of dress and appointment he had the undoubted appearance of being one to whom no door might be safely closed.

'"Alas!" exclaimed Quen, "how inferior and ill-contrived is the mind of a person of my feeble intellectual attainments. Even at this moment, when the near approach of one who obviously commands every engaging accomplishment might reasonably be expected to call up within it an adequate amount of commonplace resource, its ill-destined possessor finds himself entirely incapable of conducting himself with fitting outward marks of his great internal respect. This residence is certainly unprepossessing in the extreme, yet it contains many objects of some value and of great rarity; illiterate as this person is, he would not be so presumptuous as to offer any for your acceptance, but if you will confer upon him the favour of selecting that which appears to be the most priceless and unreplaceable, he will immediately, and with every manifestation of extreme delight, break it irredeemably in your honour, to prove the unaffected depth of his gratified emotions."

'"Quen-Ki-Tong," replied the person before him, speaking with an evident sincerity of purpose, "pleasant to this one's ears are your words, breathing as they do an obvious hospitality and a due regard for the forms of etiquette. But if, indeed, you are desirous of gaining this person's explicit regard, break no articles of fine porcelain or rare inlaid wood in proof of it, but immediately dismiss to a very distant spot the threescore gong-beaters who have enclosed him within two solid rings, and who are now carrying out their duties in so diligent a manner that he greatly doubts if the unimpaired faculties of hearing will ever be fully restored. Furthermore, if your exceedingly amiable intentions desire fuller expression, cause an unstinted number of vessels of some uninflammable liquid to be conveyed into your chrysanthemum garden and there poured over the numerous fireworks and coloured lights which still appear to be in progress. Doubtless they are well-intentioned marks of respect, but they caused this person considerable apprehension as he passed among them, and, indeed, give to this usually pleasant and unassuming spot the by no means inviting atmosphere of a low-class tea-house garden during the festivities attending the birthday of the sacred Emperor."

' "This person is overwhelmed with a most unendurable confusion that the matters referred to should have been regarded in such a light," replied Quen humbly. "Although he himself had no knowledge of them until this moment, he is confident that they in no wise differ from the usual honourable manifestations with which it is customary in this Province to welcome strangers of exceptional rank and titles."

' "The welcome was of a most dignified and impressive nature," replied the stranger, with every appearance of not desiring to cause Quen any uneasy internal doubts: "yet the fact is none the less true that at the moment this person's head seems to contain an exceedingly powerful and well-equipped band; and also, that as he passed through the courtyard an ingeniously constructed but somewhat unmanageable figure of gigantic size, composed entirely of jets of many-coloured flame, leaped out suddenly from behind a dark wall and made an almost successful attempt to embrace him in its ever-revolving arms. Lo Yuen greatly fears that the time when he would have rejoiced in the necessary display of agility to which the incident gave rise has for ever passed away."

'"Lo Yuen!" exclaimed Quen, with an unaffected mingling of the emotions of reverential awe and pleasurable anticipation. "Can it indeed be an uncontroversial fact that so learned and ornamental a person as the renowned Controller of Unsolicited Degrees stands beneath this inelegant person's utterly unpresentable roof! Now, indeed, he plainly understands why this ill-conditioned chamber has the appearance of being filled with a Heaven-sent brilliance, and why at the first spoken words of the one before him a melodious sound, like the rushing waters of the sacred Tien-Kiang, seemed to fill his ears."

'"Undoubtedly the chamber is pervaded by a very exceptional splendour," replied Lo Yuen, who, in spite of his high position, regarded graceful talk and well-imagined compliments in a spirit of no-satisfaction; "yet this commonplace-minded one has a fixed conviction that it is caused by the crimson-eyed and pink-fire-breathing dragon which, despite your slave's most assiduous efforts, is now endeavouring to climb through the aperture behind you. The noise which still fills his ears also, resembles rather the despairing cries of the Ten Thousand Lost Ones at the first sight of the Pit of Liquid and Red-hot Malachite, yet without question both proceed from the same cause. Laying aside further ceremony, therefore, permit this greatly over-estimated person to disclose the object of his inopportune visit. Long have your amiable virtues been observed and appreciated by the high ones at Pekin, O Quen-Ki-Tong. Too long have they been unrewarded and passed over in silence. Nevertheless, the moment of acknowledgment and advancement has at length arrived; for, as the Book of Verses clearly says, 'Even the three-legged mule may contrive to reach the agreed spot in advance of the others, provided a circular running space has been selected and the number of rounds be sufficiently ample.' It is this otherwise uninteresting and obtrusive person's graceful duty to convey to you the agreeable intelligence that the honourable and not ill-rewarded office of Guarder of the Imperial Silkworms has been conferred upon you, and to require you to proceed without delay to Pekin, so that fitting ceremonies of admittance may be performed before the fifteenth day of the month of Feathered Insects."

'Alas! how frequently does the purchaser of seemingly vigorous and exceptionally low-priced flower-seeds discover, when too late, that they are, in reality, fashioned from the root of the prolific and valueless tzu-ka, skilfully covered with a disguising varnish! Instead of presenting himself at the place of commerce frequented by those who entrust money to others on the promise of an increased repayment when certain very probable events have come to pass (so that if all else failed he would still possess a serviceable number of taels), Quen-Ki-Tong entirely neglected the demands of a most ordinary prudence, nor could he be induced to set out on his journey until he had passed seven days in public feasting to mark his good fortune, and then devoted fourteen more days to fasting and various acts of penance, in order to make known the regret with which he acknowledged his entire unworthiness for the honour before him. Owing to this very conscientious, but nevertheless somewhat short-sighted manner of behaving, Quen found himself unable to reach Pekin before the day preceding that to which Lo Yuen had made special reference. From this cause it came about that only sufficient time remained to perform the various ceremonies of admission without in any degree counselling Quen as to his duties and procedure in the fulfilment of his really important office.

'Among the many necessary and venerable ceremonies observed during the changing periods of the year, none occupy a more important place than those for which the fifteenth day of the month of Feathered Insects is reserved, conveying as they do a respectful and delicately fashioned petition that the various affairs upon which persons in every condition of life are engaged may arrive at a pleasant and remunerative conclusion. At the earliest stroke of the gong the versatile Emperor, accompanied by many persons of irreproachable ancestry and certain others, very elaborately attired, proceeds to an open space set apart for the occasion. With unassuming dexterity the benevolent Emperor for a brief span of time engages in the menial occupation of a person of low class, and with his own hands ploughs an assigned portion of land in order that the enlightened spirits under whose direct guardianship the earth is placed may not become lax in their disinterested efforts to promote its fruitfulness. In this charitable exertion he is followed by various other persons of recognized position, the first being, by custom, the Guarder of the Imperial Silkworms, while at the same time the amiably disposed Empress plants an allotted number of mulberry-trees, and deposits upon their leaves the carefully reared insects which she receives from the hands of their Guarder. In the case of the accomplished Emperor an ingenious contrivance is resorted to by which the soil is drawn aside by means of hidden strings as the plough passes by, the implement in question being itself constructed from paper of the finest quality, while the oxen which draw it are, in reality, ordinary persons cunningly concealed within masks of cardboard. In this thoughtful manner the actual labours of the sublime Emperor are greatly lessened, while no chance is afforded for an inauspicious omen to be created by the rebellious behaviour of a maliciously inclined ox, or by any other event of an unforeseen nature. All the other persons, however, are required to make themselves proficient in the art of ploughing, before the ceremony, so that the chances of the attendant spirits discovering the deception which has been practised upon them in the case of the Emperor may not be increased by its needless repetition. It was chiefly for this reason that Lo Yuen had urged Quen to journey to Pekin as speedily as possible, but owing to the very short time which remained between his arrival and the ceremony of ploughing, not only had the person in question neglected to profit by instruction, but he was not even aware of the obligation which awaited him. When, therefore, in spite of every respectful protest on his part, he was led up to a massively constructed implement drawn by two powerful and undeniably evilly intentioned looking animals, it was with every sign of great internal misgivings, and an entire absence of enthusiasm in the entertainment, that he commenced his not too well understood task. In this matter he was by no means mistaken, for it soon became plain to all observers — of whom an immense concourse was assembled — that the usually self-possessed Guarder of the Imperial Silkworms was conducting himself in a most undignified

234

manner; for though he still clung to the plough-handles
with an inspired tenacity, his body assumed every variety
of base and uninviting attitude. Encouraged by this inelegant state of affairs, the evil spirits which are ever on
the watch to turn into derision the charitable intentions of
the pure-minded, entered into the bodies of the oxen and
provoked within their minds a sudden and malignant
confidence that the time had arrived when they might with
safety break into revolt and throw off the outward signs of
their dependent condition. From these various causes it
came about that Quen was, without warning, borne with
irresistible certainty against the majestic person of the
sacred Emperor, the inlaid box of Imperial silkworms,
which up to that time had remained safely among the folds
of his silk garment, alone serving to avert an even more
violent and ill-destined blow.

'Well said the wise and deep-thinking Ye-te, in his book
entitled "Proverbs of Everyday Happenings," "Should a
person on returning from the city discover his house to be
in flames, let him examine well the change which he has
received from the chair-carrier before it is too late; for evil
never travels alone." Scarcely had the unfortunate Quen
recovered his natural attributes from the effect of the disgraceful occurrence which has been recorded (which, indeed, furnished the matter of a song and many unpresentable jests among the low-class persons of the city), than the
magnanimous Empress reached that detail of the tree-
planting ceremony when it was requisite that she should
deposit the living emblems of the desired increase and prosperity upon the leaves. Stretching forth her delicately
proportioned hand to Quen for this purpose, she received
from the still greatly confused person in question the

Imperial silkworms in so unseemly a condition that her eyes had scarcely rested upon them before she was seized with the rigid sickness, and in that state fell to the ground. At this new and entirely unforeseen calamity a very disagreeable certainty of approaching evil began to take possession of all those who stood around, many crying aloud that every omen of good was wanting and declaring that unless something of a markedly propitiatory nature was quickly accomplished, the agriculture of the entire Empire would cease to flourish, and the various departments of the commerce in silk would undoubtedly be thrown into a state of most inextricable confusion. Indeed, in spite of all things designed to have a contrary effect, the matter came about in the way predicted, for the Hoang-Ho seven times overcame its restraining barriers, and poured its water over the surrounding country, thereby gaining for the first time its well-deserved title of "The Sorrow of China," by which dishonourable but exceedingly appropriate designation it is known to this day.

'The manner of greeting which would have been accorded to Quen had he returned to the official quarter of the city, or the nature of his treatment by the baser class of the ordinary people if they succeeded in enticing him to come among them, formed a topic of such uninviting conjecture that the humane-minded Lo Yuen, who had observed the entire course of events from an elevated spot, determined to make a well-directed effort towards his safety. To this end he quickly purchased the esteem of several of those who make a profession of their strength, holding out the hope of still further reward if they conducted the venture to a successful termination. Uttering loud cries of an impending vengeance, as Lo Yuen had instructed them in the matter, and displaying their exceptional proportions to the astonishment and misgivings of all beholders, these persons tore open the opium-tent in which Quen had concealed himself, and, thrusting aside all opposition, quickly dragged him forth. Holding him high upon their shoulders, in spite of his frequent and ill-advised endeavours to cast himself to the ground, some surrounded those who bore him — after the manner of disposing his troops affected by a skilful leader when the enemy begin to waver — and crying aloud that it was their unchanging purpose to submit him to the test of burning splinters and afterwards to torture him, they succeeded by this stratagem in bringing him through the crowd; and hurling back or outstripping those who endeavoured to follow, conveyed him secretly and unperceived to a deserted and appointed spot. Here Quen was obliged to remain until other events caused the recollection of the many to become clouded and unconcerned towards him, suffering frequent inconveniences in spite of the powerful protection of Lo Yuen, and not at all times being able to regard the most necessary repast as an appointment of undoubted certainty. At length, in the guise of a wandering conjurer who was unable to display his accomplishments owing to an entire loss of the power of movement in his arms, Quen passed undetected from the city, and safely reaching the distant and unimportant town of Lu-kwo, gave himself up to a protracted period of lamentation and self-reproach at the unprepossessing manner in which he had conducted his otherwise very inviting affairs.'

The Temple Builder

'Two hand-counts of years passed away and Quen still remained at Lu-kwo, all desire of returning either to Pekin or to the place of his birth having by this time faded into nothingness. Accepting the inevitable fact that he was not destined ever to become a person with whom taels were plentiful, and yet being unwilling to forego the charitable manner of life which he had always been accustomed to observe, it came about that he spent the greater part of his time in collecting together such sums of money as he could procure from the amiable and well-disposed, and with them building temples and engaging in other benevolent works. From this cause it arose that Quen obtained around Lu-kwo a reputation for high-minded piety, in no degree less than that which had been conferred upon him in earlier times, so that pilgrims from far-distant places would purposely contrive their journey so as to pass through the town containing so unassuming and virtuous a person.

'During this entire period Quen had been accompanied by his only son, a youth of respectful personality, in whose entertaining society he took an intelligent interest. Even when deeply engaged in what he justly regarded as the crowning work of his existence — the planning and erecting of an exceptionally well-endowed marble temple, which was to be entirely covered on the outside with silver paper, and on the inside with gold-leaf — he did not fail to observe the various conditions of Liao's existence, and the changing emotions which from time to time possessed 'him. Therefore, when the person in question, without displaying any signs of internal sickness, and likewise persistently denying that he had lost any considerable sum of money, disclosed a continuous habit of turning aside with an unaffected expression of distaste from all manner of food, and passed the entire night in observing the course of the great sky-lantern rather than in sleep, the sage and discriminating Quen took him one day aside, and asked him, as one who might aid him in the matter, who the maiden was, and what class and position her father occupied.

' "Alas!" exclaimed Liao, with many unfeigned manifestations of an unbearable fate, "to what degree do the class and position of her entirely unnecessary parents affect the question? or how little hope can this sacrilegious one reasonably have of ever progressing as far as earthly details of a pecuniary character in the case of so adorable and far-removed a Being? The uttermost extent of this wildly hoping person's ambition is that when the incomparably symmetrical Ts'ain learns of the steadfast light of his devotion, she may be inspired to deposit an emblematic chrysanthemum upon his tomb in the Family Temple. For such a reward he will cheerfully devote the unswerving fidelity of a lifetime to her service, not distressing her gentle and retiring nature by the expression of what must inevitably be a hopeless passion, but patiently and uncomplainingly guarding her footsteps as from a distance."

'Being in this manner made aware of the reason of Liao's frequent and unrestrained exclamations of intolerable despair, and of his fixed determination with regard to the maiden Ts'ain (which seemed, above all else, to indicate a resolution to shun her presence) Quen could not regard the immediately following actions of his son with anything but an emotion of confusion. For when his eyes next rested upon the exceedingly contradictory Liao, he was seated in the open space before the house in which Ts'ain dwelt, playing upon an instrument of stringed woods, and chanting verses into which the names of the two persons in question had been skilfully introduced without restraint, his whole manner of behaving being with the evident purpose of attracting the maiden's favourable attention. After an absence of many days, spent in this graceful and complimentary manner, Liao returned suddenly to the house of his father, and, prostrating his body before him, made a specific request for his assistance.

' "As regards Ts'ain and myself," he continued, "all things are arranged, and but for the unfortunate coincidence of this person's poverty and of her father's cupidity, the details of the wedding ceremony would undoubtedly now be in a very advanced condition. Upon these entrancing and well-discussed plans, however, the shadow of the grasping and commonplace Ah-Ping has fallen like the inopportune opium-pipe from the mouth of a person examining substances of an explosive nature; for the one referred to demands a large and utterly unobtainable amount of taels before he will suffer his greatly-sought-after daughter to accept the gifts of irretrievable intention."

' "Grievous indeed is your plight," replied Quen, when he thus understood the manner of obstacle which impeded his son's hopes; "for in the matter of taels the most diverse men are to be measured through the same mesh. As the proverb says, 'All money is evil,' exclaimed the philosopher with extreme weariness, as he gathered up the gold pieces in exchange, but presently discovering that one among them was such indeed as he had described, he rushed forth without tarrying to take up a street garment, and with an entire absence of dignity traversed all the ways of the city in the hope of finding the one who had defrauded him." Well does this person know the mercenary Ah-Ping, and the unyielding nature of his closed hand; for, often, but always fruitlessly, has he entered his presence on affairs connected with the erecting of certain temples. Nevertheless, the matter is one which does not admit of any incapable faltering, to which end this one will seek out the obdurate Ah-Ping without delay, and endeavour to entrap him by some means in the course of argument.

'From the time of his earliest youth Ah-Ping had unceasingly devoted himself to the object of getting together an overwhelming number of taels, using for this purpose various means which, without being really degrading or contrary to the written law, were not such as might have been cheerfully engaged in by a person of high-minded honourableness. In consequence of this, as he grew more feeble in body, and more venerable in appearance, he began to express frequent and bitter doubts as to whether his manner of life had been really well-arranged; for, in spite of his great wealth, he had grown to adopt a most inexpensive habit on all occasions, having no desire to spend; and an ever-increasing apprehension began to possess him that after he had passed beyond, his sons would be very disinclined to sacrifice and burn money sufficient to keep him in an affluent condition in the Upper Air. In such a state of mind was Ah-Ping when Quen-Ki-Tong appeared before him, for it had just been revealed to him that his eldest and favourite son had, by flattery and by openly praising the dexterity with which he used his brush and ink, entrapped him into inscribing his entire name upon certain unwritten sheets of parchment, which the one in question immediately sold to such as were heavily indebted to Ah-Ping.

' "If a person can be guilty of this really unfilial behaviour during the lifetime of his father," exclaimed Ah-Ping, in a tone of unrestrained vexation, "can it be prudently relied upon that he will carry out his wishes after death, when they involve the remitting to him of several thousand taels each year? O estimable Quen-Ki-Tong, how immeasurably superior is the celestial outlook upon which you may safely rely as your portion! When you are enjoying every variety of sumptuous profusion, as the reward of your untiring charitable exertions here on earth, the spirit of this short-sighted person will be engaged in doing menial service for the inferior deities, and perhaps scarcely able, even by those means, to clothe himself according to the changing nature of the seasons."

' "Yet," replied Quen, "the necessity for so laborious and unremunerative an existence may even now be averted by taking efficient precautions before you pass to the Upper Air."

' "In what way?" demanded Ah-Ping, with an awakening hope that the matter might not be entirely destitute of cheerfulness, yet at the same time preparing to examine with even unbecoming intrusiveness any expedient which Quen might lay before him. "Is it not explicitly stated that sacrifices and acts of a like nature, when performed at the end of one's existence by a person who up to that time has professed no sort of interest in such matters, shall in no degree be entered as to his good, but rather regarded as examples of deliberate presumptuousness, and made the excuse for subjecting him to more severe tortures and acts of penance than would be his portion if he neglected the custom altogether?"

' "Undoubtedly such is the case," replied Quen; "and on that account it would indicate a most regrettable want of foresight for you to conduct your affairs in the manner indicated. The only undeniably safe course is for you to entrust the amount you will require to a person of exceptional piety, receiving in return his written word to repay the full sum whenever you shall claim it from him in the Upper Air. By this crafty method the amount will be placed at the disposal of the person in question as soon as he has passed beyond, and he will be held by his written word to return it to you whenever you shall demand it."

'So amiably impressed with this ingenious scheme was Ah-Ping that he would at once have entered more fully into the detail had the thought not arisen in his mind that the person before him was the father of Liao, who urgently required a certain large sum, and that for this reason he might with prudence inquire more fully into the matter elsewhere, in case Quen himself should have been imperceptibly led aside, even though he possessed intentions of a most unswerving honourableness. To this end, therefore, he desired to converse again with Quen on the matter, pleading that at that moment a gathering of those who direct enterprises of a commercial nature required his presence. Nevertheless, he would not permit the person referred to to depart until he had complimented him, in both general and specific terms, on the high character of his life and actions, and the intelligent nature of his understanding, which had enabled him with so little mental exertion to discover an efficient plan.

'Without delay Ah-Ping sought out those most skilled

in all varieties of law-forms, in extorting money by devices capable of very different meanings, and in expedients for evading just debts; but all agreed that such an arrangement as the one he put before them would be unavoidably binding, provided the person who received the money alluded to spent it in the exercise of his charitable desires, and provided also that the written agreement bore the duty seal of the high ones at Pekin, and was deposited in the coffin of the lender. Fully satisfied, and rejoicing greatly that he could in this way adequately provide for his future and entrap the avaricious ones of his house, Ah-Ping collected together the greater part of his possessions, and converting it into pieces of gold entrusted them to Quen on the exact understanding that has already been described, he receiving in return Quen's written and thumb-signed paper of repayment, and his assurance that the whole amount should be expended upon the silver paper and gold-leaf Temple with which he was still engaged.

'It is owing to this circumstance that Quen-Ki-Tong's irreproachable name has come to be lightly regarded by many who may be fitly likened to the latter person in the subtle and experienced proverb, "The wise man's eyes fell before the gaze of the fool, fearing that if he looked he must cry aloud, 'Thou hopeless one!' 'There,' said the fool to himself, 'behold this person's power!'" These badly educated and undiscriminating persons, being entirely unable to explain the ensuing train of events, unhesitatingly declare that Quen-Ki-Tong applied a portion of the money which he had received from Ah-Ping in the manner described to the object of acquiring Ts'ain for his son Liao. In this feeble and incapable fashion they endeavour to stigmatize the pure-minded Quen as one who acted directly contrary to his deliberately spoken word, whereas the desired result was brought about in a much more artful manner; they describe the commercially successful Ah-Ping as a person of very inferior prudence, and one easily imposed upon; while they entirely pass over, as a detail outside the true facts, the written paper reserved among the sacred relics in the Temple, which announces, among other gifts of a small and uninviting character, "Thirty thousand taels from an elderly ginseng merchant of Lu-kwo, who desires to remain nameless, through the hand of Quen-Ki-Tong." The full happening in its real and harmless face is now set forth for the first time.

'Some weeks after the recorded arrangement had been arrived at by Ah-Ping and Quen, when the taels in question had been expended upon the Temple and were, therefore, infallibly beyond recall, the former person chanced to be passing through the public garden in Lu-kwo when he heard a voice lifted up in the expression of every unendurable feeling of dejection to which one can give utterance. Stepping aside to learn the cause of so unprepossessing a display of unrestrained agitation, and in the hope that perhaps he might be able to use the incident in a remunerative manner, Ah-Ping quickly discovered the unhappy being who, entirely regardless of the embroidered silk robe which he wore, reclined upon a raised bank of uninviting earth, and waved his hands from side to side as his internal emotions urged him.

' "Quen-Ki-Tong!" exclaimed Ah-Ping, not fully convinced that the fact was as he stated it in spite of the image clearly impressed upon his imagination; "to what unpropitious occurrence is so unlooked-for an exhibition due? Are those who traffic in gold-leaf demanding a high and prohibitive price for that commodity, or has some evil and vindictive spirit taken up its abode within the completed portion of the Temple, and by its offensive but nevertheless diverting remarks and actions removed all semblance of gravity from the countenances of those who daily come to admire the construction?"

'"O thrice unfortunate Ah-Ping," replied Quen when he observed the distinguishing marks of the person before him, "scarcely can this greatly overwhelmed one raise his eyes to your open and intelligent countenance; for through him you are on the point of experiencing a very severe financial blow, and it is, indeed, on your account more than on his own that he is now indulging in these outward signs of a grief too far down to be expressed in spoken words." And at the memory of his former occupation, Quen again waved his arms from side to side with untiring assiduousness.

' "Strange indeed to this person's ears are your words," said Ah-Ping, outwardly unmoved, but with an apprehensive internal pain that he would have regarded Quen's display of emotion with an easier stomach if his own taels were safely concealed under the floor of his inner chamber. "The sum which this one entrusted to you has, without any pretence, been expended upon the Temple; while the written paper concerning the repayment bears the duty seal of the high ones at Pekin. How, then, can Ah-Ping suffer a loss at the hands of Quen-Ki-Tong?"

' "Ah-Ping," said Quen, with every appearance of desiring that both persons should regard the matter in a conciliatory spirit, "do not permit the awaiting demons, which are ever on the alert to enter into a person's mind when he becomes distressed out of the common order of events,

246

to take possession of your usually discriminating faculties until you have fully understood how this affair has come about. It is no unknown thing for a person of even exceptional intelligence to reverse his entire manner of living towards the end of a long and consistent existence; the far-seeing and not lightly moved Ah-Ping himself has already done so. In a similar, but entirely contrary manner, the person who is now before you finds himself impelled towards that which will certainly bear a very unpresentable face when the circumstance becomes known; yet by no other means is he capable of attaining his greatly desired object."

' "And to what end does that tend?" demanded Ah-Ping, in no degree understanding how the matter affected him.

' "While occupied with enterprises which those of an engaging and complimentary nature are accustomed to refer to as charitable, this person has almost entirely neglected a duty of scarcely less importance – that of establishing an unending line, through which his name and actions shall be kept alive to all time," replied Quen. "Having now inquired into the matter, he finds that his only son, through whom alone the desired result can be obtained, has become unalterably attached to a maiden for whom a very large sum is demanded in exchange. The thought of obtaining no advantage from an entire life of self-denial is certainly unprepossessing in the extreme, but so, even to a more advanced degree, is the certainty that otherwise the family monuments will be untended, and the temple of domestic virtues become an early ruin. This person has submitted the dilemma to the test of omens, and after considering well the reply, he has decided to obtain the price of the maiden in a not very honourable manner, which now presents itself, so that Liao may send out his silk-bound gifts without delay."

' "It is an unalluring alternative," said Ah-Ping, whose only inside thought was one of gratification that the exchange money for Ts'ain would so soon be in his possession, "yet this person fails to perceive how you could act otherwise after the decision of the omens. He now understands, moreover, that the loss you referred to on his part was in the nature of a figure of speech, as one makes use of thunderbolts and delicately scented flowers to convey ideas of harsh and amiable passions, and alluded in reality to the forthcoming departure of his daughter, who is, as you so versatilely suggested, the comfort and riches of his old age."

' "O venerable, but at this moment somewhat obtuse, Ah-Ping," cried Quen, with a recurrence to his former method of expressing his unfeigned agitation, "is your evenly-balanced mind unable to grasp the essential fact of how this person's contemplated action will affect your own celestial condition? It is a distressing but entirely unavoidable fact, that if this person acts in the manner which he has determined upon, he will be condemned to the lowest place of torment reserved for those who fail at the end of an otherwise pure existence, and in this he will never have an opportunity of meeting the very much higher placed Ah-Ping, and of restoring to him the thirty thousand taels as agreed upon."

'At these ill-destined words, all power of rigidness departed from Ah-Ping's limbs, and he sank down upon the forbidding earth by Quen's side.

' "O most unfortunate one who is now speaking," he

exclaimed, when at length his guarding spirit deemed it prudent to restore his power of expressing himself in words, "happy indeed would have been your lot had you been content to traffic in ginseng and other commodities of which you have actual knowledge. O amiable Quen, this matter must be in some way arranged without causing you to deviate from the entrancing paths of your habitual virtue. Could not the very reasonable Liao be induced to look favourably upon the attractions of some low-priced maiden, in which case this not really hard-stomached person would be willing to advance the necessary amount, until such time as it could be restored, at a very low and remunerative rate of interest?"

' "This person has observed every variety of practical humility in the course of his life," replied Quen with commendable dignity, "yet he now finds himself totally unable to overcome an inward repugnance to the thought of perpetuating his honoured name and race through the medium of any low-priced maiden. To this end has he decided."

'Those who were well acquainted with Ah-Ping in matters of commerce did not hesitate to declare that his great wealth had been acquired by his consistent habit of forming an opinion quickly while others hesitated. On the occasion in question he only engaged his mind with the opposing circumstances for a few moments before he definitely fixed upon the course which he should pursue.

' "Quen-Ki-Tong," he said, with an evident intermingling of many very conflicting emotions, "retain to the end the well-merited reputation for unaffected honourableness which you have so fittingly earned. Few in the entire Empire, with powers so versatilely pointing to an eminent position in any chosen direction, would have been content to pass their lives in an unremunerative existence devoted to actions of charity. Had you selected an entirely different manner of living, this person has every confidence that he, and many others in Lu-kwo, would by this time be experiencing a very ignoble poverty. For this reason he will make it his most prominent ambition to hasten the realization of the amiable hopes expressed both by Liao and by Ts'ain, concerning their future relationship. In this, indeed, he himself will be more than exceptionally fortunate should the former one prove to possess even a portion of the clear-sighted sagaciousness exhibited by his engaging father."

'VERSES COMPOSED BY A MUSICIAN OF LU-KWO, ON THE OCCASION OF THE WEDDING CEREMONY OF LIAO AND TS'AIN

'Bright-hued is the morning, the dark clouds have fallen;
  At the mere waving of Quen's virtuous hands they melted away.
  Happy is Liao in the possession of so accomplished a parent,
  Happy also is Quen to have so discriminating a son.

'The two persons in question sit, side by side, upon an embroidered couch,
  Listening to the well-expressed compliments of those who pass to and fro.
  From time to time their eyes meet, and glances of a very significant amusement pass between them;
  Can it be that on so ceremonious an occasion they are recalling events of a gravity-removing nature?

'The gentle and rainbow-like Ts'ain has already arrived;
With the graceful motion of a silver carp gliding through
a screen of rushes, she moves among those who are
assembled.
On the brow of her somewhat contentious father there
rests the shadow of an ill-repressed sorrow;
Doubtless the frequently misjudged Ah-Ping is thinking
of his lonely hearth, now that he is for ever parted
from that which he holds most precious.

'In the most commodious chamber of the house the elegant wedding gifts are conspicuously displayed; let us
stand beside the one which we have contributed, and
point out its excellence to those who pass by.
Surely the time cannot be far distant when the sound of
many gongs will announce that the very desirable
repast is at length to be partaken of.'

CHAPTER EIGHT

THE VISION OF YIN, THE SON OF YAT HUANG

★

WHEN Yin, the son of Yat Huang, had passed beyond the years assigned to the pursuits of boyhood, he was placed in the care of the hunchback Quang, so that he might be fully instructed in the management of the various weapons used in welfare, and also in the art of stratagem, by which a skilful leader is often enabled to conquer when opposed to an otherwise overwhelming multitude. In all these accomplishments Quang excelled to an exceptional degree; for although unprepossessing in appearance he united matchless strength to an untiring subtlety. No other person in the entire Province of Kiang-si could hurl a javelin so unerringly while uttering sounds of terrifying menace, or could cause his sword to revolve around him so rapidly, while his face looked out from the glittering circles with an expression of ill-intentioned malignity that never failed to inspire his adversary with irrepressible emotions of alarm. No other person could so successfully feign to be devoid of life for almost any length of time, or by his manner of behaving create the fixed impression that he was one of insufficient understanding, and therefore harmless. It was for these reasons that Quang was chosen as the instructor of Yin by Yat Huang, who, without possessing any official degree, was a person to whom marks of obeisance were paid not only within his own town, but for a distance of many li around it.

At length the time arrived when Yin would in the ordinary course of events pass from the instructorship of Quang in order to devote himself to the commerce in which his father was engaged, and from time to time the unavoidable thought arose persistently within his mind that although Yat Huang doubtless knew better than he did what the circumstances of the future required, yet his manner of life for the past years was not such that he could contemplate engaging in the occupation of buying and selling porcelain clay with feelings of an overwhelming interest. Quang, however, maintained with every manifestation of inspired assurance that Yat Huang was to be commended down to the smallest detail, inasmuch as proficiency in the use of both blunt and sharp-edged weapons, and a faculty for passing undetected through the midst of an encamped body of foemen, fitted a person for the everyday affairs of life above all other accomplishments.

'Without doubt the very accomplished Yat Huang is well advised on this point,' continued Quang, 'for even this mentally short-sighted person can call up within his understanding numerous specific incidents in the ordinary career of one engaged in the commerce of porcelain clay when such attainments would be of great remunerative benefit. Does the well-endowed Yin think, for example, that even the most depraved person would endeavour to gain an advantage over him in the matter of buying or selling porcelain clay if he fully understood the fact that the one with whom he was trafficking could unhesitatingly transfix four persons with one arrow at the distance of a hundred paces? Or to what advantage would it be that a body of unscrupulous outcasts who owned a field of inferior clay should surround it with drawn swords by day and night endeavouring meanwhile to dispose of it as material of the finest quality, if the one whom they endeavoured to ensnare in this manner possessed the power of being able to pass through their ranks unseen and examine the clay at his leisure?'

'In the cases to which reference has been made, the possession of those qualities would undoubtedly be of considerable use,' admitted Yin; 'yet, in spite of his entire ignorance of commercial matters, this one has a confident feeling that it would be more profitable to avoid such very doubtful forms of barter altogether rather than spend eight years in acquiring the arts by which to defeat them. That, however, is a question which concerns this person's virtuous and engaging father more than his unworthy self, and his only regret is that no opportunity has offered by which he might prove that he has applied himself diligently to your instruction and example, O amiable Quang.'

It had long been a regret to Quang also that no incident of a disturbing nature had arisen whereby Yin could have shown himself proficient in the methods of defence and attack which he had taught him. This deficiency he had endeavoured to overcome, as far as possible, by constructing life-like models of all the most powerful and ferocious types of warriors, and the fiercest and most relentless animals of the forest, so that Yin might become familiar with their appearance and discover in what manner each could be the most expeditiously engaged.

'Nevertheless,' remarked Quang on an occasion when Yin appeared to be covered with honourable pride at having approached an unusually large and repulsive-looking tiger so stealthily that had the animal been really alive it would certainly have failed to perceive him, 'such accomplishments are by no means to be regarded as conclusive in themselves. To steal insidiously upon a destructively inclined wild beast and transfix it with one well-directed blow of a spear is attended by difficulties and emotions which are entirely absent in the case of a wicker-work animal covered with canvas-cloth, no matter how deceptive in appearance the latter may be.'

To afford Yin a more trustworthy example of how he should engage with an adversary of formidable proportions, Quang resolved upon an ingenious plan. Procuring the skin of a grey wolf, he concealed himself within it, and in the early morning, while the mist-damp was still upon the ground, he set forth to meet Yin, who had on a previous occasion spoken to him of his intention to be at a certain spot at such an hour. In this conscientious enterprise the painstaking Quang would doubtless have been successful, and Yin gained an assured proficiency and experience, had it not chanced that on the journey Quang encountered a labourer of low caste who was crossing the enclosed ground on his way to the rice field in which he worked. This contemptible and inopportune person, not having at any period of his existence perfected himself in the recognized and elegant methods of attack and defence, did not act in the manner which would assuredly have been adopted by Yin in similar circumstances, and for which Quang would have been fully prepared. On the contrary, without the least indication of what his intention was, he suddenly struck Quang, who was hesitating for a moment what action to take, a most intolerable blow with a formidable staff which he carried. The stroke in question inflicted itself upon Quang upon that part of the body where the head becomes connected with the neck, and would certainly have been followed by others of equal force and precision had not Quang in the meantime decided that the most dignified course for him to adopt would be to disclose his name and titles without delay. Upon learning these facts, the one who stood before him became very grossly and offensively amused, and having taken from Quang everything of value which he carried among his garments, went on his way, leaving Yin's instructor to retrace his steps in unendurable dejection, as he then found that he possessed no further interest whatever in the undertaking.

When Yat Huang was satisfied that his son was sufficiently skilled in the various arts of warfare, he called him to his inner chamber, and having barred the door securely, he placed Yin under a very binding oath not to reveal, until an appointed period, the matter which he was going to put before him.

'From father to son, in unbroken line for ten generations, has such a custom been observed,' he said, 'for the course of events is not one to be lightly entered upon. At the commencement of that cycle, which period is now fully fifteen score years ago, a very wise person chanced to incur the displeasure of the Emperor of that time, and being in consequence driven out of the capital, he fled to the mountains. There his subtle discernment and the pure and solitary existence which he led resulted in his becoming endowed with faculties beyond those possessed by ordinary beings. When he felt the end of his earthly career to be at hand he descended into the plain, where, in a state of great destitution and bodily anguish, he was discovered by the one whom this person has referred to as the first of the line of ancestors. In return for the care and hospitality with which he was unhesitatingly received, the admittedly inspired hermit spent the remainder of his days in determining the destinies of his rescuer's family and posterity. It is an undoubted fact that he predicted how one would, by well-directed enterprise and adventure, rise to a position of such eminence in the land that he counselled the details to be kept secret, lest the envy and hostility of the ambitious and unworthy should be raised. From this cause it has been customary to reveal the matter fully from father to son, at stated periods, and the setting out of the particulars in written words has been severely discouraged. Wise as this precaution certainly was, it has resulted in a very inconvenient state of things; for a remote ancestor – the fifth in line from the beginning – experienced such vicissitudes that he returned from his travels in a state of most abandoned idiocy, and when the time arrived that he should, in turn, communicate to his son, he was only able to repeat over and over again the name of the pious hermit to whom the family was so greatly indebted, coupling it each time with a new and markedly offensive epithet. The essential details of the undertaking having in this manner passed beyond recall, succeeding generations, which were merely acquainted with the fact that a very prosperous future awaited the one who fulfilled the conditions, have in vain attempted to conform to them. It is not an alluring undertaking, inasmuch as nothing of the method to be pursued can be learned, except that it was the custom of the early ones, who held the full knowledge, to set out from home and return after a period of years. Yet so clearly expressed was the prophecy, and so great the reward of the successful, that all have eagerly journeyed forth when the time came, knowing nothing beyond that which this person has now unfolded to you.'

When Yat Huang reached the end of the matter which

it was his duty to disclose, Yin for some time pondered the circumstances before replying. In spite of a most engaging reverence for everything of a sacred nature, he could not consider the inspired remark of the well-intentioned hermit without feelings of a most persistent doubt, for it occurred to him that if the person in question had really been as wise as he was represented to be, he might reasonably have been expected to avoid the unaccountable error of offending the enlightened and powerful Emperor under whom he lived. Nevertheless, the prospect of engaging in the trade of porcelain clay was less attractive in his eyes than that of setting forth upon a journey of adventure, so that at length he expressed his willingness to act after the manner of those who had gone before him.

This decision was received by Yat Huang with an equal intermingling of the feelings of delight and colours, for although he would have by no means pleasurably contemplated Yin breaking through a venerable and esteemed custom, he was unable to put entirely from him the thought of the degrading fate which had overtaken the fifth in line who made the venture. It was, indeed, to guard Yin as much as possible against the dangers to which he would become exposed, if he determined on the expedition, that the entire course of his training had been selected. In order that no precaution of a propitious nature should be neglected, Yat Huang at once despatched written words of welcome to all with whom he was acquainted, bidding them partake of a great banquet which he was preparing to mark the occasion of his son's leave-taking. Every variety of sacrifice was offered up to the controlling deities, both good and bad; the ten ancestors were continuously exhorted to take Yin under their special protection, and sets of verses recording his virtues and ambitions were freely distributed among the necessitous and low caste who could not be received at the feast.

The dinner itself exceeded in magnificence any similar event that had ever taken place in Ching-toi. So great was the polished ceremony observed on the occasion, that each guest had half a score of cups of the finest apricot-tea successively placed before him and taken away untasted, while Yat Huang went to each in turn protesting vehemently that the honour of covering such pure-minded and distinguished persons was more than his badly designed roof could reasonably bear, and wittily giving an entrancing air of reality to the spoken compliment by begging them to move somewhat to one side so that they might escape the heavy central beam if the event which he alluded to chanced to take place. After several hours had been spent in this congenial occupation, Yat Huang proceeded to read aloud several of the sixteen discourses on education which, taken together, form the discriminating and infallible example of conduct known as the Holy Edict. As each detail was dwelt upon Yin arose from his couch and gave his deliberate testimony that all the required tests and rites had been observed in his own case. The first part of the repast was then partaken of, the nature of the ingredients and the manner of preparing them being fully explained, and in a like manner through each succeeding one of the four-and-forty courses. At the conclusion Yin again arose, being encouraged by the repeated uttering of his name by those present, and with extreme modesty and brilliance set forth his manner of thinking concerning all subjects with which he was acquainted.

Early on the morning of the following day Yin set out

on his travels, entirely unaccompanied, and carrying with him nothing beyond a sum of money, a silk robe, and a well-tried and reliable spear. For many days he journeyed in a northerly direction, without encountering anything sufficiently unusual to engage his attention. This, however, was doubtless part of a prearranged scheme so that he should not be drawn from a destined path, for at a small village lying on the southern shore of a large lake, called by those around Silent Water, he heard of the existence of a certain sacred island, distant a full day's sailing, which was barren of all forms of living things, and contained only a single gigantic rock of divine origin and majestic appearance. Many persons, the villagers asserted, had sailed to the island in the hope of learning the portent of the rock, but none ever returned, and they themselves avoided coming even within sight of it; for the sacred stone, they declared, exercised an evil influence over their ships, and would, if permitted, draw them out of their course and towards itself. For this reason Yin could find no guide, whatever reward he offered, who would accompany him; but having with difficulty succeeded in hiring a small boat of inconsiderable value, he embarked with food, incense, and materials for building fires, and after rowing consistently for nearly the whole of the day, came within sight of the island at evening. Thereafter the necessity of further exertion ceased, for, as they of the village had declared would be the case, the vessel moved gently forward, in an unswerving line, without being in any way propelled, and reaching its destination in a marvellously short space of time, passed behind a protecting spur of land and came to rest. It then being night, Yin did no more than carry his stores to a place of safety, and after lighting a sacrificial fire and prostrating himself before the rock passed into the Middle Air.

In the morning Yin's spirit came back to the earth amid the sound of music of a celestial origin, which ceased immediately he recovered full consciousness. Accepting this manifestation as an omen of Divine favour, Yin journeyed towards the centre of the island where the rock stood, at every step passing the bones of innumerable ones who had come on a similar quest to his, and perished. Many of these had left behind them inscriptions on wood or bone testifying their deliberate opinion of the sacred rock, the island, their protecting deities, and the entire train of circumstances which had resulted in their being in such a condition. These were for the most part of a maledictory and unencouraging nature, so that after reading a few, Yin endeavoured to pass on without being in any degree influenced by such ill-judged outbursts.

'Accursed be the ancestors of this tormented one to four generations back!' was prominently traced upon an unusually large shoulder-blade. 'May they at this moment be simmering in a vat of unrefined dragon's blood, as a reward for having so undiscriminatingly reared the person who inscribes these words only to attain this end!' 'Be warned, O later one, by the signs around!' another and more practical-minded person had written: 'Retreat with all haste to your vessel, and escape while there is yet time. Should you, by chance, again reach land through this warning, do not neglect, out of an emotion of gratitude, to burn an appropriate amount of sacrifice paper for the lessening of the torments of the spirit of Li-Kao,' to which an unscrupulous one, who was plainly desirous of sharing in the benefit of the requested sacrifice, without suffering the exertion of inscribing a warning after the amiable manner of Li-Kao, had added the words, 'and that of Huan Sin.'

Halting at a convenient distance from one side of the rock which, without being carved by any person's hand, naturally resembled the symmetrical countenance of a recumbent dragon (which he therefore conjectured to be the chief point of the entire mass), Yin built his fire and began an unremitting course of sacrifice and respectful ceremony. This manner of conduct he observed conscientiously for the space of seven days. Towards the end of that period a feeling of unendurable dejection began to possess him, for his stores of all kinds were beginning to fail, and he could not entirely put behind him the memory of the various well-intentioned warnings which he had received, or the sight of the fleshless ones who had lined his path. On the eighth day, being weak with hunger and, by reason of an intolerable thirst, unable to restrain his body any longer in the spot where he had hitherto continuously prostrated himself nine-and-ninety times each hour without ceasing, he rose to his feet and retraced his steps to the boat in order that he might fill his water-skins and procure a further supply of food.

With a complicated emotion, in which was present every abandoned and disagreeable thought to which a person becomes a prey in moments of exceptional mental and bodily anguish, he perceived as soon as he reached the edge of the water that the boat, upon which he was confidently relying to carry him back when all else failed, had disappeared as entirely as the smoke of an extinguished opium pipe. At this sight Yin clearly understood the meaning of Li-Kao's unregarded warning, and recognized that nothing could now save him from adding his incorruptible parts to those of the unfortunate ones whose unhappy fate had, seven days ago, engaged his refined pity. Unaccountably strengthened in body by the indignation which possessed him, and inspired with a virtuous repulsion at the treacherous manner of behaving on the part of those who guided his destinies, he hastened back to his place of obeisance, and perceiving that the habitually placid and introspective expression on the dragon face had imperceptibly changed into one of offensive cunning and unconcealed contempt, he snatched up his spear, and without the consideration of a moment, hurled it at a score of paces distance full into the sacred but nevertheless very unprepossessing face before him.

At the instant when the presumptuous weapon touched the holy stone the entire intervening space between the earth and the sky was filled with innumerable flashes of forked and many-tongued lightning, so that the island had the appearance of being the scene of a very extensive but somewhat badly arranged display of costly fireworks. At the same time the thunder rolled among the clouds and beneath the sea in an exceedingly disconcerting manner. At the first indication of these celestial movements a sudden blindness came upon Yin, and all power of thought or movement forsook him; nevertheless, he experienced an emotion of flight through the air, as though borne upwards upon the back of a winged creature. When this motion ceased, the blindness went from him as suddenly and entirely as if a cloth had been pulled away from his eyes, and he perceived that he was held in the midst of a boundless space, with no other object in view than the sacred rock, which had opened, as it were, revealing a mighty throng within, at the sight of whom Yin's internal organs trembled as they would never have moved at ordinary danger, for it was put into his spirit that these in whose presence he stood were the sacred Emperors of his country from the earliest time until the usurpation of the Chinese throne by the devouring Tartar hordes from the north.

As Yin gazed in fear-stricken amazement, a knowledge of the various Pure Ones who composed the assembly came upon him. He understood that the three unclad and commanding figures which stood together were the Emperors of the Heaven, Earth, and Man, whose reigns covered a space of more than eighty thousand years, commencing from the time when the world began its span of existence. Next to them stood one wearing a robe of leopard-skin, his hand resting upon the staff of a massive club, while on his face the expression of tranquillity which marked his predecessors had changed into one of alert wakefulness; it was the Emperor of Houses, whose reign marked the opening of the never-ending strife between man and all other creatures. By his side stood his successor, the Emperor of Fire, holding in his right hand the emblem of the knotted cord, by which he taught man to cultivate his mental faculties, while from his mouth issued smoke and flame, signifying that by the introduction of fire he had raised his subjects to a state of civilized life.

On the other side of the boundless chamber which seemed to be contained within the rocks were Fou-Hy, Tchang-Ki, Tcheng-Nung, and Huang, standing or reclining together. The first of these framed the calendar, organized property, thought out the eight Essential Diagrams, encouraged the various branches of hunting, and the rearing of domestic animals, and instituted marriage. From his couch floated melodious sounds in remembrance of his discovery of the property of stringed woods. Tchang-Ki, who manifested the property of herbs and growing plants, wore a robe signifying his attainments by means of embroidered symbols. His hand rested on the head of the dragon, while at his feet flowed a bottomless canal of the purest water. The discovery of written letters by Tcheng-Nung, and his ingenious plan of grouping them after the manner of the constellations of stars, was emblemized in a similar manner, while Huang, or the Yellow Emperor, was surrounded by ores of the useful and precious metals, weapons of warfare, written books, silks and articles of attire, coined money, and a variety of objects, all testifying to his ingenuity and inspired energy.

These illustrious ones, being the greatest, were the first to take Yin's attention, but beyond them he beheld an innumerable concourse of Emperors who not infrequently outshone their majestic predecessors in the richness of their apparel and the magnificence of the jewels which they wore. There Yin perceived Hung-Hoang, who first caused the chants to be collected, and other rulers of the Tcheon dynasty; Yong-Tching, who compiled the Holy Edict; Thang rulers whose line is rightly called 'the golden,' from the unsurpassed excellence of the composed verses which it produced; renowned Emperors of the versatile Han dynasty; and, standing apart, and shunned by all, the malignant and narrow-minded Tsin-Su-Hoang, who caused the Sacred Books to be burned.

Even while Yin looked and wondered, in great fear, a rolling voice, coming from one who sat in the midst of all, holding in his right hand the sun, and in his left the moon, sounded forth, like the music of many brass instruments playing in unison. It was the First Man who spoke.

'Yin, son of Yat Huang, and creature of the Lower Part,' he said, 'listen well to the words I speak, for brief is the span of your tarrying in the Upper Air, nor will the utterance I now give forth ever come unto your ears again, either on the earth or when, blindly groping in the Middle Distance, your spirit takes its nightly flight. They who are gathered around, and whose voices I speak, bid me say thus: Although immeasurably above you in all matters, both of knowledge and of power, yet we greet you as one who is well-intentioned, and inspired with honourable ambition. Had you been content to entreat and despair, as did all the feeble and incapable ones whose white bones formed your pathway, your ultimate fate would have in no wise differed from theirs. But inasmuch as you held yourself valiantly, and, being taken, raised an instinctive hand in return, you have been chosen; for the day of mute submission has, for the time or for ever, passed away, and the hour is when China shall be saved, not by supplication, but by the spear.'

'A state of things which would have been highly unnecessary if I had been permitted to carry out my intention fully, and restore man to his prehistoric simplicity,' interrupted Tsin-Su-Hoang. 'For that reason, when the Voice of the assemblage expresses itself, it must be understood that it represents in no measure the views of Tsin-Su-Hoang.'

'In the matter of what has gone before, and that which will follow hereafter,' continued the Voice dispassionately, 'Yin, the son of Yat Huang, must concede that it is in no part the utterance of Tsin-Su-Hoang – Tsin-Su-Hoang who burned the Sacred Books.'

At the mention of the name and offence of this degraded being a great sound went up from the entire multitude – a universal cry of execration, not greatly dissimilar from that which may be frequently heard in the crowded Temple of Impartiality when the one whose duty it is to take up, at a venture, the folded papers, announces that the sublime Emperor, or some mandarin of exalted rank, has been so fortunate as to hold the winning number in the Annual State Lottery. So vengeance-laden and mournful was the combined and evidently preconcerted wail, that Yin was compelled to shield his ears against it; yet the inconsiderable Tsin-Su-Hoang, on whose account it was raised, seemed in no degree to be affected by it, he, doubtless, having become hardened by hearing a similar outburst, at fixed hours, throughout interminable cycles of time.

When the last echo of the cry had passed away the Voice continued to speak.

'Soon the earth will again receive you, Yin,' it said, 'for it is not respectful that a lower one should be long permitted to gaze upon our exalted faces. Yet when you go forth and stand once more among men this is laid on you: that henceforth you are as a being devoted to a fixed and unchanging end, and whatever moves towards the restoring to the throne of the Central Empire the outcast but unalterably sacred line of its true sovereigns shall have your arm and mind. By what combination of force and stratagem this can be accomplished may not be honourably revealed by us, the all-knowing. Nevertheless, omens and guidance shall not be lacking from time to time, and from the beginning the weapon by which you have attained to this distinction shall be as a sign of our favour and protection over you.'

When the Voice made an end of speaking the sudden blindness came upon Yin, as it had done before, and from the sense of motion which he experienced, he conjectured that he was being conveyed back to the island. Undoubtedly this was the case, for presently there came upon him the feeling that he was awaking from a deep and refreshing sleep, and opening his eyes, which he now found himself able to do without any difficulty, he immediately discovered that he was reclining at full length on the ground, and at a distance of about a score of paces from the dragon head. His first thought was to engage in a lengthy course of self-abasement before it, but remembering the words which had been spoken to him while in the Upper Air, he refrained, and even ventured to go forward with a confident but somewhat self-deprecatory air, to regain the spear, which he perceived lying at the foot of the rock. With feelings of a reassuring nature he then saw that the very undesirable expression which he had last beheld upon the dragon face had melted into one of encouraging urbanity and benignant esteem.

Close by the place where he had landed he discovered his boat, newly furnished with wine and food of a much more attractive profusion than that which he had purchased in the village. Embarking in it, he made as though he would have returned to the south, but the spear which he held turned within his grasp, and pointed in an exactly opposite direction. Regarding this fact as an express command on the part of the Deities, Yin turned his boat to the north, and in the space of two days' time – being

continually guided by the fixed indication of the spear —
he reached the shore and prepared to continue his travels
in the same direction, upheld and inspired by the knowledge that henceforth he moved under the direct influence
of very powerful spirits.

CHAPTER NINE

THE ILL-REGULATED DESTINY OF KIN YEN, THE PICTURE-MAKER

*

AS RECORDED BY HIMSELF BEFORE HIS SUDDEN DEPAR-
TURE FROM PEKIN, OWING TO CIRCUMSTANCES WHICH
ARE MADE PLAIN IN THE FOLLOWING NARRATIVE

THERE are moments in the life of a person when the saying
of the wise Ni-Hyu that 'Misfortune comes to all men and
to most women' is endowed with double force. At such
times the faithful child of the Sun is a prey to the whitest
and most funereal thoughts, and even the inspired wisdom
of his illustrious ancestors seems more than doubtful,
while the continued inactivity of the Sacred Dragon
appears for the time to give colour to the scoffs of the
Western barbarian. A little while ago these misgivings
would have found no resting-place in the bosom of the
writer. Now, however – but the matter must be made
clear from the beginning.

The name of the despicable person who here sets forth
his immature story is Kin Yen, and he is a native of Kia-
Lu in the Province of Che-Kiang. Having purchased
from a very aged man the position of Hereditary Instructor
in the Art of Drawing Birds and Flowers, he gave lessons
in these accomplishments until he had saved sufficient
money to journey to Pekin. Here it was his presumptuous
intention to learn the art of drawing figures in order that
he might illustrate printed leaves of a more distinguished
class than those which would accept what true politeness compels him to call his exceedingly unsymmetrical
pictures of birds and flowers. Accordingly, when the time

arrived, he disposed of his Hereditary Instructorship, having first ascertained in the interests of his pupils that his successor was a person of refined morals and great filial piety.

Alas! it is well written, 'The road to eminence lies through the cheap and exceedingly uninviting eating-houses.' In spite of this person's great economy, and of his having begged his way from Kia-Lu to Pekin in the guise of a pilgrim, journeying to burn incense in the sacred Temple of Truth near that city, when once within the latter place his taels melted away like the smile of a person of low class when he discovers that the mandarin's stern words were not intended as a jest. Moreover, he found that the story-makers of Pekin, receiving higher rewards than those at Kia-Lu, considered themselves bound to introduce living characters into all their tales, and in consequence the very ornamental drawings of birds and flowers which he had entwined into a legend, entitled 'The Last Fight of the Heaven-sent Tcheng' – a story which had been entrusted to him for illustration as a test of his skill – were returned to him with a communication in which the writer conveyed his real meaning by stating contrary facts. It therefore became necessary that he should become competent in the art of drawing figures without delay, and with this object he called at the picture-room of Tieng Lin, a person whose experience was so great that he could, without discomfort to himself, draw men and women of all classes, both good and bad. When the person who is setting forth this narrative revealed to Tieng Lin the utmost amount of money he could afford to give for instruction in the art of drawing living figures, Tieng Lin's face became as overcast as the sky immediately before the Great Rains, for in his ignorance of this incapable person's poverty he had treated him with equality and courtesy, nor had he kept him waiting in the mean room on the plea that he was at that moment closeted with the Sacred Emperor. However, upon receiving an assurance that a rumour would be spread in which the number of taels should be multiplied by ten, and that the sum itself should be brought in advance, Tieng Lin promised to instruct this person in the art of drawing five characters, which, he said, would be sufficient to illustrate all stories except those by the most expensive and highly rewarded story-tellers — men who have become so proficient that they not infrequently introduce a score or more of living persons into their tales without confusion.

After considerable deliberation this unassuming person selected the following characters, judging them to be the most useful, and the most readily applicable to all phases and situations of life:

1. A bad person, wearing a long dark pigtail and smoking an opium pipe. His arms to be folded, and his clothes new and very expensive.

2. A woman of low class. One who removes dust and useless things from the rooms of the over-fastidious and of those who have long nails; she to be carrying her trade-signs.

3. A person from Pe-ling, endowed with qualities which cause the beholder to be amused. This character to be especially designed to go with the short sayings which remove gravity.

4. One who, having incurred the displeasure of the sublime Emperor, has been decapitated in consequence.

5. An ordinary person of no striking or distinguished

appearance. One who can be safely introduced in all places and circumstances without great fear of detection.

After many months spent in constant practice and in taking measurements, this unenviable person attained a very high degree of proficiency, and could draw any of the five characters without hesitation. With renewed hope, therefore, he again approached those who sit in easy-chairs, and concealing his identity (for they are stiff at bending, and when once a picture-maker is classed as 'of no good' he remains so to the end, in spite of change), he succeeded in getting entrusted with a story by the elegant and refined Kyen Tal. This writer, as he remembered with distrust, confines his distinguished efforts entirely to the doings of sailors and of those connected with the sea, and this tale, indeed, he found upon reading to be the narrative of how a Hang-Chow junk and its crew, consisting mostly of aged persons, were beguiled out of their course by an exceed-ingly ill-disposed dragon, and wrecked upon an island of naked barbarians. It was, therefore, with a somewhat heavy stomach that this person set himself to the task of arranging his five characters so as to illustrate the words of the story.

The sayings of the ancient philosopher Tai Loo are indeed very subtle, and the truth of his remark. 'After being disturbed in one's dignity by a mandarin's foot it is no unusual occurrence to fall on the face in crossing a muddy street,' was now apparent. Great as was the dis-advantage owing to the nature of the five characters, this became as nothing when it presently appeared that the avaricious and clay-souled Tieng Lin, taking advantage of the blindness of this person's enthusiasm, had taught him the figures so that they all gazed in the same direction.

In consequence of this it would have been impossible that two should be placed as in the act of conversing together had not the noble Kyen Tal been inspired to write that 'his companions turned from him in horror.' This incident the ingenious person who is recording these facts made the subject of three separate drawings, and having in one or two other places effected skilful changes in the writing, so similar in style to the strokes of the illustrious Kyen Tal as to be undetectable, he found little difficulty in making use of all his characters. The risks of the future, however, were too great to be run with impunity; therefore it was arranged, by means of money — for this person was fast becoming acquainted with the ways of Pekin — that an emissary from one who sat in an easy-chair should call upon him for a conference, the narrative of which appeared in this form in the *Pekin Printed Leaves of Thrice-distilled Truth*:

'The brilliant and amiable young picture-maker Kin Yen, in spite of the immediate and universal success of his accomplished efforts, is still quite rotund in intellect, nor is he, if we may use a form of speaking affected by our friends across the Hoang Hai, "suffering from swollen feet." A person with no recognized position, but one who occasionally does inferior work of this nature for us, recently surprised Kin Yen without warning, and found him in his sumptuously appointed picture-room, busy with compasses and tracing-paper. About the place were scattered in elegant confusion several of his recent masterpieces. From the subsequent conversation we are in a position to make it known that in future this refined and versatile person will confine himself entirely to illustrations of processions, funerals, armies on the march, persons pursued by others, and kindred subjects which appeal strongly to his imagination. Kin Yen has severe emotions on the subject of individuality in art, and does not hesitate to express himself forcibly with reference to those who are content to degrade the names of their ancestors by turning out what he wittily describes as "so much of varied mediocrity."'

The prominence obtained by this pleasantly composed notice — for it was copied by others who were unaware of the circumstance of its origin — had the desired effect. In future, when one of those who sit in easy-chairs wished for a picture after the kind mentioned, he would say to his lesser one: 'Oh, send to the graceful and versatile Kin Yen; he becomes inspired on the subject of funerals,' or persons escaping from prison, or families walking to the temple, or whatever it might be. In that way this narrow-minded and illiterate person was soon both looked at and rich, so that it was his daily practice to be carried, in silk garments, past the houses of those who had known him in poverty, and on these occasions he would puff out his cheeks and pull his moustaches, looking fiercely from side to side.

True are the words written in the elegant and distinguished Book of Verses: 'Beware lest when being kissed by the all-seeing Emperor, you step upon the elusive banana-peel.' It was at the height of eminence in this altogether degraded person's career that he encountered the being who led him on to his present altogether too lamentable condition.

Tien Nung is the earthly name by which is known she who combines all the most illustrious attributes which have been possessed of women since the days of the divine

Fou-Hy. Her father is a person of very gross habits, and lives by selling inferior merchandise covered with some of good quality. Upon past occasions, when under the direct influence of Tien, and in the hope of gaining some money benefit, this person may have spoken of him in terms of praise, and may even have recommended friends to entrust articles of value to him, or to procure goods on his advice. Now, however, he records it as his unalterable decision that the father of Tien Nung is by profession a person who obtains goods by stratagem, and that, moreover, it is impossible to gain an advantage over him on matters of exchange.

The events that have happened prove the deep wisdom of Li Pen when he exclaimed 'The whitest of pigeons, no matter how excellent in the silk-hung chamber, is not to be followed on the field of battle.' Tien herself was all that the most exacting of persons could demand, but her opinions on the subject of picture-making were not formed by heavy thought, and it would have been well if this had been borne in mind by this person. One morning he chanced to meet her while carrying open in his hands four sets of printed leaves containing his pictures.

'I have observed,' said Tien, after the usual personal inquiries had been exchanged, 'that the renowned Kin Yen who is the object of the keenest envy among his brother picture-makers, so little regards the sacredness of his accomplished art that never by any chance does he depict persons of the very highest excellence. Let not the words of an impetuous maiden disarrange his digestive organs if they should seem too bold to the high-souled Kin Yen, but this matter has, since she has known him, troubled the eyelids of Tien. Here,' she continued, taking from this person's hands one of the printed leaves which he was carrying, 'in this illustration of persons returning from extinguishing a fire, is there one who appears to possess those qualities which appeal to all that is intellectual and competitive within one? Can it be that the immaculate Kin Yen is unacquainted with the subtle distinctions between the really select and the vastly ordinary? Ah, undiscriminating Kin Yen! are not the eyelashes of the person who is addressing you as threads of fine gold to junk's cables when compared with those of the extremely commonplace female who is here pictured in the act of carrying a bucket? Can the most refined lack of vanity hide from you the fact that your own person is infinitely rounder than this of the evilly intentioned looking individual with the opium pipe. O blind Kin Yen!'

Here she fled in honourable confusion, leaving this person standing in the street astounded, and a prey to the most distinguished emotions of a complicated nature.

'Oh, Tien,' he cried at length, 'inspired by those bright eyes, narrower than the most select of the three thousand and one possessed by the sublime Buddha, the almost fallen Kin Yen will yet prove himself worthy of your esteemed consideration. He will, without delay, learn to draw two new living persons, and will incorporate in them the likenesses which you have suggested.'

Returning swiftly to his abode, he therefore inscribed and despatched this letter, in proof of his resolve:

'To the Heaven-sent human chrysanthemum, in whose body reside the Celestial Principles and the imprisoned colours of the rainbow.

'From the very offensive and self-opinionated picture-maker.

'Henceforth this person will take no rest, nor eat any but the commonest food, until he shall have carried out the wishes of his one Jade Star, she whose teeth he is not worthy to blacken.

'When Kin Yen has been entrusted with a story which contains a being in some degree reflecting the character of Tien, he will embellish it with her irreproachable profile and come to hear her words. Till then he bids her farewell.'

From that moment most of this person's time was necessarily spent in learning to draw the two new characters, and in consequence of this he lost much work, and, indeed, the greater part of the connection which he had been at such pains to form gradually slipped away from him. Many months passed before he was competent to reproduce persons resembling Tien and himself, for in this he was unassisted by Tieng Lin, and his progress was slow.

At length, being satisfied, he called upon the least fierce of those who sit in easy-chairs, and requested that he might be entrusted with a story for picture-making.

'We should have been covered with honourable joy to set in operation the brush of the inspired Kin Yen,' replied the other with agreeable condescension; 'only at the moment it does not chance that we have before us any stories in which funerals, or beggars being driven from the city, form the chief incidents. Perhaps if the polished Kin Yen should happen to be passing this ill-constructed office in about six months' time —'

'The brush of Kin Yen will never again depict funerals, or labourers arranging themselves to receive pay or similar subjects,' exclaimed this person impetuously; 'for, as it is well said, "The lightning discovers objects which the paper-lantern fails to reveal." In future none but tales dealing with the most distinguished persons shall have his attention.'

'If this be the true word of the dignified Kin Yen, it is possible that we may be able to animate his inspired faculties,' was the response. 'But in that case, as a new style must be in the nature of an experiment, and as our public has come to regard Kin Yen as the great exponent of Art Facing in One Direction, we cannot continue the exceedingly liberal payment with which we have been accustomed to reward his elegant exertions.'

'Provided the story be suitable, that is a matter of less importance,' replied this person.

'The story,' said the one in the easy-chair, 'is by the refined Tong-king, and it treats of the high-minded and conscientious doubts of one who would become a priest of Fo. When preparing for this distinguished office he discovers within himself leanings towards the religion of Lao-Tse. His illustrious scruples are enhanced by his affection for Wu Ping, who now appears in the story.'

'And the ending?' inquired this person, for it was desirable that the two should marry happily.

'The inimitable stories of Tong-king never have any real ending, and this one, being in his most elevated style, has even less end than most of them. But the whole narrative is permeated with the odour of joss-sticks and honourable high-mindedness, and the two characters are both of noble birth.'

As it might be some time before another story so suitable should be offered, or one which would afford so good an opportunity of wafting incense to Tien, and of displaying her incomparable outline in dignified and magnanimous attitudes, this was eagerly accepted, and for the next week this obscure person spent all his days and nights in picturing the lovely Tien and his debased self in the characters of the nobly born young priest of Fo and Wu Ping. The pictures finished, he caused them to be carefully conveyed to the office, and then sitting down, spent many hours in composing the following letter, to be sent to Tien, accompanying a copy of the printed leaves wherein the story and his drawings should appear:

'When the light has for a period been hidden from a person, it is no uncommon thing for him to be struck blind on gazing at the sun; therefore, if the sublime Tien values the eyes of Kin Yen, let her hide herself behind a gauze screen on his approach.

'The trembling words of Tien have sunk deep into the inside of Kin Yen and become part of his being. Never again can he depict persons of the quality and in the position he was wont to do.

'With this he sends his latest efforts. In each case he conceives his drawings to be the pictures to the written words; in the noble Tien's case it is undoubtedly so, in his own he aspires to it. Doubtless the unobtrusive Tien would make no claim to the character and manner of behaving of the one in the story, yet Kin Yen confidently asserts that she is to the other as the glove is to the hand, and he is filled with the most intelligent delight at being able to exhibit her in her true robes, by which she will be known to all who see her, in spite of her dignified protests. Kin Yen hopes; he will come this evening after sunset.'

The week which passed between the finishing of the

pictures and the appearance of the eminent printed leaves containing them was the longest in this near-sighted person's ill-spent life. But at length the day arrived, and going with exceedingly mean haste to the place of sale, he purchased a copy and sent it, together with the letter of his honourable intention, on which he had bestowed so much care, to Tien.

Not till then did it occur to this inconsiderable one that the impetuousness of his action was ill-judged; for might it not be that the pictures were evilly printed, or that the delicate and fragrant words painting the character of the one who now bore the features of Tien had undergone some change?

To satisfy himself, scarce as taels had become with him, he purchased another copy.

There are many exalted sayings of the wise and venerable Confucius constructed so as to be of service and consolation in moments of strong mental distress. These for the greater part recommend tranquillity of mind, a complete abnegation of the human passions and the like behaviour. The person who is here endeavouring to bring this badly constructed account of his dishonourable career to a close pondered these for some moments after twice glancing through the matter in the printed leaves, and then, finding the faculties of speech and movement restored to him, procured a two-edged knife of distinguished brilliance and went forth to call upon the one who sits in an easy-chair.

'Behold,' said the lesser one, insidiously stepping in between this person and the inner door, 'my intellectual and all-knowing chief is not here to-day. May his entirely insufficient substitute offer words of congratulation to the inspired Kin Yen on his effective and striking pictures in this week's issue?'

'His altogether insufficient substitute,' answered this person, with difficulty mastering his great rage, 'may and shall offer words of explanation to the inspired Kin Yen, setting forth the reason of his pictures being used, not with the high-minded story of the elegant Tong-king for which they were executed, but accompanying exceeding base, foolish, and ungrammatical words written by Klan-hi, the Pekin remover of gravity – words which will evermore brand the dew-like Tien as a person of light speech and no refinement'; and in his agony this person struck the lacquered table several times with his elegant knife.

'O Kin Yen,' exclaimed the lesser one, 'this matter rests not here. It is a thing beyond the sphere of the individual who is addressing you. All he can tell is that the graceful Tong-king withdrew his exceedingly tedious story for some reason at the final moment, and as your eminent drawings had been paid for, my chief of the inner office decided to use them with this story of Klan-hi. But surely it cannot be that there is aught in the story to displease your illustrious personality?'

'Judge for yourself,' this person said, 'first understanding that the two immaculate characters figuring as the personages of the narrative are exact copies of this dishonoured person himself and of the willowy Tien, daughter of the vastly rich Pe-li-Chen, whom he was hopeful of marrying.'

Selecting one of the least offensive of the passages in the work, this unhappy person read the following immature and inelegant words: –

'This well-satisfied writer of printed leaves had a highly distinguished time last night. After Chow had departed to see about food, and the junk had been fastened up at the lock of Kilung, on the Yang-tse-Kiang, he and the round-bodied Shang were journeying along the narrow path by the river-side when the right leg of the graceful and popular person who is narrating these events disappeared into the river. Suffering no apprehension in the dark but that the vanishing limb was the left leg of Shang, this intelligent writer allowed his impassiveness to melt away to an exaggerated degree; but at that moment the circumstance became plain to the round-bodied Shang, who was in consequence very grossly amused at the mishap and misapprehension of your good lord, the writer, at the same time pointing out the matter as it really was. Then it chanced that there came by one of the maidens who carry tea and jest for small sums of money to the sitters at the little tables with round white tops, at which this remarkable person, the confidant of many mandarins, ever desirous of displaying his priceless power of removing gravity, said to her:

' "How much of gladness, Ning-Ning? By the Sacred Serpent this is plainly your night out."

'Perceiving the true facts of the predicament of this commendable writer, she replied:

' "Suffer not your illustrious pigtail to be removed, venerable Wang; for in this maiden's estimation it is indeed your night in."

'There are times when this valued person wonders whether his method of removing gravity be in reality very antique or quite new. On such occasions the world, with all its schools, and those who interfere in the concerns of others, continues to revolve around him. The wondrous sky-lanterns come out silently two by two like to the crystallized music of stringed woods. Then, in the mystery of no-noise, his head becomes greatly enlarged with celestial and highly profound thoughts; his groping hand seems to touch matter which may be written out in his impressive style and sold to those who print leaves, and he goes home to write out such.'

When this person looked up after reading, with tears of shame in his eyes, he perceived that the lesser one had cautiously disappeared. Therefore, being unable to gain admittance to the inner office, he returned to his home.

Here the remark of the omniscient Tai Loo again fixes itself upon the attention. No sooner had this incapable person reached his house than he became aware that a parcel had arrived for him from the still adorable Tien. Retiring to a distance from it, he opened the accompanying letter and read:

'When a virtuous maiden has been made the victim of a heartless jest or a piece of coarse stupidity at a person's hands, it is no uncommon thing for him to be struck blind on meeting her father. Therefore, if the degraded and evil-minded Kin Yen values his eyes, ears, nose, pigtail, even his dishonourable breath, let him hide himself behind a fortified wall at Pe-li-Chen's approach.

'With this Tien returns everything she has ever accepted from Kin Yen. She even includes the brace of puppies which she received anonymously about a month ago, and which she did not eat, but kept for reasons of her own—reasons entirely unconnected with the vapid and exceedingly conceited Kin Yen.'

As though this letter, and the puppies of which this person now heard for the first time, making him aware of the existence of a rival lover, were not enough, there almost immediately arrived a letter from Tien's father:

'This person has taken the advice of those skilled in extorting money by means of law forms, and he finds that Kin Yen has been guilty of a grave and highly expensive act. This is increased by the fact that Tien had conveyed his seemingly distinguished intentions to all her friends, before whom she now stands in an exceedingly ungraceful attitude. The machinery for depriving Kin Yen of all the necessaries of existence shall be put into operation at once.'

At this point, the person who is now concluding his obscure and commonplace history, having spent his last piece of money on joss-sticks and incense paper: and being convinced of the presence of the spirits of his ancestors, is inspired to make the following prophecies: – That Tieng Lin, who imposed upon him in the matter of picture-teaching, shall come to a sudden end, accompanied by great internal pains, after suffering extreme poverty; that the one who sits in an easy-chair, together with his lesser one and all who make stories for them, shall, while sailing to a rice feast during the Festival of Flowers, be precipitated into the water and slowly devoured by sea monsters, Klan-hi in particular being tortured in the process; that Pe-li-Chen, the father of Tien, shall be seized with the dancing sickness when in the presence of the august Emperor, and being in consequence suspected of treachery, shall, to prove the truth of his denials, be submitted to the tests of boiling tar, red-hot swords, and of being dropped from a great height on to the Sacred Stone of Goodness and Badness, in each of which he shall fail to convince his judges or to establish his innocence, to the amusement of all beholders.

Some other Oxford Paperbacks for readers
interested in Central Asia, China and
South-east Asia, past and present

CAMBODIA

GEORGE COEDES
Angkor

CENTRAL ASIA

PETER FLEMING
Bayonets to Lhasa

LADY MACARTNEY
An English Lady in
Chinese Turkestan

ALBERT VON LE COQ
Buried Treasures of
Chinese Turkestan

AITCHEN K. WU
Turkistan Tumult

CHINA

All About Shanghai: A
Standard Guide

HAROLD ACTON
Peonies and Ponies

ERNEST BRAMAH
Kai Lung's Golden
Hours*

ERNEST BRAMAH
The Wallet of Kai Lung*

ANN BRIDGE
The Ginger Griffin

CARL CROW
Handbook for China

PETER FLEMING
The Siege at Peking

CORRINNE LAMB
The Chinese Festive
Board

W. SOMERSET
MAUGHAM
On a Chinese Screen*

G. E. MORRISON
An Australian in China

PETER QUENNELL
Superficial Journey
Through Tokyo and
Peking

OSBERT SITWELL
Escape with Me! An
Oriental Sketch-book

J. A. TURNER
Kwang Tung or Five
Years in South China

HONG KONG

The Hong Kong Guide
1893

INDONESIA

S. TAKDIR ALISJAHBANA
Indonesia: Social and
Cultural Revolution

DAVID ATTENBOROUGH
Zoo Quest for a Dragon*

VICKI BAUM
A Tale from Bali*

MIGUEL COVARRUBIAS
Island of Bali*

BERYL DE ZOETE AND
WALTER SPIES
Dance and Drama in
Bali

AUGUSTA DE WIT
Java: Facts and Fancies

JACQUES DUMARÇAY
Borobudur

JACQUES DUMARÇAY
The Temples of Java

GEOFFREY GORER
Bali and Angkor

JENNIFER LINDSAY
Javanese Gamelan

EDWIN M. LOEB
Sumatra: Its History and
People

MOCHTAR LUBIS
Twilight in Djakarta

MADELON H. LULOFS
Coolie*

COLIN McPHEE
A House in Bali*

HICKMAN POWELL
The Last Paradise

E. R. SCIDMORE
Java, Garden of the East

MICHAEL SMITHIES
Yogyakarta

LADISLAO SZÉKELY
Tropic Fever: The
Adventures of a
Planter in Sumatra

EDWARD C. VAN NESS
AND SHITA
PRAWIROHARDJO
Javanese Wayang Kulit

ALFRED RUSSEL
WALLACE
The Malay Archipelago

MALAYSIA

ABDULLAH ABDUL
KADIR
The Hikayat Abdullah

ODOARDO BECCARI
Wanderings in the Great
Forests of Borneo

ISABELLA L. BIRD
The Golden Chersonese

PIERRE BOULLE
Sacrilege in Malaya

MARGARET BROOKE
RANEE OF SARAWAK
My Life in Sarawak

C. C. BROWN (Editor)
Sejarah Melayu or Malay
Annals

K. M. ENDICOTT
An Analysis of Malay
Magic

HENRI FAUCONNIER
The Soul of Malaya

W. R. GEDDES
Nine Dayak Nights

JOHN D. GIMLETTE
Malay Poisons and
Charm Cures

JOHN D. GIMLETTE AND
H. W. THOMSON
A Dictionary of Malayan
Medicine

A. G. GLENISTER
The Birds of the Malay
Peninsula, Singapore
and Penang

C. W. HARRISON
Illustrated Guide to the
Federated Malay States
(1923)

TOM HARRISSON
World Within: A
Borneo Story

DENNIS HOLMAN
Noone of the Ulu

CHARLES HOSE
The Field-Book of a
Jungle-Wallah

SYBIL KATHIGASU
No Dram of Mercy

MALCOLM MacDONALD
Borneo People

W. SOMERSET
MAUGHAM
Ah King and Other
Stories*

W. SOMERSET
MAUGHAM
The Casuarina Tree*

MARY McMINNIES
The Flying Fox*

ROBERT PAYNE
The White Rajahs of
Sarawak

OWEN RUTTER
The Pirate Wind

ROBERT W. C. SHELFORD
A Naturalist in Borneo

J. T. THOMSON
Glimpses into Life in
Malayan Lands

RICHARD WINSTEDT
The Malay Magician

PHILIPPINES

AUSTIN COATES
Rizal

SINGAPORE

PATRICK ANDERSON
Snake Wine: A
Singapore Episode

ROLAND BRADDELL
The Lights of Singapore

R. W. E. HARPER AND
HARRY MILLER
Singapore Mutiny

JANET LIM
Sold for Silver

G. M. REITH
Handbook to Singapore
(1907)

J. D. VAUGHAN
The Manners and
Customs of the
Chinese of the Straits
Settlements

C. E. WURTZBURG
Raffles of the Eastern
Isles

THAILAND

CARL BOCK
Temples and Elephants

REGINALD CAMPBELL
Teak-Wallah

MALCOLM SMITH
A Physician at the Court
of Siam

ERNEST YOUNG
The Kingdom of the
Yellow Robe

Titles marked with an asterisk have restricted rights